Descending Circles

Ascending Earth

John Eric Ellison

Sixth Edition

978-1-63821-446-5

Contents

Heisenberg Uncertainty Principle

There is a finite probability that seemingly implausible events can happen anywhere and anytime.

"Seminars will include lectures on hyperdimensional physics, dark matter, esoteric research in recombinant DNA, magic, alarming reports of otherworldly interlopers…"

Melvin Gray Eagle paused in his reading. *"Interlopers,"* he mused. It was curious the way this article mentioned every one of these seminar topics in one breath as if they related to one another. The following phrase caught his eye:

"Don't forget your dark glasses and amulets."

Smiling, he drew one last puff on his cigar and thought, *"Amulets." I haven't heard that word used in a while. It's all about crystals these days. Physics and amulets…odd.*

The cigar died in a puddle next to his well-worn black boots. Mel stepped on it out of habit and reread the article one more time. He squinted at the address given in the news piece. It was late in the evening. Reading was mostly by streetlight. He bought the newspaper for job ads and ran across this unique little piece in the "On The Town" section. Judging by the article, this convention occurred every year, strange he'd never heard of it and was gathering in a couple of hours within walking distance.

Mel breathed deeply, enjoying crisp ocean air from the Puget Sound. First, he'd get out of the light drizzle that passed for rain in today's weather forecast and then grab a bite to eat across the street. After that, he'd walk up there and check out the convention. He had little else to do these days.

Another happy thought crossed his mind. He was wearing a Nez Perce neckpiece he'd made. He thought, might do as a sample to sell a few custom jobs at the convention. I could use the money right about now.

An old man was sitting on a bench a few yards away. Mel walked over and offered him the paper. As he handed it to him a gust of wind whipped the cover spread out of the old man's hands and carried it down the street. It nearly wrapped itself around an alley cat, followed by fervent feline indignation. Before Mel could think to go after the paper section, an updraft caught it and carried it up and over the roof of a low building. Oh well. The old guy blinked and nodded a thank you for the rest of the paper.

Mel produced another thin cigar from his vest pocket, which he lit up while cupping his hands around the flame. With a shake, the match was discarded.

He squinted through a puff of smoke at a red neon sign across the street. The café had recently changed ownership, and he understood the new cook to be marginal at best. He was famished, and hunger drove a hard bargain.

***

Somewhere a woman's prolific swearing followed a cat's howl of pain. Mel stepped to the curb, waited for a couple of cars to pass, and then crossed the street. The door of the café was suddenly wrenched open, and an angry, well-dressed drunk stumbled out. He turned back around, swore, and shook his fist at what appeared to be the cook before slamming the door shut. Mel stood aside while the man stumbled past him. He heard blaring horns and yelling. Had the drunk been hit? No. What is it about madmen and drunks? They always seem to survive.

The smell of garlic hit him as he entered the café and moved in front of the cashier's counter. Just behind the bar, he saw the kitchen window. Unfilled orders were clipped to a rusty wire above the window frame.

The cook spotted him and shouted, "Hey, jerk! Put that damn thing out! Can't you read?"

Mel blew smoke in the cook's direction and then reached in front of an unkempt coffee-sipping patron to extinguish his cigar in the nearest ashtray. Dim lighting, he thought, then noted that all of the patrons now seated in the café were wearing dark glasses.

The place seemed filled to capacity with a wild assortment of humanity. There were two tables full of rock-and-rollers, several booths seating well- dressed men and women, one booth held a couple of construction workers still dirty from the day's job, and then there were the tourist types. Mel would have placed a large bet that most of these people were waiting for the convention to start. That's why everyone was wearing sunglasses.

Jenny

He felt someone staring into the back of his neck. Glancing over his shoulder, he saw the cook glowering at him. He'd been watching Mel ever since he entered the café. The cook wiped sweat from his own forehead with the back of a hairy hand.

A booth was available with a single occupant. She was young, Mel guessed about twenty-five or so, cute with short blue hair and five amulets, or charms, pinned to the chest of her fluffy pink sweater. The amulets allowed him to gracefully distract himself from her well-endowed shape.

Mel cleared his throat. "Hi. Mind if I join you? There doesn't seem to be anywhere else to sit."

She studied him for an uncomfortable moment, then gave him a warm smile and pointed at the seat opposite her. She had beautiful teeth behind inviting lips.

"Sure, I'm good company, although I clearly see you're more interested in my body than my mind."

At this point, he had to admit to himself that she was right about that, but he avoided the outright admission by nodding at her chest and remarking, "I was just admiring your charms." He smiled and thanked her, then took the proffered seat.

Mel had noticed the actual charms pinned on her sweater.

He said, "Look, I'm not going to apologize for the fact that you are an attractive woman. Does that bother you?"

Her knowing smirk answered his question. This girl was more than a little familiar with attraction.

The painted black birthmark on her left cheek added to her mystery. He couldn't see her eyes because of her sunglasses. She'd just finished an order of fish and chips. Mel asked her if she was waiting for the convention.

"Yeah. How did you guess?" However, before Mel could answer she said,

"You look like an interesting man. What's your name?" She was direct, and he liked that in people.

"Mel Gray Eagle…and yours?"

"Jenny, Mayor."

He tapped at the cigars in his shirt pocket.

"Listen, Jenny, this might sound funny, but would you mind hanging around just long enough for me to grab a burger to go? I'm sure your company is preferable to anyone else who might happen by."

She didn't like the way he worded that.

"Yeah, sure," she said. "I like mysterious men, and I suppose any other Native American who comes through that door could be more of a problem than you have been."

He felt bad.

"What makes you think I'm Native American?" he asked.

"Let's see…headband with Native American design-work, long straight black hair, high cheek-bones, strong facial features. It all adds up. By the way, I love that necklace you have on. It looks like it has some history. Did you make it?"

He nodded.

"Nez Perce, it's a family thing. I was taught how to make these when I was a kid."

Jenny leaned forward and studied the neckpiece.

Distracted, Mel glanced around at the chatter-filled booths. This convention had drawn the interest of old folks and teenagers alike, and variations in between. He was fascinated and had a few questions that were begging to be asked.

Just then, the waitress arrived.

Jenny ordered a soda, but when Mel ordered, the waitress said, "I'm sorry, sir. He won't make anything to go. You might want to try one of the fast-food places down the street."

"Thanks, but never mind. I'll eat it here. Jen, thanks anyway. I guess I'll see you around."

"No way. Forget about it. I'm staying. I can't believe this place. I mean, the previous owners were cool. No questions, no opinions, no hassles, and all the food 'to go' if you wanted it that way. What is this asshole's problem?"

Mel didn't know what to tell her. He agreed with her and said so.

"I run into idiots like that everywhere, but that uppity chef routine is definitely out of place. Geez, look at him. That expression on his face says he thinks he's an irate French chef, but the rest of him screams that he's got a shotgun handy for stray pet stew."

Jenny chuckled at Mel's comparison and noticed that the cook kept lancing their table with facial expressions filled with unveiled contempt. Mel enjoyed her appreciation for the absurd and wished he could see her eyes for the full effect. Several moments passed without a word while Jenny studied the cook, and her expression morphed from amusement to a frown.

Finally, Jenny turned her attention back to Mel and said, "Let's change the subject. Are you hanging out for the convention?"

"Well, I was thinking about it." He nodded at the room around him and added, "Looks like it could be interesting."

Jenny was excited by his interest.

"It is! Really, Mel, you have to come! What do you know about it?" She was practically bouncing in her seat.

Mel said, "Only what I read in a newspaper article. I guess you listen to lectures and sell things."

Now she was really worked up.

"Oh, no…it's much more than that! Yes, we do have booths where you can buy and sell things, but there are also live demonstrations of some really cool conjuring techniques. I understand there's even going to be a display of some heavily-guarded pieces from that recent UFO crash up on Mt. Rainier last month. I don't know how they got those. I think they've even invited that physics guy, Michio Kaku to speak on his books Hyperspace and Visions. Come on, Mel, you've got to come!"

Mel was encouraged by her mention of what he'd always referred to as trading stalls. He was considering the idea of running up to his apartment to get a few supplies for making his neckpieces when their orders arrived with a practiced flourish. In fact, record time for the burger, enough of a record to cause suspicion. Was it fresh, or had it been sitting on the back burner for a while?

Both Jenny and Mel stared at the plate and what was on it, a small, misshapen sandwich, dripping with grease.

"Mel, you are not going to eat that thing, are you?"

"Absolutely not."

Checking out the cook, they found him staring straight at them and smirking, triumphant in a grease-clotted apron.

"Indian scum!"

Everyone in the place heard the cook's racial slur. Sunglasses everywhere oriented onto the cook. Mel's eyes roamed the scene, and he liked what he saw.

The waitress winced and seemed apologetic. She shrugged and whispered to Mel that the cook was new and from out of town. He felt sorry for her. Everyone else, including Jenny, remained weirdly intent on the cook.

Mel fished into his chest pocket and pulled out a cigar. Clenching it between his teeth, he lit up after striking the table with a wooden match. He felt himself grin, a showman at heart, as he rose to leave.

"Sorry, Jen. Gotta get some real food."

Without warning, Jenny jumped to her feet, looked around, and shouted,

"Let him have it!"

She grabbed Mel's hand and pulled him toward the door.

He threw five dollars on the table and told the waitress to keep it. On the way out, they ducked under a flying cheeseburger, parts of a tuna fish sandwich, and at least twelve orders of fried potatoes, all targeted for the cook. They paused for one last look as the door swung shut behind them. The cook was bobbing and threatening retaliation. They both broke into uncontrolled laughter.

***

Mel was relieved that the light rain had stopped, for now at least. He told Jenny that he had decided to go to the convention.

"You know, I think I will go to the gathering of yours. Hyperspace, huh?" She patted him on the arm.

"Yeah, Hyperspace. You want to go with me?" she asked. "You don't have anyone with you, why not come with me, I'll introduce you around. You'll sell a lot more neckpieces that way. Forget about going back to your place right now. You can take orders."

Mel was stunned. How on earth had she known that he was planning on running home for supplies? He was about to ask her when she held up a hand for him to be quiet and then knelt down by the sidewalk curb.

There was a cat by the curb when they left the café, and it was still there but was now preparing to run across the street when Jenny stopped it with a friendly little purring sound and a gesture to come to her. The cat noticed Mel, but ignored him, and stole up to Jenny as she knelt to pet it.

Mel recognized this to be the same cat that nearly caught his newspaper only a little while earlier.

Jenny continued to purr and looked into its eyes, then cast a playfully stern glance back at Mel. He returned her look with a confused one of his own. She bent conspiratorially close to the cat and whispered, "He was probably trying to wrap you up in a newspaper like a fresh salmon down at the market."

Although she was reticent, Mel heard enough to raise an eyebrow. How had she known about the newspaper? For that matter, he still wanted to know how she knew he planned to sell his handcrafts at the convention. He definitely had to know more about Jenny. He didn't know why, but he decided to hold off on asking her about the mind reading thing for a little while. Also, she seemed to be empathetic.

Once Jenny was back in step with him, they strolled in the direction of the convention center.

Mel playfully asked, "So, how did you get involved in all this, were your parents into crop circles or something?"

Jenny shot him a curiously, knowing glance.

"Wow, you're amazing! How did you know about that? Can you read my mind?"

That took Mel off guard, but before he could respond, she continued.

"Yeah, my parents are great. They remind me about this convention every year. I'm supposed to meet some nice guy, settle down and have kids. But I move around a lot, so I can't get tied down like that. Still, they keep trying to fix me up. I don't blame them for trying though. It's kind of cute."

She went silent a moment and looked over at Mel, then said, "Mom usually calls me with Dad on the extension. She's always working on some new aphrodisiac to sell at the convention. Dad says…,"

"Hold it. Back up. Aphrodisiac?"

"Yeah. What? You don't know what that is?"

"Sure, I know what they are…but, why does your mother push sex recipes on you?"

"Well, there's some things you'll understand a lot better once you get to know me a little more."

Mel shook his head, snorting this out.

"Jenny, look, I'm a little confused. Why don't you tell me about it? Don't look at me that way." Mel pleaded. "I'm really interested."

"You are?"

"I am."

"Okay, here goes. We live in Kansas. Why are you smirking?"

"Are you a country, girl?"

"Kansas City. Why?"

"Forget it."

She hesitated before continuing.

"Dad is a highly esteemed research scientist. He's known for his writings and some pretty amazing inventions he's built at home, like a combination time machine and flying saucer."

"Really? Does it work, I mean, is it functional?"

"Functional? Well, that depends on your point of view."

"Is the entire neighborhood in on that shit?" She glared at him.

"Shit?" she exclaimed.

Suddenly she looked ready to hit him.

"Jenny, come on, I didn't mean that the way it sounded. You must have heard worse."

She still looked angry, but it passed quickly. Then she answered his question.

"Maybe half the neighborhood."

***

They walked around a drug-related street sale and stepped over the grisly remains of a dead alley cat lying next to a parking meter. Mel stopped and looked down at it and felt a little sick. He asked Jenny to hold that thought, then knelt down for a better look before extinguishing his cigar on the meter. Standing up, he nodded and started walking again. Jenny grabbed him by the arm and stopped him.

"Wait a minute. What was that all about?"

"The cat?"

"Yeah, I mean, you looked upset or something."

He drew a deep breath and appeared distracted by fleeting thought. He glanced back down at the cat.

"Well, that old boy was beaten to death. It was a pointless, meaningless way to go. I just tried to give his death; some meaning is all."

Jenny cocked her head a little, listening. She really was trying to understand. Mel liked her.

He continued. "I've been meaning to stop smoking, so I dedicated that cigar to him, as my last smoke. I told him that I would think of him if I ever considered picking it up again. I think he feels good about that."

Jenny's smile was heartfelt. She brushed her hand across his cheek.

Mel ignored a Taco Time on the next block. He wasn't interested in Mexican food. While scanning for another fast-food place, he felt a different need. There was a Texaco on the next block, and he excused himself.

"Don't go away now. I'll be right back."

As he made for the men's room, he paused long enough to notice a young man about one-half block down Jenny's side of the street. He called out to a young woman directly across from him on the other side. She yelled something in response and ran randomly through traffic to meet him halfway. Miraculously unscathed, they embraced and kissed, then backed away from each other before removing amulets from one another's chests. Amid the sound of catcalls and blaring horns, they kissed again and then removed each other's dark glasses. They both pocketed their prizes and locked in another kiss before reality hit them. They laughed and crossed to Jenny's side of the street.

Shaking his head to clear it from what he'd just seen Mel entered the restroom. As the zipper fell, he heard Jenny's voice. She called out a welcome, followed by two gleeful replies. There was a loud exchange of glad tidings, and by the time he returned, the young couple was well down the road, on a dead run to wherever.

Jenny was moon-eyed watching the couple run hand in hand back toward the greasy spoon café. She had a soft and longing smile on her face. Mel hated to break her reverie, but…

"Who were the lovebirds?"

Jenny spun around and answered his question by nailing him with the most passionate kiss he'd ever experienced.

Mel was reeling from the effects by the time she allowed their lips to part company.

"Those two always make me feel envious and desperate," she said. "Oh, I'm sorry. I didn't mean that the way it sounded."

"Uh..." he managed.

"They are a scorching item. They used to rip off concert posters together. She would do a slow striptease while he pulled off the heist. That girl has a body that could stop a trucker on crank."

"I noticed." She continued.

"The police would fight their way to her through the pre-concert mob but could do little else. She never went further than her underwear. I mean, Madonna gets away with it, right?"

They resumed their walk.

Jenny continued, "They both used to work in a cookie factory, somewhere around here, until she quit to work the Alaskan pipeline for a year. She wanted to save enough money so that she could work junk sculpture for a while. Julie is a fine artist and can earn an easy living if she goes for it. Eddie still works at the cookie factory. He'll probably run the place one day."

"Why did they remove amulets and glasses from each other?"

"They are lovers."

"I assumed that much."

She paused and studied him with that penetrating stare of hers.

"Mel, you don't read the tabloid magazines, do you? There are some truths in those tabloids if you know where to look."

She read Mel's expression and continued. He thought, Thank God

I didn't have to say anything.

"We won't be seeing those two at the convention," she explained. "Some things are more important. I'm sure they're going back to his place, although she really wanted to surprise him with her return during the convention. It's too bad the way things worked out. Ritual reunions are always exciting."

"I prefer things private," he interjected.

They passed a telephone pole covered as far as could be reached with little pieces of paper stapled to it. These were the remains of concert posters. For the longest time, Seattle telephone poles were thick with these little posters. Now, the city did its best to clean up the poles.

"Why are you so interested in me, Mel?"

"I like unusual women."

Two punkers passed on Jenny's side. One of them had a purple Mohawk and wore black plastic chains around his neck. On his way by, he pinched Jenny's rear and howled. To Mel's surprise, Jenny spun and caught the offender on his back with a blow hard enough to bring a bruise later.

His friend, wearing eyeliner and black lipstick, called out over his buddy's shoulder.

"Got any spare change?"

Mel noticed an unsettling fiery blue flash behind Jenny's sunglasses. Except for the diffuse glow of the street lighting, they were surrounded by darkness. He wondered where the spark came from. The guy wearing eyeliner and black lipstick looked back at Jenny and snickered, but when he turned back around again, he ran face-first into the papered telephone pole.

Jenny shouted, "Get a life, asshole!"

After that, Mel gave Jenny a few moments of quiet space. They passed under a streetlight and Mel turned his attention to something that was really annoying him.

"What is it with the shades?"

"It has to do with swapping minds or casting spells on each other.

Be grateful that I'm wearing them now, Mel, or maybe with a brief glance, I could turn you into my willing love slave."

She looked serious.

He pointed to her chest. "What about those?"

"These?"

"Am I staring again?"

She smiled and replied, "Amulets are wards against gestured enchantments. They can't hang from a single chain, because each of them must be clearly visible. Sometimes we wear them as a guardian of the heart. Ed and Julie, remember?" She frowned. "You really know nothing about this?"

"Let's just say we travel in different circles. Do any of those things protect you against horny strangers?" When he realized that she might think he was referring to himself, his face flushed and he said, "I don't mean me, I…"

She held her hand up to silence him, then stopped walking and cocked her head to one side. Curiosity washed over her face as she studied his sincerity.

"Go ahead, Mel. Take my glasses off. I dare you."

Relishing the moment, he slowly removed her glasses and handed them back to her. She tucked them into the neck of her sweater so that they hung down in front of her chest.

"Nice. Very nice. I love brown eyes. Have I told you that?"

"Mel, you haven't revealed much about yourself at all. Are you married?

Or do you have a girlfriend? Where do you work, live, and what do you like to do?" She tapped his chest with her index finger for emphasis, then added,

"That kind of stuff."

That was quite a list, but he gave it his best shot.

"Let's see. I'm an out-of-work printing press operator. I live in one of those up-town high rises you can see from here, and I like to watch the pier from my porch. I shop at Pikes Place Market a lot, and I hate that oversized moving black statue of The Hammering

Man outside the Seattle Art Museum. I also like to bug my neighbor Ted with articles about earthquakes. Our flats are pretty high up, and that bothers him a lot. Not enough to move, though." He considered a moment and then continued. "I'm divorced, and no, I don't have a girlfriend." He took a deep breath just for drama.

She looked wistful and said, "No luck in Seattle, huh?"

"Well, I wouldn't go so far as to say that," he said, "but you are close." In the next block, something grabbed his attention.

Finally! Here's a fast-food place where I can sink my teeth into some real food.

He bought an all meat Vegetarian Nightmare sandwich.

When they returned to the sidewalk, he asked her a question that he felt would keep him out of the conversation long enough to eat.

"So," he began, "how about telling me more about your dad, the mad scientist?"

Jenny looked at Mel and smiled with pride.

"My father, yeah, sure, but wait a minute."

She stopped him from walking any further with a hand on his chest and then pointed to a spot against a brick wall. A young couple was sitting against the wall with their legs stretched out on the sidewalk, and they looked homeless. The woman looked up Mel, then at Jenny. She flashed a faint but warming smile. Jenny returned her smile, but then, as Mel watched Jenny, there was another expression on her face for a fleeting moment. It reminded Mel of someone intently eavesdropping on a whispered voice. The couple said nothing and yet Jenny seemed intense, as if listening.

Jenny broke the moment and spoke to Mel.

"Look, let's stop here so you can eat."

Mel agreed, and they slid down the wall next to the couple. To Mel, they looked like a couple, because they occasionally crossed legs with each other and because of the way they spoke to one another. Sad, he thought, that these two are on the street instead of in front of a beautiful fireplace somewhere together.

Despite her best intentions, Jenny wasn't going to let him eat in peace. She said, "Before I say anything more, I want you to tell me a little more about yourself. I've been doing all the talking."

"Now?"

"You don't talk much, so I figure you can make it brief. Yeah, right now…then eat."

She winked and added, "Clock's ticking on that burger."

He lowered the burger into his lap and flicked a bug away from it. Mel spoke reluctantly.

"My family lives mostly in Idaho, but I don't get out there much. I haven't seen my family since the return of some ancestral relics to the Nez Perce National Park, in '79, for…"

"Relics?"

"Well, there is an old collection of items that were traded to the pioneers, Whitman and Spalding, back around 1836. The relics found their way back home to my people in '79, and there was a lot of ceremony over it. I went back home for that. My people finally raised the money to buy them outright

in '96."

"Mel, that's almost twenty years ago. When you said you don't get out there much, you should have said 'ever.'"

Jenny was close to her family. She asked, "Don't your family members miss you?"

"Most of them are down-and-outers. They really aren't aware of too much anyway, outside of their own problems. Besides, I like not having family strings. I move around a lot. Family expectations would cramp my style."

She was looking at him with an obvious question in her mind.

"Twenty years. You know you don't look old enough for that. You must be well over forty."

"Forty-something, yes."

"Boy, you sure age well. You look maybe thirty-five, or so."

"Thank you."

"In fact," she added, "I think you're handsome."

Jenny screwed up her face in a cute little grimace, eyes sparkling, and touched her finger to the end of his nose.

She said, "So, will you tell me how you got your name?"

Then she motioned toward his sandwich. "Go ahead and eat if you want, I don't care if you talk with your mouth full."

"Thanks," he said and ate a bite, then continued.

"Gray Eagle. I'm named after the father of In-Who-Lise. She's famous among my people. She was the only survivor after a brutal attack on her family. Soldiers at the Big Hole Battlefield murdered them. Her father Gray Eagle was killed in his own lodge during that attack. Some of the old ones among us say I resembled him in spirit when I was a child. I can't tell you how they knew that. I mean, descriptions of Gray Eagle are scarce. I do know that some of the old ones just 'see' things like that, which is good enough for me."

"Cool."

"My people fought bravely for their homeland and spiritual beliefs during the last of the great Indian battles. They were spread out from Idaho and Montana through Washington, Oregon, and parts of Canada. They traveled with the seasons."

Mel could tell that Jenny wanted some little personal detail to sink her teeth into…so he gave her one.

"I have a picture of Chief Joseph at home, hanging on the wall. He often negotiated for peace between native and white people, although there was some confusion about that since Joseph also led many battles himself."

"So, is he kind of a mentor for you, then?"

"Not really, how could he be?" He winked. "He's dead." Jenny cuffed him.

"You know what I mean." She paused and looked thoughtful.

"Are you religious about your tribal heritage?"

"If you mean do I practice tribal rites and that kind of thing, no, I do feel close to the earth, and have a pretty strong belief system of my own."

She perked up.

"Let's hear it, I want to hear about your beliefs."

He swallowed hard on a rather large mouthful that polished off the sandwich and then wiped his mouth.

"No, please, not right now, Jenny. Thank you for being so open about yourself, but I don't think now is the right time for me. Don't look so down. There will be another time, and when the student is ready, the teacher will appear."

Hair had fallen into her eyes, Mel brushed it aside and then added,

"Anything else you want to know?"

He rather hoped she'd make it quick. The concrete was uncomfortable.

"OK, let's see. You're a warrior and a lover of peace and a reluctant shaman. That's cool."

He was looking down and fidgeting with the hamburger paper. His head snapped up.

"Reluctant shaman. Where did you get that?"

"I can see it in your eyes, besides, what do you call that thing hanging around your neck?" She pointed. "It looks like a totem to me."

The necklace was undoubtedly a spiritual symbol. He made it from shell, bone tubes and beads, and some elk's teeth interspersed with small ornaments made by wrapping porcupine quills and cornhusk together with rawhide thongs.

He fingered it absently.

"Well, it is traditional, and I believe it holds power, but I don't think you could understand that unless I were to give you a course in Nez Perce lore. Mother Earth wore a necklace similar to this."

That little bit of information satisfied her. She stood up, dusted herself off, and Mel gratefully followed.

Then Jenny did the genuinely inexplicable. She reached into one of her pockets and produced a twenty-dollar bill. Then she handed it to the homeless woman, who thanked her profusely, as did her male companion. Jenny said they were welcome, and that it would be a shame if they could not find a friendly fire to sit in front of together. She then continued to walk toward the convention center. Mel was stunned by her generosity but did not say a word.

What he felt was another matter, and Jenny seemed to sense some of that in him. She told him that she knew what he was feeling and that there was no need for her to regret, or even question, her generosity. She explained that the couple was probably afraid to ask for help, for their own reasons.

Mel was struck by another weird notion, the fire. Had Jenny reread his thoughts? No, he dismissed that idea, but then he remembered her speaking to the cat and her remark about selling his necklaces. He dropped the subject, for now, making another mental note to bring it up later. Jenny started talking about her dad again as if she'd never left the subject.

"I really love my dad, and I am proud of him. Last year the convention coordinator invited him to fly out here, expenses paid, to speak on his book Secondary Narcissism."

Mel cleared his throat. He knew something about this topic.

"Wait a minute, Jen. Let me guess. The book is about loving others, so they love you, and you love yourself all the more."

She was impressed.

"Right. Have you read the book?"

He shook his head. "No, but I had a cat like that once. I found her on my doorstep, and she stayed four days. She would rub her head on my leg to get my attention. I'd pet her a couple of times before she would run off and lick herself silly. On the third day, she went out to pee and never came back. I haven't seen her since."

"That's sad. What was her name?"

"Sybil."

Jenny watched his face for a moment. She was looking for something meaningful. Finding nothing but catsup on his face, and no great revelations, she continued to speak about her father.

"Dad's book has helped me a lot. I understand myself better, and yet it's difficult not to use people to build myself up inside. Do you know what I mean?"

He realized that he still had the wrapping paper in his hand. He threw it into a curbside garbage can, then put his arm around Jenny's shoulder, and tickled her ear with his thumb.

"I've sensed a little cynicism in you, Jen."

"You're getting awfully friendly, Mel."

Abashed, he dropped his arm, although she tucked a hand into his back pocket.

Suddenly kids were everywhere. Some were wearing sunglasses.

"Do you like kids, Mel?"

"Sure. Doesn't everyone?" Jenny shook her head.

"I don't. At least I don't think I do. Kids freak me out."

Jenny caught his sarcastic expression and cuffed him on the arm. He dropped into a mock defense posture. She reached to put on her sunglasses and then thought better of it.

Mel was amused and asked, "So you either don't like or don't trust kids. Why tempt fate by screwing around?"

"Birth control. It's a touchy subject, propagation of the species and all that. You are right, though. I am cynical. I mean, how many of us are sincere. Odds are against being picked up by an…"

Her voice trailed off, leaving something out.

"Jen, what are you telling me?"

She looked up at him, but it was apparent she would keep whatever she was going to say a secret. Mel had the nagging suspicion she was going to say something weird like "Odds are against being picked up by an alien," but he kept this suspicion to himself. Of course, if she could read his mind, she'd already know what he was thinking. Maddening. Mel reconsidered the provocative question about the mind reading thing. He thought I might as well get it out of the way.

"Look, Jenny, please don't take this the wrong way. I'm not prying into your secrets, but you seem, well, back there with the cat you knew about the newspaper, and then a few minutes ago you told that young couple the same thing I was thinking about a warm fire. Now that might be coincidental, but then again …"

She picked up the thread he left trailing. "Yeah, sometimes I feel strong emotions in other people and see vivid mental pictures they see, in my own head. It just happens. Usually, I can kind of control it, and other times, I can't. It works with animals too. Is that what you wanted to know?"

Mel looked relieved at not having to spell it out.

"Yeah, right. Thanks. You don't have to tell me anymore. It's probably a personal thing."

She shrugged and told him she didn't mind, after which she studied him for an awkward moment, which was something he'd experienced several times that evening.

Jenny grabbed his hand.

"Come with me, Mister Gray Eagle."

For nearly twenty minutes, she led him, by the hand, through several blocks of old buildings. It was dark, and streetlights were now few, or non- existent. Add to that, the drizzling rain was back. For some reason unknown to Mel, Jenny refused to talk for a while or reveal where she was taking him. No amount of prodding got any verbal response. Once, she did turn to him and place a finger on his lips. When she did that, he noticed a distant look in her eyes, something preoccupied. Mel felt the creeps despite himself. She was so intent on whatever purpose she had in mind that she was temporarily beyond all reach. One thing was for sure; the convention hall was in the opposite direction.

Finally, they arrived at an old corner house, and she led him through a backyard gate to a basement apartment that she claimed was hers. Large rose bushes were growing on both sides of the darkened entrance. She unlocked the door with a key she had hidden on the inside of one of her boots.

Her place was dark and stuffy with incense. The only source of light came from a colorful glow, down a short hallway, leaking around a poorly hinged door. This was the only other door in the apartment. Her living room also seemed to be her kitchen. Bright light suddenly enveloped her as she opened her refrigerator. It was full of sandwich stuff, pizza, and…

"Beer?" she offered, finally dissolving her silence.

"Great. Thanks."

She cracked it and took a sip before handing it to him. She asked him if he wanted to listen to some music. Mel could see her extensive collection of CDs and tapes. Jenny apparently enjoyed collecting demos from local bands, which was something he enjoyed as well, so he said, "Sure."

Her collection included little known works by The Chinese Girls, Echoplex, Plan Orange, Phatt Pharm, and Nehalem Blue. Nehalem Blue's demo had a mutilated deer on the cover, which reminded Mel of pictures of reported cattle mutilations he'd seen. Mel saw a selection he enjoyed and was about to suggest "White Trash Heros"—misspelling intended—by The Archers of Loaf, when she picked one of the heavier bands, Harkonen. After the music started, she did a cute little bump and grind, then took Mel by his free hand and led him down the hall and through the mystery door.

There were nearly two dozen lava lamps of varying colors placed on top of anything and everything all over the room…in fact, there were so many of them that it was bright enough to read. The ambiance and subtle movement produced by these lamps was mesmerizing. There was a ceiling light, but he guessed she never used it. Mel was amazed and said so.

"Wow."

She wandered around the room while letting her hands nearly touch and linger over several of the lamps. There were a couple of bookshelves lined with books, a dresser, a computer desk and computer, several unpacked moving boxes, and a mattress on the floor. Jenny walked back up to Mel and brought her hand to rest on his chest.

"They're pretty cool, huh?"

He playfully ignored her hand.

"You should turn these things off when you leave. Conserve energy." She began to unbutton his shirt.

She said, "I forgot." Then she cocked her head, looked up at him, and performed something like a pensive pout with her lips.

"Mel?"

"Yeah?"

"When I dared you to take off my glasses, did it scare you?" He nearly choked on a mouthful of beer.

"No. Why?"

"Good."

She started unbuckling his belt.

"You know, Jenny, I'm beginning to believe that you have some of your father's mad scientist traits in you."

She looked up at him with a sultry smile. "I still think you have some reluctant shaman in you. Let's find out if you have anything to teach me."

Jenny's brown eyes began to sparkle and flash with little blue highlights. They missed the convention.

Some things are more important.

Postscript

"Regarding the Alien Convention held last Friday night in downtown Seattle, the gathering of at least three hundred people was both entertaining and hard to describe. Among other things, there were four ritual reunions, one mass wedding involving several unconventional groupings, a large display of UFO hardware, and five herbalist booths. Many of these people profess to be, in part, extraterrestrial. After meeting several convention attendees, this writer can't help imagining this to be true. For those of you who missed the festivities, see you next year."

Specter

Mel was asleep in the front row, between acts, during a popular freak show in Seattle, Washington. "The Hose Monster" was next on stage, and someone kept shaking Mel's shoulder to wake him. He did not want to awaken. He knew he would start to gag as The Hose Monster swallowed gallon after gallon of anything and everything through a length of rubber tubing. He hadn't the slightest clue how he was able to remain sleeping through all this retched absurdity. Lurid lighting accentuated a nauseating stage set. The audiences around him drifted in and out of his consciousness through waves of disjointed conversation, sweet smoke, and people smell. Someone, he was sure it was a woman, continued to insist that he awaken.

"Wake up. Wake up, Mel!"

She shook him again.

"Will you please get up, and turn that VCR off before I throw something at it!"

His eyes blinked open. He was in his own bed, it was Saturday morning, and the voice belonged to his girlfriend. He'd set the VCR to wake them early in the morning, and chose a tape guaranteed to keep him from falling back to sleep. Marla wasn't pleased with his choice in tapes. He rolled out of bed and hit the steam heater next to the bed with his shoulder. It burned him, and he jumped to his feet with a moan of pain. He stumbled to the end of the bed and bumped into the footboard with his right knee. Finally, he managed to reach over and turn off the VCR. It was on top of the dresser, next to the TV.

Marla's voice was always raspy in the morning.

"I thought you said you were not going to use that freak show tape again." Mel sat on the edge of the bed and couldn't decide what ache to rub first, the shoulder or his knee.

"Yeah. I know. It's an obsession."

Marla groaned a little and then smiled. She rolled over onto her back.

She said, "You saw that show with Jenny the day after you met her last year; in fact, a year ago today. This is not just a coincidental fixation. I should be upset about a preoccupation like this."

She wore an impish frown and added, "Instead I'm viewing it like the professional psychiatrist I am."

Mel shot her a glance.

"And your prognosis is?"

She threw her hands over her head.

"Clinical enamor. Jenny still has you under a spell of some kind. I'm charitable because she's my cousin. As far as what you need to do about it…, I'd say Mr. big shot publisher heal thyself."

Mel traced her navel ring with a finger. Marla caressed his hand and said,

"Nez Perce means pierced nose, so why don't you have anything pierced? You'd look good with one in your ear."

His finger left her navel and circled slowly up between her breasts.

"Actually," Mel corrected, "my people were originally a Shahaptian tribe that some French traders called nay pearsay. Others called them nez presse,' and that means 'pressed nose.'"

He kissed her stomach, and she prankishly held onto his ears and pushed his face into her stomach.

She spoke softly.

"You mean like this?"

His reply was a little muffled.

"Not exactly."

She let him go and changed the subject.

"That story you wrote about you and Jenny and how you met is still being circulated around the convention circuit. You're both celebrities. You really should attend one of them and find out how famous you are. Jenny's been soaking it up."

He grumbled and nipped at her wrists. She laughed and let go of his ears. He got up and disappeared into the adjoining bathroom to wash.

The phone rang.

Marla rolled over and reached under the covers near the foot of the bed. She extracted the cordless phone after fishing for it and flipped her long straight black hair over her shoulders. She knelt on the end of the bed and cradled the phone to her ear.

"Hello…yes, I'll accept the charges."

Mel reached out through the shower curtain and pushed the bathroom door open.

"Who is it?"

"Who do you think?"

"Be right out."

He really had expected Jenny to call before the VCR came on. That would have been more like Jenny's pattern over the last week. When she received Marla's invitation to take her with them into the mountains, Jenny was extremely excited. She'd said, "This is perfect. I was going to call you anyway about a trip to Rainier! I'll explain when I get there." That was her cryptic message in a nutshell. After that, she called nearly every day during the week before her two-week trip to Seattle. She kept asking probing questions about how much time Mel and Marla could take away from their work. She also said things like "I've got a surprise for you both," or "wait till you see what I've arranged…you'll both love it!" Also typical to Jenny was the fact that no amount of prodding would convince her to reveal any answers until she was ready to divulge them. Exasperating.

By the time Mel wrapped a towel around himself and dripped into the bedroom, Marla had hung up the phone.

"She just flew in. She'll be here in about an hour."

Mel replied, "I'll start breakfast." He shook his head and added, "I can't believe we're up at five a.m. on a Saturday."

***

When Jenny arrived, the entire upstairs smelled of sausage and eggs, hash browns, and pancakes with maple syrup. Jenny walked right in through the front door, put down several pieces of luggage in the entryway, and then entered the kitchen. She hugged Marla, and then tapped Mel on the nose and winked at him. She asked, "Are you sure you don't want me to remove that glamour I placed on you the night we met? I can see in your eyes that you are still attached to me."

Mel blinked.

He suddenly felt oddly relaxed.

She impishly looked him up and down.

"I like your new look."

Mel changed his appearance to match his new business profile. He now wore conservative clothing, and an occasional suit and tie, just for the fun of it. His hair was shorter but longer on top and combed a little rough. It was a Brad Pitt or Brian Ferry look. He was now wearing Dockers shorts, and a loose long sleeve white cotton shirt. His feet were bare.

Mel's eyes glazed for a moment. He shook his head, and then his mind returned to what she had said about the glamour. Jenny no longer appeared to be interested in the subject, but Mel pursued it anyway.

"Jen, are you absolutely certain that I am not descended from off-world somewhere? That glamour seemed to have worked, and it could have been an off night for you. Let's try it again." He winked. "With a year behind us, who knows."

"You are awful, Mel. Marla may be broad-minded, but she has her limits." Mel held up his hands and said he was only kidding.

Marla interrupted while she took Jenny's blue wool coat and cap. Underneath, Jenny wore a durable no frills hiking outfit. Marla playfully bumped into Mel on her way to hang up Jenny's coat.

"Thanks again for introducing us, Jen. I won't give him back to you, even if you do reconsider your gypsy ways. Besides, I want kids, and you don't." Marla winked at Mel.

"Kids?" Mel asked. "You want kids now?"

"Someday," Marla replied.

Mel raised an eyebrow. He felt a wisecrack coming, and said, "According to Jenny, all Native American blood is indigenous to

Earth, but I don't buy it.

I feel right at home with the two of you."

Both women caught the good-humored jab and laughed.

Mel chuckled, then added, "I'll bring breakfast out to the porch. You two go out and get comfortable. Looks like it's going to be a nice morning, and a beautiful day."

Marla drew conspiratorially close to Jenny as they walked through the living room. She whispered to Jenny as she opened the sliding glass door.

"Would you please remove that spell. He's driving me crazy with the fixations he developed after you cast that glamour on him."

Jenny winked.

"I already did when I touched his nose in the hall."

***

The house was a large two-story structure, built on the side of a gentle slope, and overlooked the suburbs of north Seattle. Its natural wood exterior was designed to blend in with the tall pine trees around it so that it might be barely noticed from the property below. After breakfast, their conversation drifted from general pleasantries to the trip at hand. Mel was the first to raise the subject.

"We'll take the Suburban and a couple of tents. Jenny, from the looks of what you brought with you, we should be able to get all of your photography equipment in the back seat. The rest of our stuff should fit in the back, with the tents tied on top."

Jenny wasn't listening. She was staring at the table, and quite obviously troubled or distracted. She began tracing a knot in the wood surface. She spoke softly.

"When was the last time you had a sighting around here?"

Marla answered. "You mean alien craft...around here? I don't remember, but where we're going there was a craft reported yesterday, at about the same time the convention was in full swing. Which reminds me, why didn't you fly in earlier? You missed a great convention. The Claiborne twins brought several dozen jars of Yulan's apricot jam and sold them all." Jenny looked crushed. Marla smiled, "Don't look too disappointed, Jen. I bought some for you."

Jenny returned her smile but still looked lost in thought.

"Thanks, Marla. You know the twins told me he stopped making it. He told everyone he'd lost his touch. I'm glad he changed his mind."

She looked up at the treetops and watched them sway in a gentle morning breeze.

"I've missed three or four gatherings around the states this year. My light sculptures are selling pretty well over the Internet, so I guess I've gotten kind of production oriented. I don't have the travel time I used to have, although I've got a lot more money to travel on. Odd the way that works."

She shrugged and then returned to the subject of yesterday's sighting.

"What did it look like, and who spotted it?"

"The usual saucer shape. Tim Jensen spotted it on his way into Seattle, over in the Rainier foothills. He snapped some Polaroids and drove like crazy to get them back to the convention before ten. We all got the chance to check them out by overhead projector. That's when we spotted the open portal, in two of the photographs, suspended between the trees just below the craft."

Jenny was excited. "So that's what Donovan was so worked up about when I called him before I left."

Marla remembered something.

"Did you bring that book you told us about?"

"Yeah. It's in the brown backpack."

Marla quickly left to retrieve the book. Mel took that opportunity to clear the table. When Marla returned with a thin album, they all crowded over it together. Jenny opened it and showed them several black and white drawings of what appeared to be round black blotches hovering in the air. The locations varied. There were nameless wooded areas, rocky terrain, or several other unidentified sites. Jenny explained.

"You know, these hyperdimensional openings, or spatial rifts, are frequently reported by people attending the conventions. They show up during, and just after, craft sightings. I don't know of anyone ever attempting to enter one, but what's to say that nobody has ever tried. Perhaps they couldn't return to tell the tale."

Mel pointed at the drawing.

"Who drew these?"

"Lots of people," Jenny answered. She opened the book to a page where the portal appeared within an abandoned warehouse.

"I met the artist that drew this one. This one opened in a warehouse somewhere back east. Here it is, in Illinois. The artist seemed credible enough to me, and she was with two other people at the time who verified it. They were driving through an industrial district when they spotted a glowing green sphere floating over one of the buildings. The sphere flew off, but they were also interested in what the craft might have left behind, or perhaps what it was looking for. They found this thing and got close enough to see something dark moving around inside it. Thankfully, nothing came out. It was frightening." She shook off a shiver. "Creepy, huh?"

Marla picked up the book and started flipping through it. She was frowning when she said, "You're sure you want to look for one of these things?"

"Absolutely. Are you kidding? We're going to be up there anyway. Oh, by the way, I've got a surprise for you both."

Marla said, "That's right, you mentioned a surprise."

When Jenny seemed reluctant to reveal the secret just then, Marla continued.

"You know we really had it in mind just to take you for a casual camping trip, to take your mind off your parents' death."

Jenny's loss, though temporarily forgotten, now rushed in upon her. Sudden tears gave away her feelings, and Marla felt her loss. She scooted her chair closer and put her arms around her.

"I'm sorry, Jenny."

It was common knowledge that an updraft pulled her parent's Ultralight glider into the path of a black helicopter. They swerved to avoid it and hit a downdraft. At least they died while enjoying a favorite pastime. They were spotting crop circles.

Unpleasant memories were interrupted by the sound of a heavy vehicle pulling into the driveway out front. They couldn't see the road from the patio, so Mel got up to check it out.

"I'll see who it is. Probably the newspaper guy."

He paused before opening the front door and listened for a moment. He had this old habit of listening before acting. Caution, and quite often over- caution, was in his blood.

The stained-glass panels on either side of the door did not allow him to see out, yet he could clearly hear the sounds outside in the driveway. The vehicle had come to a stop, and the engine was off. Doors were opening, and closing, and several enthusiastic voices approached his door. He pressed his eye to the peephole but couldn't see a thing. Odd. The peephole was utterly dark. He rubbed the tiny glass lens and tried again. Nothing. He threw open the door and found himself nearly nose to nose with a man wearing a leather flight cap like those worn by early fighter pilots. Grinning, the man who had been blocking the peephole by looking through it from the other side drew back for a better look at Mel. Consequently, Mel got a better view of the crowd standing on his doorstep.

Including the sky pilot, there were seven of them. No, wait…six. Three of them were women, but then he suddenly realized there were seven of them…four men. One of the men kept disappearing out of the corner of Mel's eyes. Very strange.

All seven were from Jenny and Marla's cult of friends, although they were not wearing sunglasses or amulets. He knew by now, thanks to Jenny and Marla, that they seldom wore their trappings outside convention sites. Sky pilot leaned forward. He pinched Mel's shirt and introduced himself.

"I'm Donovan Diggs, you must be Mel. Nice fabric."

He grabbed Mel's right hand with both of his own and shook it.

"Cool to finally meet you in the flesh. You've got to get out more often, everyone loves you, man."

He peered around Mel, and into the house.

"Jenny, here yet?" Mel found his voice.

"Yes, she is. Wait a minute, what are you people doing here?"

He turned around and shouted through the house.

"Hey, Jenny! Will you come out here, please!"

Jenny obviously knew they were coming because she bounced into the entryway with all the excitement of a child receiving a coveted Christmas toy.

"Sorry, Mel. I wasn't sure they would come, so I didn't want to bother you with the possibility, but here they are! Isn't it great?" Then she kissed him on the cheek and added, "Surprise!"

She beamed and invited them all inside.

Mel was annoyed, and looked it, as they paraded into his house. He indicated Jenny's guests and asked, "What are they here for?"

"They're coming along. They'll take their own bus, of course."

He could see that they had come in a bus...a small school bus actually...and it was loaded with stuff. Mel sighed, relaxed a little, and lifted his hands in resignation.

"OK. Why not."

He gestured them into the living room.

"Well, might as well get acquainted before we leave."

***

The entire upstairs portion of the house held a pleasant aroma of coffee and breakfast intermingled with cedar construction. There was also a trace of last night's candles and a wood fire in the air. The living room was spacious and decorated in red cedar, soft hunter green and burgundy fabrics with tasteful brass fixtures and track lighting. A brick fireplace graced one wall. Morning sunlight reflected in from skylights. Several pieces of northwest native art decorated the walls and fireplace mantle.

Mel's neckpieces were represented throughout the house, but in the living room, wood masks and brightly painted carvings were displayed. There was a giant killer whale and raven carving, a bear fetish, a wall hanging featuring several fish and an eagle, masks of a raven and "Hramsem" the trickster, a mosquito mask and a one featuring the winter moon. The most affecting piece of all was a dark mask with red eyes and a fluid outline called "Otter Woman." In Native American lore, Otter Woman could possess people and drive them insane. Also, Native American folklore often held otters in association with the end of the world.

The floor was a polished natural wood. An expansive Native American throw rug covered most of the level, with at least four feet of wood exposed around the circumference of the room. This space kept the carpet out of heavy traffic and provided an excellent area to wander in while enjoying the artwork.

The colors used in the rug were livelier than most earth tones and really enhanced the bold flowing designs parading outward from the center of the carpet. Matching furniture arranged in an open ring faced an entertainment center. A substantial round glass coffee table sat in the middle of this circle.

Jenny placed her book about "Portals" in the center of the coffee table so everyone could get a look at it. For the most part, everyone was more interested in the morning news.

Someone had turned on the wall-mounted wide-screen television. Every news station was covering one story of common interest to the entire planet right now. There was something significant going on in orbit around the planet Mercury. Donovan seemed especially agitated by this subject. They all watched in rapt attention while the President held a news briefing over what was being called "The Mercury Event."

Jenny offered them all some breakfast, as though she owned the place, and there were a few takers for toast and coffee. Mel took this opportunity to put off introducing himself to everyone until after he went back into the bedroom to put on some deck shoes. By the time he emerged, everyone was seated comfortably in the living room. No one spoke until the briefing had ended. As the news moved to another topic, Marla clicked the television off with a remote.

By now, the "Mercury Event" was not news to anyone. Several weeks ago, a metal object appeared in orbit around the planet Mercury. It was a craft or probe of some kind, and scientists could tell that it was scanning the solar system for some unknown purpose. The only cause for alarm, so far, was the fact that it was growing in size. This was significant indeed, and there were no indications as to how it was accomplishing this feat. Some scientists guessed at hyperdimensional physics and the possibility of its drawing substance from outside the confines of our own known universe. Earth scientists were investigating as best they could. It was all preliminary stuff so far. Interest around the room quickly turned to introductions and Jenny's book.

Jenny sat forward in a rocking chair and flipped through the book. She commented on several pictures while everyone listened or nodded in confirmation at some point or another. Mel sat down beside Marla in one of two matching loveseats. He lifted one arm over the back of the chair and accidentally bumped Marla's arm, nearly spilling her coffee. He apologized.

A blond woman on Jenny's right said, "You two have wonderful taste in decor. Everything blends so well."

Mel responded with a nod. "Thank you. Cooperative effort."

An uncomfortable moment passed. Still, Mel had not been introduced to these people, and Marla took the hint.

"Let me introduce you to everyone," she offered.

She indicated the man seated in the recliner on Mel's left. A tall, handsome man with long blond hair pulled back in a ponytail. He wore blue jeans, a dark green flannel shirt, and brown work boots. He had light blue eyes, which regarded Mel in a friendly manner.

"This is Dane Claiborne." She continued. "He is a licensed naturopath, practicing in Lynnwood."

Dane took a sip of coffee and then gave Mel a cordial greeting and asked to speak for himself.

"Actually," he said, "that is more a hobby of mine. I prefer to dabble in the elemental powers of the earth, and how these powers bond with the creatures that live with her. Marla tells me that you are Nez Perce so you can understand a passion for these things."

Mel nodded in agreement.

Dane continued, "As a child, I did enjoy plants and gardening. I still do. Hence, my interest in the healing powers of nature and naturopathy. You should see the greenhouse I built for my youngest sister." He took a deep breath before continuing. "She was twelve when I finished it. Sara was thrilled. She loved it." He lifted a hand in dismissal. "Please forgive my meandering mind just now. Memories of my youth were of much simpler times, and I was an average young man. I enjoy traveling back to them, occasionally…in my mind."

Mel asked him where Sara was now. Dane regretted that she could not join them just yet. Perhaps in time, she would.

Continuing left around the circle, Marla indicated the man that Mel had nearly pressed noses with at the front door. He was seated next to a woman in the other loveseat.

"That's Donovan Diggs, he writes expensive software out of his home…must be nice…and his wife, Lin. She's a reporter for the Times, and her piece about the sculpture in front of the Seattle Art Museum was wonderful."

Mel winced but didn't think anyone noticed.

"They just got married last night. Nice ceremony…simple, though." She glanced over at Jenny and added, "Lin is related to Jen and me. She's a distant cousin."

Lin smiled and took Donovan by the arm. Both Donovan and Lin were middle aged. She was small and curvy, with long thick dark hair and an attractive face. She looked like a cross between Betty Page and Ann Margaret. Her hiking outfit failed to detract from her well-endowed figure. In fact, it accentuated it. By contrast, Donovan wore gear suited to the Australian post-apocalypse science fiction genre. This emphasized his tall, lanky frame, and significantly contributed to the visual contrast between him and his wife. The difference between Donovan's appearance and Lin's kept Mel glancing back and forth between the two, as though he could not believe they were a viable couple.

Moving on, Marla introduced a tall blond woman. Her name was Andrea, and the woman seated next to her on Andrea's left was her twin sister, Carmen. They were both stunning women. The only apparent difference between them was their individual choices in clothing. Andrea preferred blue jeans and pastels, with a soft feminine selection of boot wear.

On the other hand, her sister wore black jeans, heavy boots, a black tank top, and a worn-out blue Levi jacket. Apart from that, they wore their make-up and long, straight, blond hair precisely alike. Mel also became aware of one other odd fact. They resembled the first man he'd met, Dane, right down to the glittering blue eyes.

Marla continued.

"I see you've made the connection. Yes, Dane is their older brother." Andrea and Carmen flashed Mel, a disarming smile.

They spoke in harmony with one another, which was a little weird.

"It's nice to finally meet you, Mel."

Their voices blended beautifully. He imagined tuning forks on crystal glasses.

Jenny was seated next to Carmen, and she picked up the introductions.

"Andrea and Carmen are both anthropologists, although their fields of specialty are vastly different from one another. Andrea goes for earth studies, while Carmen's expertise runs into more classified materials. She works with the government now."

"How do you mean 'classified'?" Mel asked.

"Well, ask her sometime," Carmen interjected.

"I might tease you with a little of it…as much as I can anyway. Why not?"

Mel felt something undeniable crawl up his spine as she spoke. Jenny's little love taps on his nose suddenly came to mind. Odd. Stranger yet, he unexpectedly felt compelled to talk with Carmen, ask her lots of questions, study up on her interests, find out about her on a personal level, carry her equipment, and meditate on her eyes. He felt a little dizzy. He suddenly became aware that he'd been staring at her, and she was looking squarely, and frankly, back at him.

How much time had passed? Marla shook him.

"Hey. Stare, much?"

"Sorry…, I'm really sorry."

Carmen aroused Mel with a sultry smile. She softened the moment with a not-too-terribly-apologetic glance at Marla and said, "We'll talk later, Mel." He felt as though he'd been pulled inside out, and then he realized just what had happened. Carmen had been flirting with him…mentally. Jenny used to have that effect on him. For some reason, his fascination with Jenny was no longer a fixation, but he was now able to recognize what Carmen was doing to him. Live and learn. The thought of engaging in this kind of heavy mental foreplay was staggering, to say the least. Had anyone else in the room noticed it, or was he the only one unaware of it? If Marla did, she didn't seem to care.

Dreamily, Mel now recognized that Jenny was talking about the Claibornes.

"They live further up the coastline in a wonderful old mansion. They've invited us all to visit. Would you like that, Mel?"

"I guess so…yeah, sure."

Jenny continued the introductions with the man seated on her left. His name was Yulan Van Maldergem. Judging by his name, he could have been of Belgian descent. Mel figured that this was the apricot jam guy. He looked to be about the same age as Dane, about thirty. He wore clothing and boots that suited a colder climate. In Mel's opinion, Yulan, because of his choice in clothing, would be the most comfortable among all of them during the outing.

The first detail about Yulan that grabbed Mel's attention were his eyes. They were a disturbing white in color. They suggested blindness, and yet he most certainly could see. Mel thought that perhaps he was an albino, and then dismissed that idea because nothing else about

Yulan would bear that out. He decided that Yulan's eyes must be the result of a birth defect. He was well-tanned and ruggedly built. There was a hint of aristocracy in his face, and his hair was strikingly peppered with premature gray.

Yulan frowned at Mel's shoes and spoke in a questioning, almost rude, tone of voice.

"Please tell me that you are not going to wear those deck shoes into the mountains. Are you prepared with extra clothing for this trip?"

Mel cleared his throat.

"Absolutely."

He felt a little disturbed by the man's demeanor.

Yulan's scowl broke into a broad smile and a hearty laugh. He pointed at Mel.

"You know," he said, "I've been watching you. You're very vulnerable around our women. I must imagine that you are just as open to anyone. You have the delightful quality of trust in you. That's rare these days, and dangerous."

Yulan measured Mel with his eyes, then added, "I should think you will need some amount of protection. I've seen some interesting neck pieces around here, on the walls, but they won't work as well as this."

He fished into his pants pocket, then stood up and leaned across the table while handing Mel an ornate talisman on a leather thong. Mel guessed it to be Celtic in design.

"Here, wear this around your neck…go ahead, put it on now. It should prevent any further distractions." He chuckled and openly gestured at Carmen and Jenny. Yulan's attitude was, at the same time, severe and prankish. He sat back down, leaving Mel, unsure how to take him. Mel studied the necklace and placed it around his neck.

Jenny said, "Yulan is the caretaker at the Claiborne estates, and a great deal more, from what I'm told. He's been living with their family nearly all his life."

Yulan interjected.

"I was a friend of Dane's when we were young men, and when I was orphaned, the Claibornes took me in. I offered to care for the estate," he shrugged, "and they let me."

Mel guessed there was much more to the story than that. This was obvious by the way Yulan interacted like family around the Claibornes. Mel noted the way the twins touched him from time to time, the way a sister might. Mel suspected an intimate relationship somewhere, but he could not pin down where, just yet. Mel remembered that Dane had mentioned another family member, Sara. Perhaps that was the link.

That left one more member of the group to be introduced. He was the most disquieting of the lot. This man was of medium stature and the type of individual that would fail to stand out, even in a small group. His brown hair was combed in a short collegiate hairstyle, and his hiking attire was most likely purchased at some yuppie outdoor store. He bore no distinguishing marks and had a very average Anglo-Saxon facial structure. Mel thought that this guy could quickly disappear moments after you met him, and nobody would notice his absence.

Jenny introduced him almost apologetically.

"I'm afraid I know very little about Ben here." She looked at him and asked, "Sorry, Ben, would you mind introducing yourself?"

He replied with a wink and a boyish smile.

"No, not at all. I'd be glad to." Jenny looked relieved.

As far as any of them knew, Ben was Dane's friend. Yulan appeared to know him as well. Ben was the guy that Mel failed to notice right away on the porch, although Ben and Yulan were engaged in casual banter right in front of him.

Ben cleared his throat. It sounded unnaturally dry and forced, or contrived.

"I'm only here because I own the school bus."

He laughed, which also sounded strange, then added, "Well, I guess that is a trifling lie. Dane did invite me, and I am here with a purpose in mind. The portal expedition, and inviting all of you, was indeed Jenny's idea. She picked individuals that she knew or that corresponded with her father. You may not recognize me right now, Jenny, but I did know your father. In fact, I drew several of the anonymous drawings in that book you brought. These portals are more significant than you know right now, especially with that alien probe out there."

Jenny cast a questioning look at Dane, who was taking all of this in with the kind of disquieting composure one came to expect from Dane.

Ben gestured around the room.

"Except you, Mel, I think everyone here knows me at least by reputation."

Everyone was looking at Ben with some questioning discomfort. Now that they thought about it, he did look familiar…but didn't guys that look like him always look familiar?

Ben continued.

"I apologize for being so antisocial on the way up here. I guess you could say that I'm not feeling very comfortable in my own skin right now."

He smiled at some private thought, and absently slid his gaze over one of the art pieces on the wall. It was the dark mask with red painted eyes and fluid features.

"Except Dane," he continued. "I've never formally met any of you, although I do get around a lot."

He paused, seemingly for effect.

"I'm also known as Specter."

The reaction in the group was immediate.

There was a sharp intake of breath as all the women reacted with alarm. Lin began poking Donovan, and saying, "See, I told you he's not a myth."

The Claiborne twins stared at Ben in mute disbelief.

Yulan stood up and quickly urged Marla out onto the porch with him. Mel watched in stunned fascination while Yulan shut the doors behind them and then began some kind of animated lecture while repeatedly pointing at her and occasionally at Mel.

Dane sighed. He sat up in the recliner, leaned forward, and then whispered to Mel.

"Better leave the house until this is sorted out. I knew this would happen." Mel looked at Ben, then back at Dane. He shook his head in disgust, then pushed himself out of the chair. Now seemed a great time to investigate the bus.

***

An hour passed until one of the visitors came out to find Mel sitting on a large rock on the other side of the bus. It was Carmen's twin, Andrea. She motioned to him to move over a little so she could sit down.

Mel remained silent and more than a little upset.

Andrea said nothing for a minute, listening to the wind, and then spoke.

"Dane should have told us that Specter was here, for your sake… if nothing else. Pureblooded humans are not supposed to know he exists, on Earth, at all. We would have found a way to keep you insulated. Sometimes, Specter is perverse. He did not have to divulge himself with you in the room. He may now try to kill you. I can't be sure."

Mel jumped to his feet and twisted his foot on a rock, throwing himself off balance. He barely noticed the pain.

"What in God's name do you mean by that!" He felt nauseated. "Kill me for what?"

She explained, "For knowing of his existence."

Mel buried his face in his hands, then shook his head, moaned, and looked over at the trees. He imagined Ben hiding behind one of them, aiming a forty-five straight at his head. This was crazy.

"You mean to tell me that I am not supposed to know that Mr. Ordinary is alive and walking the earth? Come on, Andrea. You'd better do better than that!"

"He came through one of those portals, over a thousand years ago, or so they say. He was the first of his kind, from the enemy race, the Varr. They're the ancient enemies of the race of beings called the Megal that have coexisted with us on Earth for thousands of years. Didn't Jenny or Marla tell you any of this."

Mel just shook his head. He couldn't quite get the words out. Andrea's voice was compassionate, as usual.

"Specter is a traitor to his own race. He swore to see the military arm of his people die during the coming invasion while crossing between portals…and there definitely will be an invasion. He believes the probe is part of the first wave."

Mel shifted his feet and staggered again, then fixed her with a glare.

"Why are you telling me this?" Waving his arm toward the house, he continued. "You people are all deranged. Why am I even listening to all of this cult crap?"

"Please, sit down and listen to me, Mel." Reluctantly, he sat back down.

"Dane just now explained it all to us, while he had you waiting out here. Dane and Specter are together on this, although Specter has his own agenda and no loyalties except to his own vengeance. I don't even think Dane trusts him completely. If you live past the next hour, it's a safe assumption that you will learn all you need to know."

She looked thoughtful a moment, then added, "I think he needs you, that is, Specter needs you."

"Why?"

"Just an educated guess, but I think it has something to do with being genetically pure. He mentioned something about needing someone he can trust, with untainted blood. Jenny just now vouched for you. She said she knew you were of pure blood the moment she met you."

He covered his face in his hands again and muttered something she couldn't hear, although it sounded like "Thanks, Jenny."

He looked up at her.

Mel said, "For a year this whole thing has felt like some kind of cult joke to me. I don't know what came over me after meeting Jenny."

He pondered a moment.

"Strange. Today I felt free of it for the first time in a year, and then with

Carmen…I…I don't know, I just…"

He let his words trail off into nothing. He was staring at the treetops when Andrea placed her hand on his shoulder and excused herself to go back inside.

Mel sat alone in sad contemplation.

About five minutes later, his skin started to itch for some reason. The air felt suddenly charged with static electricity. He sat looking around for an explanation when the silence was broken by the sound of the front door opening and then closing.

Mel nearly died on the spot when Specter casually walked out the front door and started in his direction. There was a buzzing sound, and simultaneously, the itching increased horribly. Specter appeared to float rather than walk toward him, and then he altered in shape briefly, into something black and amorphous. For a moment, he glimpsed Specter's eyes as glowing hot and red. They tracked in the air from side to side as he moved, like time-lapse photography. Mel blinked away what seemed like a brief illusion, and then Ben, Specter, was standing right in front of him.

Mel started to get up when Specter motioned with his hand to remain seated. He knelt down in front of Mel, looking like a thirty-something out of-uniform boy scout. When he spoke, Mel could sense a controlled guise in his voice. At least the itching had stopped.

"Mel?"

"What."

"Andrea has told you all you really should know right now. Please try to not fear me. If you help me, when the time is right, you will be rewarded. You have my word."

Mel wasn't comforted or fooled by Specter's calm tone of voice.

He knew that if Andrea was right, then, Specter was placating him, for his own reasons.

Mel felt his own defiance stiffen in his voice.

"How come none of the others knew you were Specter?"

Specter made a noise like a sigh, but Mel couldn't see his chest, shoulders, or neck move. In fact, Specter did not look as though he genuinely breathed at all.

"Dane knew me to be Specter, but none of the others did. That was by my own choice really, although I think Yulan more than suspected. I would have been surprised if he hadn't."

He paused to gauge how Mel was reacting, then added, "Now this trip takes on a whole new meaning."

Specter stood and asked, "Do you agree?"

"Do I have a choice?"

"Only one other."

Specter brightened suddenly. He clapped his hands and then rubbed them together. All of a sudden, he'd taken on the air of a man that's ready for a backyard barbecue. He walked back to the house with a bounce in his step. It was surreal. He called out over his shoulder, without looking back.

"What do you say we get on the road, huh?"

***

Mel drove the Suburban with Marla beside him. Jenny rode in the back seat next to Donovan and Lin. Jenny held the directions to the Rainier portal. Specter's bus followed behind Mel with Yulan and the twins as uneasy passengers. Dane alone seemed comfortable seated behind Specter.

It was decided that turns would be taken riding with Mel. It was in Specter's best interest for Mel to get to know all of the key players. He encouraged them all to become better acquainted with Mel. Specter had his reasons for this. Right now, it was Donovan and Lin's turn to share a story with Mel. Why was Specter confident that those two would open up to Mel? Because Specter knew how talkative Donovan could be. In the thousand plus years that Specter had walked the Earth, he'd met individuals like Donovan Diggs before. If given the opportunity, and a little encouragement, Donovan would gladly unload his story on Mel. He almost wished he could hear it himself.

OBE (Donovan's story)

At two in the morning, on the Saturday before his meeting at Mel and Marla's place for the trip to Rainier, Donovan Diggs left his body for the most critical OBE of his life. Out of body experiences occurred for him without forethought nearly every time he so much as dozed off. As one might imagine, this was both a blessing and a curse. He also had the power to enter and ride another being's mind…to see, hear, taste, and feel what that individual was experiencing. He might even share their thoughts, although he determined early on not to reveal himself, if possible.

He learned the secret behind his talent through the minds of beings, not of this earth, creatures that called themselves "Megal." He was what they referred to as a "Changeling," or, those human beings that resulted from extraterrestrial experiments in recombinant DNA. The Megal knew he was observing them and did not mind, so they spoke to him. Because of this, he discovered the truth behind the myths of monsters and magic.

Most of those phenomena were directly the result of cross-breeding between the inhabitants of two hyperdimensional realms, and two wildly different sets of physics. In the nineties, research in theoretical physics began to postulate on the possible existence of such things. Donovan's gift came as the result of sub-cellular, transdimensional manipulation. In other words, Donovan was an "abductee" and the product of alien experimentation. He could clearly remember being taken from his bed as a child and subjected to careful study before being injected through his chest with a syringe full of brown fluid.

Donovan's most satisfying experiences out-of-body were strictly ethereal. This night he decided to soar above Earth for a better look at what famous astronomers recently dubbed "The Mercury Event." This was not so much an event as an object of considerable size that had parked itself in orbit around the planet Mercury. It materialized, rather than arrived, only two weeks ago. He sped through space well beyond the speed of light until Mercury loomed in front of him. Not far from him was an asymmetrical body of unknown metal that appeared to be reshaping itself while he watched.

It was seamlessly unfolding from within itself, drawing from an extra-dimensional source or from a tremendously condensed nucleus. He studied it for some time, from several angles, when without any warning a beam of light shot out at him from the object. The light carried a message within it of distinct patterns, which formed and reformed within his mind. Harmonic resonance followed. He felt it rather than so much as heard it. He knew he had been located, and they were...

"...focusing on me," Donovan muttered to himself as he fell back into his physical body and sat straight up in bed. It was four in the morning.

"Can't let them focus on me."

What he'd seen and felt stunned him. That object was an entity of some kind, a living spacecraft, and it was the source of the probe that he and others like him had felt passing through the Earth at regular intervals over the last several days. He needed to hide from them... he knew this...and toward that end, he decided to completely wrap his suburbia home with insulated wire.

*****

Donovan paced in his home waiting for the stores to open in town. He spent the remainder of that day locating large industrial size spools of insulated wire, which he then purchased from several vendors so that he would not have to deal with questions about what he was going to do with so much wire. When he returned home, he started winding the cord around his home. The next morning, he scoured a twenty-mile radius for dead animal carcasses. He returned home with a small Chevy pickup load covered with flies, and worse, with which he cautiously decorated the doorframe around his front door and along the porch railing. He lifted the carcasses up and onto the wire by hanging them on coat hangers. By noon that same day, Donovan stood in his driveway wavering with exhaustion.

While in town, he purchased an outfit he felt might work to confuse "them" into believing he was someone else, so "they" might not be able to "focus" on him. He was now wearing an old leather flight helmet, and he rubbed dust from off the thick goggles he chose to wear. Donovan was dressed in the only manner that now made him feel safe. As he perceived it, this was vitally important for his survival. Under the circumstances, he needed to be satisfactorily out of character.

He stood with his fists on his hips while critically surveying his creation. His well-kept colonial style home was neatly tucked away within a dense stand of evergreens. Built several years before, it was comfortable and isolated.

The whole of his property was developed after the style of homes preferred in the Deep South. Donovan was a devout student of the Civil War era, and he collected all sorts of Civil War memorabilia. His home embodied a unique blend of southern charm and gracious living. Anyone visiting Donovan at home inevitably felt a deliberate sense of history all about the place. He was very proud of the effect it had on guests.

From outside, this showcase home now resembled an electrician's nightmare. He'd managed to wind the wire three times around his house, and even coiled some around the porch railing. Donovan thought he still had so much yet to do and so little time to do it in. From now on he thought sleep would be out of the question until he'd finished insulating and disguising his home. He repeatedly muttered to himself, "Can't let them focus---don't let them focus---on me."

Despite discrete precautions, Donovan's privacy crumbled to the prying eyes of birds, circling in the heat of the mid-day sun. Donovan became aware of them and realized what new measures must be taken. He raced up the porch and into the house. Some wire above the doorframe had slipped, and the body of a dead raccoon now hung down too low. To enter the front door, he had to lift the tail of the dead raccoon out of the way. Soon he emerged with several rolls of plastic wrap from the kitchen pantry. He immediately set about on the apparent mission of wrapping the animal carcasses with it. He was frustrated by not having enough to do the job correctly.

Somewhere in the back of his mind, Donovan registered the approach of an automobile. He dismissed it with a shake of his head and concentrated on staying awake. He decided to pause in his labors long enough to get another quick look at the place from the driveway. He put down the roll he had in his hands and backed down the front steps, all the while staring up at the birds and watching for dive-bombers.

"Gotta do this right. Can't let them focus."

The soft sound of footsteps from behind caused him to spin around and stumble. He collapsed onto the driveway. Thoroughly embarrassed, he glared accusingly at the woman that had crept up from behind him.

"Do I have to put up signs!" he shouted. "What do I have to do to keep a little privacy for myself?"

The woman was shocked, her eyes flitting back and forth between Donovan and the gruesome fruits of his labor.

"Dono, I'm your fiancé for God's sake!" Shaken by the sight, she cried in alarm, "Remember me? I'm the woman you're marrying in a few days. What have you done to this place?" She looked him over. "Look at you! What have you done to yourself…and what are you wearing?" She was angry, disgusted, and confused. "I fly out to visit my mother for a week and return home to this?"

Donovan remained kneeling on the pavement. She bent to help him stand and found herself deeply disturbed by the distracted distance in his eyes. He glanced over his shoulder at the house and wagged his head with dissatisfaction. He accepted her help in standing and then dusted himself off before stumbling toward the front porch.

Lin followed him.

"Donovan slow down, you're going to fall again!"

His reply was so quiet it was nearly drowned out by the sound of birds, and a few cats, making noises of interest over his home's decor.

"Sorry, Lin. I love you, but I can't stop now. I'm not finished."

Lin caught up to him and helped him recover from another stumble.

"Not finished with what? Destroying our home? What's wrong with you?" The front door was still partially blocked by the raccoon's body. Donovan tenderly shook off Lin's support and then opened the door while lifting the raccoon out of the way. As he entered, Lin heard Donovan whisper, "Not finished---needs more work---don't let them focus on me."

Lin followed him into the house and covered her nose and mouth with her hand while carefully avoiding the raccoon.

"Who's focusing on you? What is that supposed to mean?"

***

All of that day and into the next Lin felt wholly helpless and disoriented by Donovan's deteriorating frame of mind. He would babble incoherently about dreams he'd experienced for years but especially about the ones he had since the Sunday Lin had left for Minnesota.

He called the power company and canceled the electrical service. Lin overheard the phone call and took him by the arm as he hung up the phone. She was more distressed than angry.

"What did you need to do that for?"

Donovan did not hear the question because he was already set to lecture her again. He said, "I know why I've always been able to read people's minds and sometimes predict the future. Did I tell you that I once tried to levitate a pencil?" He chuckled to himself and shook his head, then threw himself into more frenzied activity. He added, "That probably won't mean so much to you since you can lift small objects with your mind anytime you want."

He began unplugging all of the lamps in the living room. "Got to do this to everything in the house. Don't just stand there, give me a hand."

Lin ran up to him and took him by the shoulders. She shook him and raised her voice, hoping to be heard above his delirium.

"I can't take this anymore, Donovan! I should have called someone to help you when I saw you in the driveway. I can't stand the intolerable stench of all those dead animals any longer." She grimaced. "Speaking of smell, how long has it been since you've had a bath and a shave?" She hesitated only a moment. "What were you doing with all that cellophane? You weren't going to do what you looked like you were going to do, were you? I mean, wrap the front porch up in it?"

He straightened and gently removed her hands from his shoulders. When he spoke, it was in that insufferably superior tone of voice that Lin had come to hate in the last couple of days.

"Yes, I was, and I am sorry I let you stop me, Lin. The cellophane was to protect our home from intrusion, not to mention the smell. For all, I know, birds and animals can become messengers for the enemy. We have to do whatever we can to avoid allowing the enemy race to focus on me. I've figured out what they want with the human race, and now they'll come for me so I won't tell the world where they are and what they're planning do to s-o -o-o m-a-a-n-y people."

Lin backed away from him. She started for the front door, fuming and disgusted.

"Bullshit…you've never acted this way before, and besides, if you really felt this way, you should have used your gift and sought out Specter's help. Maybe he, or she for all I know could have helped you sort this out. I think your gift has driven you right off the edge. Remember what that old woman said at the convention last year?" Not waiting for a reply, she went on: "She said that there was a profound disturbance in your aura."

Donovan shouted back, "Specter is a myth, Lin. You might as well ask me to consult with Santa Claus." He added, "As for that old woman…that was all drivel, and you know it!"

She opened the front door and gagged at the sight of the dead raccoon as it swung toward her from the suction caused by the opening door. Grabbing her mouth to stifle her gag reflex, she ducked under it on her way out. She didn't bother to close the door.

"I'm leaving, Donovan, but I'll be back soon. I can't deal with this. I'm bringing someone out to help you. Please promise to stay here until I get back."

Donovan dropped to his knees in the middle of the room, sobbing.

"No, please, don't. Don't betray me. Please don't go. Just let me finish up here, then everything will be fine…I think."

"Bye, Donovan, I'll be back soon. Don't worry."

Donovan looked up at the ceiling and said, "I've wasted too much time, and there's still so much to do."

After he heard her car leave the driveway, he sullenly wandered into the kitchen. He took a potpie out of the freezer to thaw. He'd have to eat the pie cold…no electricity.

Three hours later Donovan muttered in self-contentment. He felt he was on the road to the successful completion of his project. He disobeyed Lin's request, drove into town and bought as many television antennae as he could fit into the back of his Chevy pick-up. On the way back, he watched the sky for birds while listening to the radio for any news that would confirm his visions.

He felt certain that eventually, Lin would understand. He only wished he hadn't listened to her about the cellophane. He dressed in the warmest clothes he could find and then spent all night mounting antennae all over his home. He then carefully hung magnets from them. Loss of sleep was a necessary price to pay. He even went so far as to erect a few inside—for good measure.

***

Sunrise found him asleep on the roof, curled around one of the more giant antennae. He was awakened by the sound of crunching gravel and the diesel purr of Lin's Mercedes. Donovan carefully stood up while Lin climbed out of the driver's side. A hesitant young man in a business suit emerged from the passenger side.

"Dono, you remember Doctor Anthony Tool? He's here to help you." Donovan shivered among the antennae before stabilizing with a reply.

"I remember you from a convention. Tony, am I right?"

Tool shrugged. "You can call me Tony if you wish."

Donovan waved him up. "Climb up here, and we'll talk. It's vital that someone hears what I have to say before hell decides to vacation on our beautiful world."

Lin moved to the front of the car, but before she could say anything, Donovan spoke again.

"Stop where you are, Lin, you brought him into this. Let him be the hero. Besides, I wouldn't want you to fall."

Doctor Tool shifted his weight nervously. He'd been scanning the house with professional interest, but now his eyes were fastened on Donovan. He cleared his throat.

"Mister Diggs. May I call you, Donovan?"

"Suit yourself."

"You do understand that I really have no intention of climbing up there with you, don't you? Why don't we all go inside where we can be comfortable. Lin has told me a great deal about you already. You seem to have a lot on your mind so this could take some time."

Donovan raised his eyes and smiled while shaking his head.

"I like it up here. In fact, I believe I'll stay up here for a while. It doesn't matter."

Donovan stared at the sky and treetops as though he expected more company.

"I had another dream last night…more revealing than any I've had before. The final piece in a puzzle I've been fighting all my life. I thought I could hide if I surrounded myself in dreamscape images while disconnecting myself from the world. I had hoped to dispel the forces within me, cutting myself off from what I fear the most. I can feel their eyes on me."

Tool appeared more at ease with the situation, and he visibly relaxed the more Donovan spoke. Delirium was quantifiable.

"Donovan, Lin and I want to believe you. Can you be more specific?" Donovan lowered his eyes regarding the doctor with pity.

"I'm now painfully aware of the fact that I've been crazy and out of control for the last several days, but I've snapped out of it, more or less. Lin wants to understand, I believe that, but you don't really give a shit. Do you?" Shaking his head in disapproval, he continued. "Don't try your pathetic psychology on me, doctor. The only reason I have for telling you anything is because it makes little difference if I do or don't. Our real enemy has planted a seed near the heart of our solar system."

Lin interrupted.

"Dono, it's cold out here, and my neck is going to get stiff if you insist on a running a narrative from the roof. Meet us in the living room. We're going inside. Come in, doctor. I wish I could offer you some coffee, but I believe the electricity has been turned off."

Donovan shrugged his shoulders and replied, "Yeah, all right. I'll be right down."

By the time Donovan entered the living room, Lin had all the windows open. Morning sunlight flooded the room. Doctor Tool had settled into a rocking chair and was studying Donovan over crossed arms.

Donovan remarked on the doctor's relaxed composure.

"I see the doctor has made himself right at home. Lin, I apologize for the electricity. I'm glad I didn't disconnect the phone. I'll call and have the power turned back on if you like."

"Later, sweetheart. Right now, all I care about is you. Sit down and tell us what this is all about, and please don't talk in riddles."

Donovan settled into his favorite overstuffed chair. Lin sat on the sofa with her legs tucked under her as if she were a young girl about to hear a bedtime story. Only the worried expression on her face belied that impression.

"As you already know, Lin and I are the products of an experiment. In my case, I was taken from my bed as a child and altered in some way that gave me my special talents."

Again, Donovan's mind flashed back to memories of alien examination rooms, invasive procedures performed on him, and a hypodermic syringe filling his body with a brownish fluid.

He continued.

"I can't think of it as 'alien' abduction because the creatures responsible have been with us on our world for countless centuries. Are they aliens, or do we consider them resident immigrants?" Donovan hesitated a moment before going on. "They watch their experiments as closely as any of our scientists would, but as far as I can tell, they have little interest in us apart from what they can learn through manipulation."

Doctor Tool cleared his throat.

"We understand this, but what of your current state of mind?"

"You haven't been listening! I told you that I have dreams, and not the kind of dreams you're used to, doctor. For that matter, they are more like out-of-body experiences than dreams. I go to places and see things through other people. I could write volumes about other individuals as though I vicariously lived their lives myself. I travel without a body, like mist, a creature from myth, capable of assuming any form. Perhaps I can assume any form, but it would seem more likely that I project myself rather than transform, because I awakened in the same spot in which I fell asleep. I've been traveling the earth in that manner since the time I was altered as a child, learning and collating what I've seen, heard, and felt through the minds of others. I've learned a great deal through the mind of a man by the name of Dane Claiborne. He and his family live a few miles from here. I'm sure I could find his place if I look, but I'm afraid to try. However, I would not be a bit surprised if he chose to track me down."

Tool cleared his throat and shifted uncomfortably. He'd been doing that a lot since coming into the house.

"Lin and I are interested in hearing more about this man Dane Claiborne. If you'd like t..."

Donovan interrupted.

"Forget Dane! Soon everything I've just told you will seem insignificant and stop speaking for Lin?"

Lin got up, crossed over to Donovan's chair, and sat on an armrest.

She placed a hand on his shoulder.

"Dono...it's all right. Just tell us the bottom line."

Donovan turned his tired eyes toward her, then back toward the doctor. He sighed.

"For the last week, a psychic ripple has been passing through all of the sensitives on this planet. I believe the immigrant alien race, the Megal, has a great enemy pursuing them, perhaps in another dimension. That's about all I've been able to piece together. I do know this, that enemy race knows about what the aliens have accomplished here through generations of experimentation, and they covet the results. Their war has caught up to us." Tool was sitting on the edge of his chair, wild-eyed with interest. When he spoke, it was as though he'd caught a portion of Donovan's delirium with his own mind. He looked as though he wanted to stand for emphasis.

"It's true. You must be referring to the 'Mercury Event.' I've heard something about it on the news. There is something out there, growing to moon-sized proportions, in orbit around Mercury just as you said. It appears to be circling the planet Mercury while increasing its size. There's some kind of bluish glow around it. No one knows for sure where it is getting the raw materials to grow in size the way it is. The only thing anyone can determine is that it is a machine of some kind, and unmanned...as far as they can tell. A crewed mission to investigate is out of the question right now due to logistics and financing."

Tool's eyes moved to the window, and he seemed lost in thought for a moment.

Donovan was about to speak when Tool continued. "There are rumors," he said, "at the conventions, about a powerful man they call Specter. Some say he is not human or even one of our alien relatives. They say he is one of the enemies, in disguise, and walks among us for some evil purpose we will not know until it is too late to do anything about it. They say that he's a shape-shifter."

Tool became irritated and waved his hands in front of himself in dismissal, then continued. "Have you heard of Specter?"

Donovan nodded.

"Lin mentioned something about Specter, although I'd never heard anything much myself, and nothing in my dreams."

Tool pursued the issue.

"OK, so you don't believe in Specter, but certainly you cannot be ignorant about the object in space. It's all anyone is talking about. At the very least, you must have heard some of this while you were in town buying antennas for y..."

"I don't give a damn what you think about all this, doctor! I will tell you what I suspect, and then you might as well leave because we're all going to find out the truth sooner than later."

Tool raised his hands again, in resignation, and sat back in his chair.

"I apologize for offending you. Please, I'd like to hear more."

"Fine, …but, you won't believe me. Not now, anyway." There was an uncomfortable silence before he resumed.

"I believe that thing out there is a probe, and it's analyzing our solar system. I don't think its interests are limited to our world alone. Its eye penetrates the Earth and then moves on, scanning everything, including the sun. Do you remember that psychic ripple I mentioned before? Each time the Earth is in its focus, sensitives the world over feel its violation like a spiritual rape. No doubt the 'crackpots' have been coming out of the woodwork lately. Am I right?"

Silence.

"I thought so."

Donovan leaned forward, fixing the doctor with a cold stare.

"Call it an insightful hunch, doctor, call it insanity if you like, but I believe that thing is somehow thinning the walls between worlds."

Lin and Tool exchanged an uneasy glance.

She apologized and excused herself on nature's behalf. Donovan relaxed a little. After she'd left the room, he fixed Dr. Tool with a calculating eye and spoke softly.

"Please don't take what I'm about to say as an affirmation that Donovan Diggs might have been out of his mind. I've already admitted to being crazy as a June bug the last few days. Just listen to what I have to say, and try to keep an open mind."

Donovan hesitated again before continuing. His eyes nervously scanned the room while following a twitch in his nose, as though he was searching for some new fragrance. By the time he resumed his train of thought, the doctor had begun to suspect that Donovan had slipped into a paranoid stupor.

"Insanity does not cause isolation; it presents you with a host of new friends."

Tool snapped out of his fascination long enough to feel disoriented by

Donovan's last statement. His professional veneer had irrevocably cracked. He faltered when he spoke.

"That sounds a bit, well, what I mean to say is that…what you just said sounds a little…"

Donovan launched himself from the chair and stood glaring down at Dr. Tool.

"Paranoid. That's what you were about to say, wasn't it?"

Tool cowered while Donovan quivered above him. Lin burst into the room.

"Dono, stop it!"

She ran over to him, not knowing what she intended to do next.

Donovan pushed her away and lanced her with an icy stare before demanding, "What do you want…to have me committed? Love hasn't a clue, does it? And neither do you."

Donovan forced his way past Lin on his way to the front door. He then spun on his heels long enough to make one last declaration.

"When the eye of death passes over us for the last time, the reality we've come to expect will be undone."

Lin moved to take Donovan by his hands. Donovan avoided her by opening the front door and moving onto the porch.

"I might as well go to find Dane before he comes looking for me. I don't know what it will accomplish, but I feel compelled, nonetheless. I don't know when I'll be back."

Donovan stopped and turned. He suddenly felt weak. His eyes fastened on the woman he'd fallen in love with. He returned to Lin and embraced her. She hesitated a moment before placing her arms around him. There were tears in both of their eyes.

"Lin, I've been putting you through hell, and I'm sorry for that."

He gently pulled away from her and reached for the raccoon above the door. There was a bird perched on its head, pecking at one of its eyes. Donovan grabbed the roadkill by its tail and yanked it down. The bird flew off in disappointment—only to return to it the moment after it landed in the bushes. Donovan left the porch and moved to the driver's door of his pickup.

He hesitated before opening it.

"You'll understand everything all too soon. I'll be back for you when it all begins. Please stay here and wait for me."

Lin ran after him.

"Oh no, you don't, I'm coming with you. Besides, we're getting married at the convention. Remember?"

Donovan watched Lin pull open the passenger door and climb in. He shrugged and smiled. Donovan picked up the cellular phone while they closed the doors.

"I just remembered something. I've got to call Jenny. She's supposed to be on her way out here within the week. I'd like to remind her to bring me some things her father left to me in his will."

She brightened. "Can I talk to her when you're done?"

"Sure, she's your cousin."

He started the engine. Lin spotted Tool, now standing on the porch with his hands held in a where do you think you're going gesture. She motioned to Donovan to wait a minute, then climbed out of the truck's cab long enough to throw her keys to the doctor.

"Go ahead and take it. I'll get it later, and thanks."

He deftly caught the keys, then smiled, and waved goodbye.

She turned back to Donovan, frowned, and then held his gaze as she indicated the front porch with a wave of her hand.

"OK, now, come on, why the dead animals?" Donovan shrugged.

"Why not?"

Doubts and Dreams

Mel and Specter drove through Buckley, on Highway 410. It was almost noon, and they were ready for a break. They decided to press on to the next town before stopping for lunch.

In Mel's suburban, all during the trip, there were the usual family bulletins to discuss. Jenny's father left his entire library on the subject of dreaming to Donovan, although he'd have to take delivery by truck because this included a great deal of reading material and charts. Lin was enthralled while listening to Jenny's account of her father's recent studies on the topic of dreams. Donovan heard most of what Jenny said, but kept nodding off to sleep.

Specter's bus didn't enjoy any light-hearted banter between the house and their lunch stop. There was also a last minute check on supplies. This stop would be the last place to buy anything they might have forgotten. The twins sorted through seismic and photographic equipment. Dane and Yulan took inventory of items with less apparent purposes. These included objects and mechanisms mostly made of copper. Dane also inspected a fascinating collection of live bugs; beetles to be exact, of varying sizes, shape, and color. There were tools for measuring electrical activity, for excavation, and clearing underbrush—such as knives, pickaxes, machetes, and a couple of chainsaws.

There was plenty of food and adequate beverages. They had already established that the Suburban would not carry provisions, so it appeared that all was well in hand.

At one point, Donovan startled everyone in the Suburban by jolting awake from a dream. He hastily pushed his flight helmet up and out of his eyes, then frantically glanced back at Specter who glared back at him from several car lengths away through the windshield of the bus. In the bus, Yulan, Dane and the twins heard Specter mutter under his breath, "Never go there again," and then watched as Donovan freaked out and ducked down behind the back seat of the Suburban.

What had just happened? As far as the others were concerned, no explanation could be forthcoming, and none felt the need to ask. Apparently, Donovan saw something in his sleep that Specter did not appreciate. After that, there was a lull in all conversation, in both vehicles, until they arrived at Wilkeson, a mining town nestled in the Cascade foothills. Mel slowed the Suburban, then pulled off onto the gravel and dirt shoulder just outside of town. He got out and walked back to the bus to confer with Specter. They both agreed to stop at a little diner on the Mt. Rainier side of town.

When they reached the diner, Mel parked and stepped out of the Suburban. Neither the road dust nor the gas exhaust fumes could hide the refreshing scent of evergreens and a hint of the summer's wild blackberries. He also detected the charred smell of overcooked hamburgers. He stretched and breathed deeply, then scanned the sky with a hand over his eyes.

"Oh yeah," he exulted. "What a beautiful day this is." He heard footsteps beside him. It was Dane.

"Hey, Mel looks like there was a grill fire inside. They're airing the place out. Let's give 'em about twenty minutes or so before we go in."

"Sounds good to me," Mel agreed.

Dane nodded and then wandered over to a tree under which Specter was speaking with the twins. Yulan was on his way over there as well. Mel suddenly felt left out, but then he noticed Donovan standing alone on the restaurant porch. His hands were cupped around his face, and he was peering into one of the restaurant windows. Mel watched him for about a minute. Donovan put his hands down, stepped away from the window, and turned to look at the group gathering under the tree. Something none-too-subtle and troubling crossed Donovan's face. Specter waved Donovan over to join them under the tree, but Donovan only frowned and declined, by shaking his head. What was bothering Donovan?

Marla and Jenny thought Mel looked a little lonely. He was still contemplating Donovan when they stepped up next to him. He turned his attention toward them.

Jenny smiled and waved to Donovan, who sullenly waved back. She quietly remarked at how odd he was acting, and then told Mel, "Specter wants everyone to call him Ben when we're in public."

Marla interjected, "By the way, back at the house he urged us all to share as much of our background with you as we wanted before we get to the portal site. He said he has plans for you, and that you should get to know the group as quickly as possible. He also said something weird about how important you may be to the entire world…or something like that, and that we should get our requests in while we can. He has a creepy sense of humor, and I don't think I like him at all. I wonder what he meant by all that."

She remembered Mel's few moments alone with Specter in the driveway and asked, "Did he explain much to you?"

Mel shrugged, and said, "No."

Marla studied Mel's face for a moment but didn't find any hidden answers. Then she added, "I guess we'll find out soon enough, huh?"

Jenny touched Mel's shoulder. She had a playful expression on her face.

"Hey, I've got an idea. Let's play some games while we wait." She called out to Lin.

Lin was busy chatting like an old friend with a young mother and son who sat on a bench waiting to go inside. The boy was playing in the gravel with a couple of toy tanker trucks. Lin looked the part of a friendly Midwestern neighbor, ready to invite the other woman over for coffee and rolls. When she saw Jenny waving her over, she excused herself from her new friends and joined Mel, Jenny, and Marla. Jenny asked Mel if he had anything light in his pockets.

"Like what?" he asked.

"Anything. A pen, a coin, anything."

"Well, here's a quarter."

"Perfect!"

Lin stood next to Jenny, and she knew what Jen had in mind. When Jenny handed her the coin, she handed it back to her with a confident smirk.

"No, thanks, Jen. That's kid stuff. I'm beyond that now." Jenny was delighted.

"Really? What can you do?"

"Well, let's see."

Lin looked past Marla and caught a glimpse of two teenage boys playing Frisbee dangerously close to the road.

"OK," she said. "Watch this."

The boys were just goofing around. Neither of them was any good with the Frisbee. When the Frisbee skidded to a halt just in front of one of the boys, Lin went to work on it. She concentrated on the Frisbee; it then shot straight up into the air and eventually disappeared into the blue. The teenagers were not stupid enough to write it off as wind and knew something unnatural had just happened. They were more curious than pissed off. They looked over and saw Lin with her hands held palms up. She was looking up into the sky, and something bright kept flashing from her eyes. Inquisitiveness got the better of them.

Lin lowered her eyes and watched them walk over to her. When they asked her how she'd done that, she lifted her hands again, only this time with an innocent look on her face. She was enjoying this. She mischievously explained with a smile that she'd been injected with alien DNA. They didn't laugh, but they did roll their eyes and shook their heads before shuffling off down the street.

Mel was amazed.

"Levitation?" he asked.

"No," she explained. "It's more like energy and matter manipulation, by a sort of mental request. I essentially told the air to carry it away. Something in me was altered, and I'm getting better at knowing how to use the new me. That's all. It's not so much that physics are up for grabs, just redefinition. Tell me, after what you've just seen who decides what is natural and what isn't?"

Marla agreed with Lin's explanation of what was happening to a lot of people, like her, that were abducted for Megal experimentation. She added,

"Specter says that's why the Varr want this world. The combinations of Megal and human DNA have brought wonderfully unexpected results. He says the Megal call them 'Changelings,' and that they operate within redefined laws of nature and hyperspace … having talents that differ, not unlike our own personalities. A recent school of physics proposed a simplified, more elegant, theory for hyperdimensional reality called the superstring theory. Boiled down, it equates to vibration, or as some say, 'movement and repose.'"

Marla paused in front of a frustrating thought and then frowned with a pout before explaining that she hadn't noticed any powers in herself. Lin replied that she would when the time was right. She further told that she found the secret of tapping her own abilities by going within her intuitive self and not the cognitive.

Mel listened carefully to everything these women said. Every one of these women amazed him with their understanding of abstract concepts. He was learning things that fit right in with what he understood from his own Native American beliefs. The last thing Lin mentioned stuck with him and popped unbidden into his mind from time to time, like a whispered voice, that part about her intuitive self.

*****

Specter conferred with his group about what he planned to do once they got to the portal site. There were three sites to choose from in the western United States. However, it did not matter which portal they chose, because they were all linked.

The Varr had recently started tracking the movements of the Megal here on this world through the object they planted in the solar system. Its scanning and tracking abilities increased every time it enlarged itself. Dane guessed that it might be possible to destroy the probe, but Specter doubted that possibility. Besides, even if they did succeed in destroying the probe, it would only result in a temporary setback for the Varr. They would come back, more formidable to be sure. However, he did not rule the idea out.

Specter's plan was based on his knowledge of how the Varr used probes like this one to manipulate time and space, given that this one was like the ones he remembered. For some reason, understood only to Specter, his homeworld cut him off after he became a perceived security threat. It was possible that the millennial delay before the invasion was due to the development of new invasive techniques.

He really had no idea what new technologies they might now possess. That alone worried him. What if this was not a probe? Before he left his homeworld on assignment to this place, he heard rumors from one or two Varr research and development teams of a new drive system that would be capable of warping more than time and space—much more. The new designs were said to provide a tap into the void, or "ether," between worlds and allow artificial manipulation of hyperdimensional space. If this was a resulting design from one of those Varr research and development groups, Specter suspected that anything could happen. They'd have to take things as they came.

He knew how to disable and shut down a simple pre-invasion probe. The Changelings would have to secure this side of the portal as best they could. Yulan asked him about the other portals. Specter explained that once he went through with Mel, all of the Varr would rush to the portal through which they entered. Those on this side would have to do their best in dealing with the Varr that came through, at least until he accomplished what needed to be done on that end. Again, he would not explain in detail the subject of how Mel fit into his plans. He did not want any such information to influence Mel in any way. He kept repeating that when the time was right, he wanted Mel to act as instinctively as possible. This was crucial. Specter was uniquely qualified to understand the Varr, and none of them questioned any of his decisions on this. In spite of that, they were anxious, to say the least.

***

Mel, Marla, Jenny, and Lin sat down at a picnic table and watched the smoke clearing out through the restaurant windows.

Mel asked, "What is Specter's story anyway? Do any of you

know it? Why does he hate his own race to the point of wanting to destroy it?"

Between the three women, they pieced together what they knew for Mel. They drew on myths about Specter and upon everything that Specter told them back at the house.

Jenny said, "We've got a lot of myths, mostly. Stories were passed around within the human/alien groups for so many years that nobody remembers where any of them originated. It's not so much that he hates his own race but that he despises the regime that currently defines it. A hive-minded society like Specter's can be ruled from the top in much the same way that ants order their insect colonies, and that is also one of the Varr's strong points. Moreover, the Varr could conceivably become genuinely benign, if ordered to become so in the same way."

Lin said, "All this hive-minded stuff really goes only so far, though. I mean, unlike a true hive-minded society, the Varr can retain an individual sense of self once removed from close proximity to larger groups of Varr. If anyone, or even two or three, Varr should find themselves segregated from the others, they could easily develop divergent views, which is exactly what happened to Specter."

Marla remembered something else she heard about Specter that neither Lin nor Jenny remembered. She asked, "Didn't we hear something about him falling in love with the wrong female, or something like that? Wasn't she from a politically incorrect strain of Varr? I know that sounds like a human thing, but who is to say what is universal and what isn't?"

Jenny did remember something her father told her once about Specter. She added, "Dad once told me that Specter's own father ostracized him, and forced him into exile. That not only included Specter, but also his wife and their children. How sad. Dad had said that Specter's father offered him an opportunity to 'make good' with 'the family' and the Varr race. That's how Specter got his assignment here on Earth."

Marla added a bit of what Specter told them back at their place before they left. "The Varr discovered another Megal incursion into a promising new planet, right here. Earth offered new possibilities for the Varr's covetous need for knowledge. In fact, they routinely followed the Megal for this very reason. The Megal had an insatiable thirst for new experiences and a lust for learning. As far as either the Varr or the Megal knew, this was the only perceived commonality the two races shared."

Lin added, "Another thing Specter told us was that on his homeworld, his race has an average life expectancy of just over two hundred years. Here, they might live to reach over one thousand. That fact was startling, and yet the Megal did not have enough data to know why, or just how long they might actually live. Specter himself is well over a thousand."

Mel could no longer keep silent through all this.

"Hold it. Let me guess." He tipped his head and fluttered his hands like a mischievous jester. "This longevity factor is one of many delightful discoveries under study by the Megal, and is also going to get us all killed when they fight it out with each other for this new theoretical fountain of youth." Mel became suddenly serious. "Right?"

Every one of the three women shrugged with raised eyebrows and with questioning expressions.

Marla offered what she thought.

"Well, current theories on hyperdimensional physics suggest that Earth could exist in a section of space that operates under a different set of physics from the Varr's. Space is transitional by nature. It's in constant flux and flow, and as such has endlessly diverse sets of rules. They may have discovered that beings created under one set of rules may not be affected by all, or any, of the rules in another realm, even if they travel into that sector of space and remain there for any number of years. In some cases, this has given rise to monstrous, and or even superhuman anomalies in our world." Jenny remembered something else her father had told her.

"Hey, check this out." She was excited. "Dad had said that visitors from another dimension or sector of space might possess the powers of shape- changing…maybe incredible speed or the ability to move through the air with little regard for gravity. Possibly even strengthened powers of the mind, or the ability to form and shape plasma fields by drawing the raw energy from the much-debated ether between worlds. In some cases, he said, interracial mutations could have given rise to some of the creatures found in earth mythology. The list goes on and on."

Mel was staring at her, blank-eyed. He said, "Geez, it sounds like comic book stuff to me."

Jenny remained enthusiastic.

"Everything we imagine as fantasy might really come from truth gathered within our collective consciousness. Don't you see?"

Lin brought it back to a more compact issue.

"The most important by-product affecting both the Varr and the Megal is extreme longevity. Specter reported this particular benefit to his home race while he spied on the Megal. It was only after that fact was discovered that talk of invasion, and plans to carry it out, began in earnest on his homeworld. Apparently, at that point, not much else here interested them enough to follow the Megal here."

Mel wondered out loud, "Kind of makes you wonder what else, in space, is out there that the Varr consider more interesting."

Lin nodded, and continued, "So, whoever discovered the reason for this longevity might rule in virtual immortality. What a prize that would be."

Jenny said, "It didn't take long for Specter to find out about the longevity thing, and he thought that would buy him his ticket home, and acceptance back into his clan. It didn't happen. For some reason, he was denied his request and was refused the codes required for making the return jump home. He grew angrier as time went by, but never received the codes. The only reason he was given was that 'national security' would not allow his return." Marla said, "Specter won't say for sure, but we think the reason they wouldn't let him back was that the Varr believed Specter's intimate knowledge about possible immortality could become a threat to the existing Varr regime. In other words, politics."

Lin held up a hand for them to wait a minute before speaking. She nodded toward the tree under which Specter was standing. Specter appeared to be engaged in an in-depth discussion with the twins, so she felt it was safe to whisper, "We can't know all of Specter's motives for stopping the Varr from coming here. That's why no one trusts him. We can guess that his own mate, at home, is long dead from old age, and his children as well. Politics aside, perhaps the Varr share another common trait with other life-forms—a need for vengeance, or justice."

Mel said, "Well, that would be enough to make me want payback on a few people myself."

Jenny said, "He's had all the time in the world to observe the human race, and he says that after a while, he grew to like us and even respect us. Who can say? Maybe he's telling the truth. He knew what would happen to us if his own people were to invade. They would use Earth for experimentation until they stripped it of knowledge and assimilated it into their collection of planets. This would definitely destroy Earth's civilization…to say the least."

Marla added, "So Specter said he decided to stop them during their jump to invade. He said that perhaps this would slow them down long enough to buy Earth some time to grow into a relationship with the Megal and learn how to prevent future attacks."

Mel felt cynical. All of this sounded rather selfless on the surface. Jenny did add that, for now anyway, Specter cared very little for his return home. As far as they all knew from Specter himself, this world had become his home, for now.

Jenny snapped her fingers.

"Oh yeah, Dad did say something else. There was one other issue to resolve before Specter could rest easy for a while. He needed to release others of his kind being held prisoner by the Megal. POWs, I guess. If Specter could find a way home, he wanted to return with a small army of his own. He might attempt an assassination of the current Varr ruler, and a coup d'état, and then he'd try to overcome the Varr population's hive-minded ambivalence and bring down the entire dynasty governing his homeworlds. If he could do that, he, himself, would try to fill the political vacuum left as a result."

Mel listened to Marla, Jenny, and Lin as they alternated speaking between each other. By Specter's own admission, he knew Jenny's father.

Mel held up a hand.

"Wait a minute," he objected. "If you know all this, then why was Specter such a shock to you?"

Jenny answered, "Very few other than my father and Dane believed that Specter really existed at all. Yulan knew him only as Ben, as did quite a few people."

Mel wasn't through.

"How about Specter's revelations about the portals, or hyper-windows? Why was that such a shock?"

Jenny answered. "The portals always seemed to show up around saucer sightings. We thought the saucers created them. We had no idea that it was due to the Varr's attempt to penetrate our world. The truth is, from what Specter told us after you went outside, the Varr could occasionally locate Megal spacecraft using several means at their disposal. Now, those earlier portals are crude by comparison to what they can do with this Mercury probe thing. Specter did refer to what the probe was doing as 'focusing.'"

Mel nodded thoughtfully and said, "You mean like what Donovan called it—'focusing'?"

Mel's eyes widened in realization. "Hold up." He glanced nervously over at Specter, who still seemed engaged in conversation with the twins. "If I'm supposed to remain naive, then you've all just blown it. I'm as good as dead."

Lin answered, "No, I don't think so. We've only told you what little we do know, but we still have no idea how Specter intends to use you—only that he will. In a sense, you are still what he might call 'naïve.' Why Specter is playing it this way, we don't know. Again, this is one of the reasons no one completely trusts him. Maybe he is guarding something within his own motives. If he is, it's strictly need-to-know. He has a perverse sense of logic. But then, after all, he is only a Varr."

Only a Varr.

Boy, that brought a sudden flood of bad memories into Mel's mind. When Lin said, "he is only a Varr," Mel remembered an old pressroom adversary of his. He ran a new computerized press, and he loved to rub Mel's face in it. He used to say things to goad Mel into an argument. At one time, he went so far as to say that the print shop owners would never trust an Indian with one of the newer presses and that Mel was only a "dumb Indian," that he would never understand that fact. After hearing that, Mel calmly walked over and knocked him bloody cold with a blanket cylinder wrench. It didn't kill him, thank God, but Mel did lose his job, which is what led up to his wandering the streets the night he met Jenny. Mel blinked himself back to the present.

"OK," he said, "supposing all this is true. How do I prepare?" The women looked at each other.

Jenny said, "We don't know."

"Great."

At that moment, the restaurant owner called them in.

***

The diner, restaurant, was just the usual roadside stop with burgers, fries, and other assorted greasy spoon fares. There were also a few local specialties like pies and cookies. The walls were lined with Northwest trivia and a few local antiques. Hunting trophies were frowned upon these days, mostly because of the X-generations lack of understanding for such things. At least that was how Yulan explained it. Mel retained an uneasy feeling around Yulan. The man radiated tension.

They seated themselves as the other patrons entered the diner.

It was interesting to note how little attention anyone paid to Ben

71

(Specter). In fact, the waitress had to be reminded twice that Ben had not placed his order and would like a cheeseburger with fries. Odder yet was the fact that nearly everyone else in the place ordered the same thing, and still she could not remember Ben's order.

She returned to the table and apologized when she claimed to have neglected to write it down again. Mel waited for the cook to forget to fill Ben's order. His mind flashed back to a particular Seattle grease pit, and how this whole thing reminded him of the time, he first met Jenny. He noticed Donovan avoiding Specter's eyes. No doubt about it, Donovan had developed a defiant dislike that went beyond the familiar unease they all felt around Specter.

Specter cultivated his "non-existence." His race had a talent for mind control as well as shapeshifting. As long as he retained a human guise, the disquieting effects his race had on other life forms did not prove to be a problem. In fact, neither he nor any of his race preferred to wear an alien form. It was taxing to maintain and frequently slipped during times of stress or preoccupation. However, it did have its conveniences and offered some amusements.

He supposed the majority of his people could occasionally enjoy taking human forms and even vacation on this beautiful world if he had his way. In fact, if all went according to plan, he intended not only to stop this ridiculous war of misunderstanding between his people and the Megal but also to further the Varr's endless pursuit of knowledge by integrating with, rather than assimilating, other worlds. My God, he thought, what a paradigm change that would prove to be…and indeed the next step in their collective evolution.

That inspiration comforted him. The idea of bringing about the revolution he desired for well over one thousand years excited him to no end. Because of his politically incorrect standard of ethics, Specter had always suspected that his own father had chosen him for this assignment to get him out of the way. His family, and whichever one was currently ruling his race, would soon be in for a cultural surprise.

He scanned the room and eavesdropped on several conversations. His companions ate and ignored him. Well, all but one ignored him.

Donovan was pretending not to pay attention to him, but he kept peeking up at him over his sandwich. Specter noted to himself that the incident on the road was the start of all this. He knew that sooner rather than later he was going to have to straighten Donovan out. Fear like his, not the respectful fear Specter cultivated, would prove treacherous. He hoped he could keep a lid on Donovan for now.

Specter did eat his burger when it finally arrived. He could absorb and enjoy, nearly anything. There were several groups of customers in the place. The diners were mostly adults, except one child. He felt discomforted by this fact because children frequently penetrated his disguises, despite his substantial control over the reality they perceived. His human appearance was tangibly authentic. However, children do possess some natural skill at "seeing" things for what they really are. Elderly humans do occasionally share this same talent with children.

The mother and her young son sat in a corner by the front window, some distance from where his group was seated. The child paid little attention to anything but his food and his two toy trucks. One table held three bikers. Two men and one female. An elderly woman sat at the counter, sipping coffee while watching a television broadcast. One young couple sat next to a window, and a loud group of good-old-boys occupied the other half of the restaurant. At the moment, only one customer interested Specter...the old woman. He was picking up something she was muttering under her breath. It was a chant of some kind, in a tongue unknown to him.

His attention shifted from the woman and then riveted on the television. She was watching another news broadcast on the seemingly ever-present topic of "The Mercury Event." The unknown object had stopped increasing in size after achieving what scientists had calculated to be 19.5 miles across. It was difficult to describe its shape and size because it was asymmetrical in design. Earlier fears that this would become moon-sized were ridiculous, and he'd known that and yet this was vastly larger than he remembered from previous invasion accounts. As Specter took careful note of the broadcast, he observed with significant discomfort that this was not, at all, the size and configuration he expected the probe to take. The beginnings of doubt crept into his Varr mind. This object was taking on the look of a staging vessel…but no, the configuration was all wrong for that. On the other hand, was it?

The news anchor introduced a guest by the name of Richard C. Hoagland. Dane quieted everyone at the table and listened carefully to Hoagland's references and theories on hyperdimensional physics. Hoagland claimed that this would explain the presence and structure of the alien device, or craft. However, he did not pretend to guess at their motives.

Yulan remarked, "Richard hit another one on the head this time. By the time all this is over, he'll have a world full of converts." He smiled at Specter.

Specter returned Yulan's gaze for a moment, following Yulan's commentary, but he did not return his smile. He said, "Yulan, the fewer acolytes Hoagland has right now, the better. We don't want his best intentions in our way…and he does tend to complicate things."

Yulan's own smile disappeared. He nodded agreement and finished his burger.

Suddenly, to everyone's surprise, the old woman at the bar abruptly slid back and off her stool. Her head dropped, and her arms rose over her head. She began chanting aloud in that unknown tongue Specter heard under her breath. All conversation within the room stopped, as attention shifted in her direction.

Donovan turned to Lin and whispered, "That thing in space is scanning us again. Do you feel it?" She nodded. The old woman cut off her chant in mid-chorus and then spun around. She leveled a finger at Specter. The room's tableau seemed to freeze. All eyes were now on Specter.

The old woman declared, "He is one of them!"

Specter played the only card he could, under the circumstances, he laughed with a Boy Scout look of innocence on his face. That seemed to send an atmosphere of relief through the room. Everyone shrugged off the old woman. Andrea showed concerned for the woman, but before she could decide whether to speak with her or not, the old woman quickly ran out the front door and avoided meeting anyone's eyes on her way out.

Specter watched the woman leave. There was some sadness in his assumed human features. Some in the diner took this for compassion. What he really felt was fear. That probe was not functioning according to the way he was briefed before coming through to this world. This one was much larger and more powerful. The usual methods for an invasion might be turning into something worse. He was told from the start that a probe would be sent to prepare the way for attack and would open portals, or windows, which would allow them to trickle through directly from their homeworld. He could already tell that this was much more than that…much more. If this was a staging vessel of some kind, then they could come through all at once. There was also the possibility that they might choose to "soften" this planet by manipulating Earth's geomagnetic fields before they would come through. He shook himself away from any more speculation on that subject.

***

When they left the restaurant, Specter moved close to Donovan and stopped him from hurrying away. Once outside, he pulled him off to one side of the front door. Donovan objected and tried to pull away, but Specter prevailed.

None of the others wanted to interfere.

Donovan said, "What do you want?" and then added, "if you hurt anyone, Specter, I swear I'll pull the plug. I don't trust you any more than I trust any of your kind. I saw what was in your freaking alien brain." Specter held up a hand.

"Despite what you think you saw; you are wrong in your conclusions. Don't make the mistake of crossing me, Donovan. In fact, you're all going to have to trust me. You don't have any choice. No one has that choice right now."

Donovan groused but said nothing more. He started for the Suburban but noticed that it was already full. It was his turn to ride on the bus. He felt his throat tighten with mindless, although not groundless, fear.

***

Carmen, Andrea, and Jenny now took the back seat of Mel's Suburban. Marla sat up front in the passenger seat. The women chattered like schoolgirls from the moment they all climbed in together. The Suburban was more comfortable by far, for more reasons than one. Andrea spoke at some length with Jenny about gardening at the Claiborne estates. Andrea spent most of her spare time when at home, working with Yulan around the grounds. She was a seemingly uncomplicated woman, and yet she was far more complex than she appeared. Occasionally she would begin a discussion on one esoteric subject or another that left Mel in the proverbial dust. All of these women had a capacity for a conversation that went well beyond small talk.

Mel took advantage of a slight break in the conversation. He glanced back at Carmen and remembered her mental promise to tell him her own story if he asked. Carmen caught his stare and read his mind. As far as she was concerned, he just "asked." She leaned toward him and responded to his thoughts. Her face was so close to his ear that he could feel her breath. He knew she got a kick out of the effect she had on him. Marla was amused more than anything else. Some women enjoy a little friendly competition.

Carmen spoke right into his ear, "That's right, I did promise, didn't I?" Mel smiled and agreed. She sat back and said, "OK, then. It was about one week before you met Jenny in Seattle, about a year ago, that some friends and I were chasing a UFO down over the North Cascades Mountain Range."

Snow Circles (Carmen's story)

Carmen described the majestic beauty of the Cascades as seen from a military helicopter, from a high altitude. Covered in thick evergreen forests they were the snow-capped backbones of the Great Northwest, looming near the coastline, and extending through the states of Washington and Oregon. Carmen's mind drifted back to the previous year—as if it were just happening.

It was an exciting month for UFO activity. During the first week of summer, there were at least a dozen UFOs reported in the skies over Washington state. Carmen and helicopter pilot Captain Nolan Philips headed a team of four to track one of these as far as possible. The Cascades had long been reported to conceal secret military operations that some believed were responsible for numerous sightings of mysterious phenomena. However, this definitely was not a classified U.S. government craft.

They passed through another patch of scattered clouds. The sun was in their favor. It shone like a beacon over the silvery surface of the saucer-shaped craft. This one was acting strangely, even for one of these things. It slowed to a one-hundred-mile-an-hour crawl, as though baiting them to pursue. There seemed to be no reason to ignore the invitation, so they followed.

Carmen had a particular interest in UFOs and possessed an uncanny skill at locating these craft. She saw events and engagements in her mind well before they appeared on any intelligence systems. Consequently, she headed this team regularly.

Nolan was the oldest member of the team and pushing retirement. He led the others by rank and experience. He was of average build, kind in the face, clean-shaven, and wore his gray hair in a crew cut. The crew cut was his wife's idea. She liked how it felt when they made love. His mild temperament was a counterpoint to the other two men on the team, Vincent Teil and Ferris Gibbs.

Teil was short and bald with a policeman's style mustache, which he dyed black. He shaved off his eyebrows for reasons of his own. It set off the fact that his left eye was the color of an unclouded sky, while the other was a light brown. This unnerving aspect caused anxiety in anyone staring at him. He knew this and enjoyed it.

Gibbs was tall and muscular with short red hair. He too had an unpleasant demeanor, but this was due to a disagreeable personality and not his appearance. His face was freckled but otherwise unremarkable and clean- shaven.

Teil and Gibbs remained close to each other like twin brothers. They had been friends since high school, and they served together as special ops in the Middle East. Few would suggest there were any improprieties implied by their close proximity to one another, and those few that said anything like that found trouble. One such person felt the need to call them "sissy freaks" during a night incursion into Lebanon. Vince and Ferris have long memories. Eventually, military police found this unfortunate person in the garbage dump behind a mess tent, unconscious and badly bruised.

The moment of his unlucky statement to Teil and Gibbs was long passed, so nobody connected the dots back to them. When the guy finally regained consciousness, he was so intimidated by the attack that there was no way he'd identify either Teil or Gibbs as his attackers.

All four members of the Blackhawk team wore loose-fitting black jumpsuits. They also wore wide belts carrying small pieces of equipment and one handgun each. Individual preference decided their choice in weapons. They all wore darkened glasses against the glare of sunlight and its blinding reflection off the gleaming surface of the craft they were chasing.

Despite his glasses, Teil held a hand up to temporarily shield his eyes. He shook his head and complained.

"Damn, that thing is bright, and there it goes into another dive. Where does it think it's going? Weird the way this one's not trying to shake us, as usual."

Gibbs echoed his friend.

"I don't like it. We're being suckered."

The craft was roughly the size of a small house, and like others of its kind, moved without regard for known aerodynamics or laws of gravity. It dipped under a cloudbank when only a second before it looked as though it would sail up and over the top of it. Was this acceptable to modern physicists? That depended upon which ones you asked.

Nolan made a few speed and altitude adjustments. He said, "Someone is wearing an awful deodorant, or we have an electrical fire somewhere. Gibbs, check it out."

"You got it, Cap."

Nolan squinted through the windows, and then double-checked the instruments. The craft became visible again just below the helicopter and above their line of acuity. It must have doubled back while in a brief cloud cover. What was going on?

Nolan turned to Carmen.

"It's slowing down again. Gibbs may be right, and it wouldn't be the first time he's smelled a rat. There's a high valley in the mountaintops ahead. Looks like it's heading that way. What do you get, Carmen?"

Carmen closed her eyes. Several moments later she told them that the craft was indeed heading for the valley. She also saw three beings aboard, and they were not of alien origin. In her mind, they looked human. This caused both Nolan and Teil to start talking at once. The upshot was disbelief.

"If not alien, then what?" demanded Teil. "Is that one of our experimental ships? If so, man, we're wasting our time. Let's get the hell out of here and chase down some beer."

Carmen kept her eyes closed and shook her head. "No, this is not one of ours. I think we should pursue it."

Gibbs overheard everything and shouted his agreement to continue the pursuit.

"I say we cruise the strip as long as there's gas in the tank!"

They continued straight on course for the valley, which was a mile-wide cleft in the mountain ridge. It was dotted with short evergreens, broad patches of snow, and assorted groundcover. Gibbs reported his findings.

"You're right about the electrical. Nothing is shorted out, yet, but we've gotta land. I want a better look."

Teil said, "I think you're about to get that chance. Looks like our pigeon is going to roost."

The saucer slowed to a standstill and hovered motionless in the air one- quarter mile into the valley. There was a flat area under and around it, and three times its size. One other detail caught their eyes as they quickly closed the distance between themselves and the craft. Two small figures were standing close to each other, watching the saucer. They wore large packs and carried walking sticks. They were dangerously close to the alien craft. Hikers.

Nolan rolled his eyes. "Can you believe this? We've got spectators."

Just then, the saucer began to change. Bright colors rotated around the rim, and it began to blur. The air around the saucer took on an agitated quality, as though it was held on a vibrating plate, suspended in transparent jelly. The disturbance then extended to the ground beneath it. A large round patch of snow and underbrush directly below the craft transformed into a spinning whirlpool of debris.

There must have been considerable seismic activity as well because everyone in the helicopter could plainly recognize that the hikers were having trouble keeping their feet. Snow appeared to be shaking off from tree branches as far as visibility allowed them to see. The hikers still had difficulty standing as the Blackhawk roared to landing several yards behind them. The faces of the man and woman were masks of terror. Nolan waited to put down until the trees stopped shaking. The Blackhawk had barely settled down before the first three UFO chasers jumped out followed by Nolan. A steady wind blew powdered surface snow into their faces, and there was a loud, high-pitched musical clamor, which competed with the dying chop from the Blackhawk's propeller blades. That sound was coming from the UFO.

The couple had been watching the helicopter land, but now they turned back to view the saucer as the four UFO chasers ran up beside them. They all watched in dumbfounded disbelief as the alien vessel abruptly dropped into the earth, seemingly swallowed up, with only settling snow and grass to indicate its ever having been there at all.

They all stood motionless and staring. Only the wind disturbed the silence. All rumbling and harmonic racket had ceased. The six onlookers scanned the ground for any sign of the craft's return. They searched the sky as well. There was always the possibility that others might be close by. After seeing what had become of this one, nobody wanted to be anywhere near if another one landed. Moreover, God forbid if one ever came up from underneath you.

Carmen was the first to break the quiet.

"You two are either at the wrong place at the wrong time or very lucky. I guess that depends on how you're taking this."

The hikers were severely shaken. The man said, "I've heard there's radiation around those things. Is that true?" He was pointing at the area where the craft had descended into the earth. Nolan, Teil, and Gibbs were inspecting that area now. The spot was marked by a classic circle formation. Carmen shook her head as she thought about what all the crop circle fanatics would think about this one. She picked up on what was said about radiation.

"I don't know, but let's get you two away from it, just in case."

Then she noticed something in the way the woman acted and how the man glanced at her midsection. It didn't take unique gifts to know that they were worried for more than their safety. She gently touched the woman's arm.

"You're pregnant." She did not state this as a question. The woman merely nodded. She was very interested in taking Carmen's advice as quickly as possible. Carmen led them back to the helicopter and got them inside. It was starting to snow.

After they closed the doors, the couple slumped against a wall and sat down. At first glance, they were young and earthy. Carmen always thought that these Generation Xers more or less resembled kids from the sixties. She introduced herself, and they did the same. Her name was Nell, and he was Tony. They felt guilty for hiking while she was pregnant, but she had insisted on going. Besides, with the baby coming soon, this was likely to be the last time that they'd be able to go on a trip like this for a long time. Carmen agreed. It was the possibility of radiation that mattered right now.

Carmen knelt down to talk with them and then raised herself up to look through the windows at the crew. They were still examining the circle. When she returned, she looked confident.

"They don't seem to be in any hurry, and Teil is using a hand-held device for monitoring all sorts of energy fields. I'd say we aren't in any real danger here."

Comforted, the couple looked relieved. They asked a lot of questions and received quick answers. Carmen could not reveal much without direct orders to do so. The answer to "What was that thing?" came quickly. That was obvious, and so was Carmen's answer: "a flying saucer." Wide-eyed, what could the couple do now but nod and stare up at the window. Tony asked for a lift down the mountain. At that moment, Gibbs opened the bay door.

"Something's up. We need you out here. Can you leave them?"

She said the hikers were "fine," then went into the cockpit. She came back and explained that she started the audio beacon. Teil knew this would transmit their status, coordinates, and flight information back to headquarters.

The couple seemed calmed for the moment, so Carmen jumped out and followed Teil into the circle. The blustery weather had really picked up. She had to raise her voice a little to be heard above the wind in their ears.

"What's up?" Nolan explained.

"We're getting some anomalous readings, coming from beneath us. Can you scan anything?"

Carmen dropped to the ground and felt the oddly flattened and mutated debris under her hands. She closed her eyes and concentrated. A few moments later, she stood up. She looked frightened.

"Yes, vibration, colors, and five men. I think something's coming. We need to get the hell out of here!"

They wasted no time, but as they started to run for the helicopter, they were thrown off their feet by a jolt from the earth. The shaking had started again in earnest, accompanied by the strangely musical harmonics. It was nearly deafening. Gibbs was shouting.

"Mother of God! It's coming up right under our feet!"

They still had several yards to go before they could reach the Blackhawk. There was not enough time. Vertigo overtook them, and the air swam in circular colorful, waves. Carmen noticed that the couple was staring at them from the helicopter windows. They were horrified.

The UFO chasers expected to be swept up and destroyed, on the top of a flying saucer. Suddenly most of the sound and vibration abruptly ceased, except for an area just behind them. They all turned to see what appeared to be five phone booth-sized vortexes erupting from the ground, in the same manner as the saucer had descended into it fifteen minutes before. Colored lights were pulsing within each torrent, and each held a vaguely human-like plasma form at their center.

The chasers flattened themselves to the ground and watched as best they could. Their eyes stung from flying dirt, and they were being pelted with small rocks thrown from the ground. Within less than a minute, the plasma forms solidified into five uniformed men standing within five smaller circle formations under their feet. These men wore semitransparent facemasks that covered their entire head. Their suits were similar in fashion to the UFO chasers, except that their uniforms were gray, and they wore more substantial belts.

On each belt, they carried two identical triangular-shaped devices and spare facemasks that matched the ones they wore. These were also partially transparent and fitted with some kind of breathing apparatus. It appeared that their heads were shaved. They were all moderately muscular in stature. Teil and Gibbs were ready for action. Gibbs reached for his gun. At that move, the one in front of their triangular formation lifted a restraining hand in warning. His voice was low and distorted by the mask. It was difficult to hear through the wind; however, his menace was easy to interpret.

"If you do that again, I will enjoy killing you."

Gibbs still had the weapon in his hand, although he had not pointed it at any of them. He remained defiant.

"Yeah?" he asked. "And how are you going to stop me? As far as I can see, you have no weapons, and I sure as hell won't let you take mine."

The spokesman removed his mask by pulling it off over his head. He was bald and had no facial hair. It looked as though he had none to grow, and yet, he appeared to be close to Gibbs's age of twenty-eight. The man was smiling malevolently.

"Would you believe me if I say I do not need a weapon?"

"Fat chance, asswipe," spat Gibbs.

The man rolled his eyes, smirked, and turned to the individuals standing behind him. He raised his hands in a "can you believe this" gesture. They still wore their headgear, but it was plain from their body language that they found the situation amusing. The apparent leader turned back and raised his hands, palms forward, disarmingly. He said, "Perhaps I can placate you a little by introducing myself. I am called Taker. It is more a title than a name, but that is the way we do things down below."

At this moment, Carmen suddenly grabbed Gibbs's gun from out of his hands with astonishing speed and strength.

Carmen spoke to Gibbs in a calming tone, although Gibbs was anything but calm.

"He is not what he appears to be, Ferris. I don't know what he is, but let it alone."

Gibbs looked into the man's smug face and saw red.

Taker raised his bald eyebrows, and sarcastically said, "That is good advice, Ferris." He shifted a little and carefully regarded Carmen. "Well, it seems the little lady conceals a surprising secret. Esha was right, and I should have sensed it. A Changeling, I believe."

Carmen lowered her guard a moment and looked confused by

what Taker had just said. That was enough for Gibbs. Angry and humiliated, he retrieved his gun away from Carmen and pointed it at Taker. He stepped forward with an aggressive posture. Taker only laughed and clapped his hands as though this was some hilarious new joke. He then pointed the palms of his hands back at Gibbs in a pushing gesture. Instantly Gibbs froze. Confusion crossed Gibbs's face, followed by a shock of pain. His face muscles began to visibly knot, and his eyes bulged.

Ferris Gibbs was in unspecified agony. His body shuddered violently. His jaws flew open, and he screamed aloud and awful sound, cut off in a moment by a gurgle in his throat. Watery blood began to stream from the corners of his eyes, and to the horror of his companions, he vomited thick gouts of fresh blood. Just as suddenly as this began, it stopped. Gibbs dropped to the ground. His eyes were squinted shut and gummy from new blood.

The team ran to his side, but they found that he was already dead. When they looked up, they saw Taker looking up into the clouds with his mouth open in ecstasy, and his fists clenched. When he looked down at them again, his eyes were literally glowing a bright blue. He cocked his head to one side, and he stopped smiling. The light in his eyes dimmed and extinguished. He asked, "Believe me now?"

Teil's eyes were as disquieting to watch as Taker's. The two men stared at each other for a long moment of understanding. Teil's eyes vowed that he would eventually kill Taker. That much was certain. Taker did not find Teil's gaze in the least bit entertaining. He demanded that the remaining chasers stand and move away from the body.

Taker gestured to his group behind him. They removed the extra masks from their belts and threw them to the chasers. Nodding at the masks, he ordered them to put them on. Three of the interlopers walked around Taker and approached the chasers. They hooked one of the triangular objects to each of the chaser's jumpsuits. Taker told them not to touch the objects. He told everyone to keep a distance of at least two feet between each other. He positioned everyone to make sure that Gibbs's body was included in the group, although it remained on the ground.

A sound emanated from Taker's facemask that now hung loosely on his chest. He pulled the mask over his head. The noise in the mask was a communications device. He responded loudly enough to be overheard.

"Eight, and one body." He listened and then again responded. "There are two more, and one child, inside the copter. You'll have to dispatch someone for them. We're coming down now."

Returning his attention to the group, he told the chasers that the body would be left halfway down. Whatever that implied.

Taker chuckled in jest. He said, "No doubt buddy Ferris's corpse will give some future anthropologist a woody. Happens all the time."

He winked.

Within a few moments, there were nine more small circle formations in the earth, or fifteen in total—if you included the biggest one. Wind and snow would soon obscure them all, then more grass would grow, and the circles would vanish.

Tony and Nell were watching from the helicopter the entire time although they stood back away from the window hoping not to be noticed. After the lights disappeared into the ground, they scrambled around looking for radio controls. They nearly jumped out of their skins when the radio chirped to life, and they struggled to figure out how to respond.

Obsidian Labyrinth

Twenty-four thousand feet below the surface of the Cascades, a dimly-lit cavern brightened when eight descending cocoons of spinning light entered through an orange vortex in the ceiling and came to rest on the cavern floor. The cavern was lined in a shiny obsidian-like black material that reflected this light, and yet this effect was visible only on the ceiling and floor because the walls were so distant they could not be seen. The only constant light source emanated from the vortex. There were a few saucer-shaped craft on the chamber floor, but nothing else.

Eerie harmonies, in seemingly random compositions, flooded into the cavern's furthest recesses. These sounds stopped and were replaced by gentler tones emanating from the vortex itself. The cocoons dissipated just after touching the glassy floor's surface, leaving their passengers standing. All eight figures stood trance-like for several seconds after their own individual vortexes dissolved.

Taker's group snapped out of it first. Taker walked over to Carmen and steadied her as her head cleared. Nolan and Teil wavered, on the verge of falling. Taker's crew helped them to lie down. A faint electric humming came from some short distance away. As it grew closer, it resolved into a small flat gray vehicle that sounded as though it had an electrical drive or some equivalent.

A tall woman dressed in a long white gown stood behind a raised dais at the front of the vehicle and steered, using an ovoid wheel. This woman was bald and did not wear ornaments of any kind. There was one other woman aboard. This woman was harder to see. She was also tall but dressed in a purple gown with a cowl pulled down over her head and face.

The vehicle came to a stop a couple of yards from Taker. The woman in purple stepped down and walked up to Carmen. She ignored the others. When she was less than two feet away from Carmen, she removed her cowl. Taker stood aside and regarded

Carmen with some amusement.

Carmen had been watching her approach, and yet she reflexively pulled back when she saw the woman's face. Her face was elongated and almost lycanthropic with long straight ebony hair. Her eyes were large, round, black, and held no visible iris. Her nose was small but wide, and her skin color was a pinkish gray. She smiled. Her teeth were human but small. There looked to be near twice as many of them. Carmen felt faint.

The woman's voice was soft and soothing, contradicting her appearance. She introduced herself as Esha and then held her hands open to Carmen. Her hands were the same color as her face. They were smooth, well groomed, and strong. She asked Carmen to try and relax. Carmen still felt dizzy and could not take her eyes off this woman's monstrous face. Especially her eyes. Numbing darkness filled her mind, and her vision swam away.

***

Teil's eyes blinked open. He did not move. Remaining very still, he scanned what little he could make out of where he lay. He was on his back. He dared to turn his head slowly to his right side. Nolan was unconscious next to him. He and Nolan had been placed on a comfortable bed and were still dressed in the same clothes. They appeared to be alone. He slowly turned his head to the left and was startled to see a sizeable impressionistic statue looming above where he lay. It was formed from gray rock, and had short humanlike appendages, with a large head, and no facial features.

He lifted himself on an elbow and avoided waking Nolan as he slipped off the bed. Their gear was nowhere in sight, let alone the weapons, which did not surprise him. He wandered quietly around the small room. It had the look of a small hotel room unless you considered the smooth black walls, ceiling, and floor. A soft light came from three small white globes on pillars located around the room. One adjoining place seemed to be a bathroom.

It held a sink and mirror, with two light globes mounted on the wall on either side of the mirror. There was also a toilet and shower, complete with toiletries and all of the usual hotel fixtures.

The place even smelled like a hotel room, although it had a decidedly different atmosphere. Teil found his dark sense of humor beginning to stir, like the time he and Gibbs were imprisoned in South America following a partially successful covert government operation. They shared a small cell with three other prisoners from the local Hispanic community and to pass the time they made up a lot of twisted stories and cracked a lot of sick jokes for each other, and all in the local native tongue.

The two men barely noticed the passage of time during their one-week detention. However, the guards failed to find any enjoyment from these sordid tales and were almost relieved when US special forces broke into the compound to liberate both Teil and Gibbs.

Teil could now imagine himself wandering around this room with a pad of paper and pen, taking notes for the Washington State Visitor's Guide magazine—assuming they were still within the boundaries of Washington state.

There was a dresser, and a couple of chairs, and a stocked kitchenette. He looked into the small refrigerator. There were sandwiches, canned beverages, and a few unidentifiable raw vegetables. He closed the door and stood up. He almost laughed. Instead, he muttered that the vegetables must be imported from France, then said, "What, no pictures on the wall or television…and, where's the view?"

Teil's voice woke Nolan. He jumped off the bed, disoriented. He looked at Teil, then the room, and finally at the bed. Teil watched Nolan's surprised expression, shrugged, and then reached into the fridge. He grabbed some of the raw vegetables and tossed some to Nolan.

"Hungry, Cap?"

***

Carmen awakened alone and in a similar hotel-like room. As

Carmen's head cleared, she noticed Esha seated in a comfortable chair across the small room. Esha sat quietly, watching her as she sat up in bed. After a moment of uncomfortable silence, Carmen spoke.

"Your name is Esha, that is all I know about this place. Are you going to tell me where I am?"

The strange woman nodded. She stood, and then said, "Will you walk with me? I'd like to answer your questions and ask you a few of my own as well."

Esha's voice had a calming effect. Carmen did not reply. She did not have to. Esha gestured to the door, and Carmen followed.

The door was constructed of the same hard black substance she'd seen everywhere. It was framed in ornately carved rock. The oblong door developed a hole in its center, and then the rift widened to allow the women to pass through into a well-lit hallway.

Carmen watched the opening with interest and asked about it. "This door looked solid. Did I just see it liquefy?"

Esha directed her to touch the door after it closed behind them.

"There, you see? Solid as a rock."

She paused long enough to smile at Carmen's evident fascination before explaining.

"The rock did indeed liquefy, and a small device in the wall here," she touched a spot to the right of the door, "controls it on a molecular level. It keys on mental commands. Because we have programmed them to recognize thought commands, we can efficiently control ingress or egress. For example, if you had been a prisoner, we would have told it to watch for a planned escape. I see by your expression that you understand. Please, follow me."

She led Carmen through several long, intersecting, black corridors. The tunnels were anything but deserted. Humans, as far as she could tell, made up the bulk of the traffic. On one occasion, however, what appeared to be a small gray gargoyle shuffle by her. It paid her only a brief glance.

Light emanated from small panels sunken into the walls and ceiling at regular intervals. Esha explained that the light energy was limitless and that no attempt need ever be made to conserve any of it. For that matter, all their energy supplies were inexhaustible and derived from geothermal and geomagnetic sources. For the most part, alien technology was used in processing these Earth energy resources, but Esha occasionally referred to the work of Nikola Tesla and a few of his experiments in harvesting free energy out of the earth itself.

As Esha chatted over several topics, one piece of information of considerable interest to Carmen was the fact that these beings now experienced total isolation from their homeworld. Esha hinted at war somewhere in a very distant part of space. This war still threatened them somehow. Carmen listened with little interruption. She felt an unquestioning acceptance within her.

Esha touched briefly on food supplies and hydroponics. These were not limitless and had to be carefully maintained. In fact, she could smell what had to be a hydroponics area not far from where they were. When she attempted to view it with her mind, Esha anticipated her effort by explaining that the materials covering the walls, and in fact the entire complex, would prevent her from penetrating with her thoughts.

Esha felt Carmen's persistent attempts and said, "Nice try, Carmen, but you won't be able to breach any of these walls with your mind without my first teaching you how to accomplish it. I pierce them all the time, but you must understand the necessity for the seemingly impenetrable quality of these walls. This material is equally effective against discovery by current Overworld technology."

They walked together for close to a half hour before arriving at another large portal on their right. Esha told her that all of their portals operated in the same manner as the room they left. Esha nodded in the door's direction.

It opened.

Esha stepped through and then offered a hand to Carmen as she followed. They entered another cavern. Profoundly resonant and relaxing tones filled this cavern with sound. Esha told her that this sound came from the vortex above their heads.

This place was identical to the first cavern she'd seen but smaller. An orange vortex capped the ceiling in this place as well, but its light was augmented by hundreds of large white globes located on pillars set strategically around the chamber. She could see the far distant walls curving down from the ceiling. This cavern's content was altogether startling by comparison to anything she had seen or heard thus far.

Esha gestured expansively, indicating the whole of the cavern.

"Our collection."

Carmen's face looked drained from shock. "My God," she breathed.

Where the first cavern she'd seen was nearly empty, this one was filled with artifacts from the surface world. There were automobiles, trucks, aircraft, weapons, children's toys, personal effects and clothing, civilian and military survival equipment and supplies, airliners from past and present, as well as several small buildings. An old B-52 Bomber was the closest to the chamber entrance, and Esha lifted a hand in its direction.

"Look familiar?"

According to Esha, this imposing museum was a diverse assemblage of anything and everything short of perishables. All were neatly sorted over the length and breadth of the expansive floor space, with lots of room between each item.

Esha gestured to the cavern walls.

"The process we used in creating this place fused the walls into what is very much like hardened lava. You might be interested to know that it is over one hundred feet thick in places and insulates us as well."

Carmen interjected.

"Let me guess, the same type of force fields generated by your spacecraft melts and shapes rock and soil."

"Well, not quite. We did, however, use the saucer craft to carve out most of this underground installation. The force fields, as you put it, can be selectively tuned to reshape what they touch. In fact, we have artists' guilds that delight in creating anachronistic formations here and there. You'll see their work from time to time. They are hard to miss."

Esha cocked her head and regarded her as a guest.

"Where should we begin? Would you care for a brief history lesson?"

"It bothers me that you are so open about all of this to an outsider."

A moment of silence followed, during which Esha considered her answer before continuing.

"From among those Taker recently captured, right now you alone will have the choice to leave. The others will be kept here with or without their consent. As far as why you will have that privilege, I only ask that you indulge me with an open mind while I explain."

She closed her eyes a moment, then reopened them and said, "I have just been informed that the young couple above ground had been rescued by a military escort. That is unfortunate. We had hoped to bring your aircraft down before they arrived to save them the trouble of having to solve the mystery of your disappearance."

Carmen took the opportunity to ask the burning question of just why her team was taken at all. Esha's answer brought little comfort.

"I sent them for you, my dear. But let's not get ahead of ourselves."

The strange woman led the way between artifacts as she spoke. They passed a small pile of stuffed animals on their left, and an elaborate display of civil war clothing and weaponry, on the right.

"These memories have been gathered from over hundreds of centuries and reflect our interest in the human race. We have been interacting with this world for several thousand years. We arrived through one of many inter- spatial 'soft-spots' found everywhere on your world, and in space around it. These places are known among your people for unexplained hauntings, disappearances, and otherworldly manifestations."

Esha paused to allow Carmen time to digest what she'd just said while they walked past an enormous stuffed wooly mammoth and then she continued.

"The race of beings I am referring to are called the Megal and are known to you as the Grays. Their interest in this world began when the Megal discovered that the laws of physics here differ radically from most of the other regions of hyperspace they've explored. The science they brought with them allowed great freedom while they concentrated on new fields of study they found possible only in this world. The technology they delivered included, among many things, control over gravity and the ability to destabilize Earth elements down to a subatomic level."

While listening to Esha, Carmen took note of a kind of symmetry in the way the exhibits were placed. Esha read her mind and remarked, "Yes, there is a geometric pattern arranged all around you? Geometry and sound play the most significant part of our higher technologies. If you were to view this room from above, you would see it as an elaborate design. To us, pattern, shape, and harmonic frequencies are like your printed circuit boards. Someday your race will be shown how to take this next leap in technology."

Esha was comforted to note understanding in Carmen's face. She tugged at a memory surfacing in Carmen's mind.

She said, "Yes, I know of your brother's studies in this same field. Dane is a remarkable man." Then she shifted her topic back to the history lesson. Only a few seconds into further revelations, Carmen stopped and redirected the conversation back to what Esha said about her brother. Esha assured her that the information she had about her and her family came from Carmen's own mind. She told Carmen that she would soon explain and asked if she might continue. Carmen reluctantly agreed.

"After a time, the Megal discovered side effects that altered them in two ways while they remained on your world. The first was that they could not successfully procreate in your dimension of space. The reasons for this are still not clear. Perhaps procreation is sacrosanct to its place in hyperdimensional space. The second was that in time, they found that their life spans had increased beyond measure as though your laws of entropy failed to have the same effect on the Megal.

"Eventually, factions developed. A third of them decided to remain indefinitely out of scientific curiosity and because of the increased life span. They remained despite the procreation problem, establishing a colony of several hundred. Once they achieved a comfortable base of operations, so deep underground as to be virtually undetectable, they returned to their procreation problem in earnest.

"There was an early attempt at breeding with human women which did result in alien/human children. These halflings came to be called simply…Progeny. I am one of these."

Carmen glanced at her briefly but continued to listen without interruption.

"The problems with these children were two-fold. They were ugly by both racial standards, and they were shunned as a result."

At that moment in Esha's narrative, the world around Carmen dissolved, and a vision unfolded in her mind with such clarity, it was as though she were living it. She could still hear Esha speaking, and Esha encouraged Carmen to concentrate on what she was being shown.

Carmen squeezed her eyes shut and concentrated on the image that formed. Esha waited, and after a few moments, Carmen said, "I see a child. It's so vivid."

Esha explained.

"I gave you that image. It is one of the Progeny, just after birth. What do you see now?"

"I see a peculiar looking young girl, with large black eyes, of about three years old, and I see a human woman cradling the child in her arms. The woman looks dazed and upset. She's crying. A small gray alien is walking up to the woman and is pulling the child away from her. The girl is also crying and wants to stay with the woman. Now the child is gone, and the woman is alone. She is sobbing and burying her head in her hands. It's so sad. What is this?"

Esha nodded.

"That child was me. The alien was what you would call my father. His DNA was inserted into that human woman's egg. Those procedures are no longer allowed and are now considered a failure. It was a cheerless time in Megal history."

Carmen began shaking her head to clear it, but Esha took hold of her face and asked her not to disengage just yet.

"Those images will come unbidden while we speak. I placed them into your mind when I first took your hand. They are pieces of our collective memory. I instantly read your mind, as well. Now you know how I came to know of your family." She paused briefly before saying, "I know everything about Yulan and Sara as well."

She watched as a complex mixture of emotion crossed Carmen's face. Before Carmen could say anything, she continued.

"Yes, I know why Sara haunts your estate. I do have answers for you, although you may not like all of them."

So much time had passed since Carmen's sister Sara died, that she thought her feelings were prolonged since healed. She was surprised when she felt tears and choking emotion rise up in her throat. Esha took her one hand and led her to the front porch of an old log cabin surrounded on all sides by exhibits that had nothing in common with it. She guided her to a swing chair. They sat together as Esha spoke.

"I know how your younger sister died and the love of the man she left behind…Yulan. I know about your brother, Dane, and how Taker's Changeling eyes reminded you of Dane's. You have those abilities yourself, although your parents told you that only men could hope to develop such powers. They were not intentionally lying. They simply did not understand that they were wrong.

"Tragically, your parents did not understand what happened the night you were abducted, and altered. They were too old to be involved in the experiment, so the Megal ignored them. They died before they could learn the truth. All they knew was that you were altered in the night somehow. They grappled with the mysteries the best way they knew how, through superstition and taboos. Ignorance taught you the inadequacies of sex. The power of suggestion is stronger in Changelings than in healthy human beings. The forces of suggestion and ignorance are what killed your sister.

"In time, your father saw that none of you seemed to age, so he told all four of you, as children, and Yulan, that you must remain virginal or the loss of it would rob you of your immortality. In that event, your longevity would instantly reverse. This was not true, but in the mind of a Changeling that thought held power."

Esha's eyes locked with Carmen's.

"Carmen, this may be hard for you to take, but Sara need not have died after she was raped. She believed she would die after losing her virginity. That belief is what killed her."

Carmen's voice caught.

"Then she and Yulan could have…" She let the thought trail and lowered her eyes.

Esha nodded.

"Yes, she and Yulan could have been wed, and became more than frustrated lovers, had your father not forbidden it."

Carmen lowered her eyes. Her sadness was interrupted a moment later by another vision. This one was aboveground, in a forest, and at night. Three spindly Megal stood some distance away from a sizeable male Progeny. This Progeny was wearing a Roman toga, and lace-up sandals with his black hair pulled back in a ponytail. There was an expression of violent satisfaction on his face. His large black eyes were wide above a tiny pug nose, protruding teeth, and a wide jaw. His arms were outstretched in front, with palms held open and away from him. Unexpectedly, multicolored flames, like lightning, encircled his chest and traveled down to his forearms. These flames gathered in his outstretched hands and then shot out and away from him in a torrent of plasma fire. That blast was directed at a tree, which was then violently uprooted by the Progeny's will. It hung suspended in the air with roots dangling above a gaping wound in the earth.

Esha was speaking throughout the vision.

"The Progeny were coldly studied from purely scientific motivations. It was discovered that they shared the longevity of their Megal parents, at least in so far as could be determined. They also seemed to be able to tap into the laws governing temporal physics and manipulate them somewhat through a mental process the

Megal could not, and still don't, understand. You call it magic. That phenomenon continued in the Changelings, but we now believe that the reason for this is that the human spirit exists in hyperdimensional space, and as such, can act much like a bridge between planes of existence, or realities…given certain conditions. We, Progeny, are part human. We share your Changeling powers but do not have the overall potential you have. In time, you will discover this yourself."

Carmen objected.

"A lot of people don't even believe in the human spirit. How do you explain any of this to them?"

Esha considered a moment, then said, "Think of it this way. You can watch subatomic particles with the naked eye, but only by viewing their passage in a particle acceleration chamber. In a like manner, evidence of the human spirit can be seen by making a note of its effect on the world around it. Speaking metaphorically—evidence of things not seen, by the shadow it may cast, by the wind it creates, or the trail it leaves behind."

Carmen stared into the woman's disturbingly black eyes and asked, "Assuming we have a 'spiritual' ingredient, why don't you have one? Aren't Progeny part, human?"

Esha nodded. "We do have a 'spirit,' or a hyperdimensional component, as far as we can tell, as confirmed by our ability to bend natural laws the way Changelings can. However, what you have not seen is our vast accumulation of data on the Changeling project gathered over a great deal of time. A fully human subject, successfully combined with Megal DNA, is capable of twisting so many established laws of physics that if you research only a few of the archives, you would soon begin to understand the difference between the Progeny and Changelings."

Carmen's vision shifted to a place in front of the male Progeny. The Megal had given him a respectable distance. He stood horrific in the moonlight with his arms and face held up to the stars, exalting in his power. Esha could see within Carmen's mind and shared her thoughts on what she saw.

"It was as though the Progeny straddled a line between two worlds and were only partially restrained by either one, as though they were organic and 'spirit' portals, or rift windows, between worlds—the 'spirit' component comprising the critical factor. Take yourself, for instance, and what you can accomplish with your mind and voice. For you, the reality is somewhat subjective.

Many out-of-body experiences result from this as well. Better yet, your brother Dane and the seeming miracles he can perform are prime examples of the way Progeny and Changelings manipulate hyperspace. Dane is a genius inventor and adventurer, and routinely bends the laws of physics to suit his imagination. Imagination and intuition predetermine his creations."

Esha now spoke softly as though the ensuing portion of her tale held some measure of pain for her. Both women kept their eyes shut as a night view of a European castle swam into their minds. Four Progeny clung to the outside walls and hid in the shadows of a medieval flying buttress. Their eyes flickered and glowed in the moonlight.

"In time, many of the Progeny managed to escape to the surface world of their human parentage to find an uncomfortable niche as gargoyles and other creatures of the night. They were at home in the darkness as is understandable from the hundreds of years they'd spent living underground. Understandably, they were considered monsters, and humans found means to destroy most of them before the remaining Progeny returned to the underground."

The vision changed yet again. Carmen felt she saw through the Earth as though from above the planet. She could see past clouds and groundcover and into underground the cities deep below the earth's surface. Towering alien structures were formed out of the shiny black rock, twisted and stretched into a variety of unusual shapes and sizes. They wove throughout the earth, at extreme depths, in wildly decorative patterns and intricate designs. Colorful lights glittered everywhere. She saw an expansive view of vast caverns lit by thousands of floating light globes. These cities had a lived-in look about them and felt to Carmen as old as Esha had described.

The view tightened and then spun back up through the Earth, higher and higher until she was well over the Western United States. Her mind flew above the Cascade Mountain Range and then flowed deep into a chamber much more extensive than anything she'd seen so far. A city spread out around her.

Esha explained that what they were seeing was the city they were now in. Carmen really had not seen any of it. Two chambers and a bedroom did not come close to describing the vast interiors of this world below ground. Esha helped her to focus on a hundred or so Progeny dressed in loosely fitted clothing and sandals. These beings were herded into areas where they were kept separate from the others. There were no children among them.

Esha sighed.

"The Megal outlawed the creation of any more Progeny. All Progeny were sterilized. This sterilization was most likely needless, as natural conceptions among the Progeny were as unsuccessful as with the Megal. Those Progeny that remained underground consigned themselves to a lonely freak life. Grossly outnumbered, they agreed to live as a separate faction, co-dependent upon their creators. The Megal crushed several violent uprisings among the Progeny by technologies withheld from the Progeny."

Carmen was disturbed by the next vision. A midnight moon softened the darkness around a peaceful farmhouse somewhere in the Great Plains states. Above it hovered a silent UFO twice the size of the house. A bright light erupted from beneath the saucer and enfolded the house in a beam of intense light. Four figures floated up and into the saucer within the beam of light. The figures appeared to be asleep. Two were children, and the others were young adults. The saucer pulled them from their beds as though the house wasn't there at all.

She felt a shiver as she watched an intense scene in which all four of the humans were taken, naked and unconscious, to be laid out on white tables. The Megal injected both parents and the children through their chests with hypodermics filled with a brownish fluid.

"These studies revealed an incredible new discovery. When

injected with Megal blood many, though not all, human bodies absorbed it rather than attacking it as they would a virus. Many of those who rejected the plasma suffered cancerous deaths. In many cases their blood filled with a poisonous gas that caused surgeons, nursing staff, and pathologists to asphyxiate during exploratory surgery.

"In those instances where human bodies accepted the Megal plasma, the happy conclusion would be that they adapted to it and combined with it in a survival move. Much like natural selection. In that event, a Changeling was born. When a successful subject was found, the rest of their family would usually be targeted as well. Success ran in families due to a genetic predisposition.

"For reasons yet unknown, breeding Changeling hosts with each other failed to transfer the Megal/Human DNA. Perhaps, the laws of physics on Earth interfere with this, in much the same way it interferes with Megal procreation. The consensus was that any mix of this DNA would be accepted only in the host."

Esha changed the subject, and the vision followed.

"In time, the turmoil over the Progeny rebellion stabilized. Despite an official ban on Progeny research, their scientific community continued into another chapter of experimentation. They stayed with trips aboveground to capture human subjects. For the most part, Changelings were left Overworld and ignorant of what happened to them. The exceptions were found to possess an unusually high aptitude for telepathy—like you, Carmen. Many of these were used in our 'Adept' program, like Taker, for instance.

"The research on integration with humans did not stop. Many people were taken only briefly and let go virtually unharmed while others were destined to remain captives underground for the rest of their lives. These became integrated with the Megal. Most found happy lives down here. Eventually, the Megal hoped the humans taken by the Megal would aid them during the final integration stage when the Megal would announce themselves Overworld.

They needed a virtual army of these humans if this was to be accomplished without much bloodshed. Remember, the Megal Grays are few in number. For their loyalty, the Megal shared their name with these underground humans, and these humans now refer to each other as Megal as well."

Carmen asked what happened to those that did not find peace underground. Esha only waved her hand in dismissal, which Carmen took to mean that they were killed. When pressed about it, Esha explained that those released aboveground had their minds wholly erased, before they were released Overworld. The Megal humans knew this would happen to them if this were their choice, but they all felt this was preferable to death if any of them refused to stay underground. Life was actually of extremely high quality for those that remained. The Megal humans were far luckier than the Progeny.

Carmen opened her eyes slowly. A mental fog lifted, and her mind cleared. She was now looking at the strange Progeny woman next to her. She wondered why this woman had been elevated to an apparent level of some status, while the rest of her kind supposedly suffered in slavery.

If Esha read her thoughts, she gave no indication of it as she continued her narrative. "Humans injected with Megal plasma became the next field of study. Changelings shared many of the traits the Progeny bore. Those were longevity and abilities that could only be described, aboveground anyway, as…magic. Shape changing is also the result of this.

A few Changelings can pull extra mass, or 'dark matter,' from the etheric void between worlds, without even knowing how they accomplish it—rather like breathing or other autonomic mental functions. Consequently, they can assume forms much more extensive than their original size. They are unthinkingly following Einstein's equations for converting raw energy into mass. When they return to their natural shape, this borrowed mass returns to the space between worlds from which it came. One Overworld musician has written an accurate description of the 'void' in a composition he called 'The Magnificent Void.' He can be paraphrased as saying that it is the source of everything and cannot itself be derived from anything else. Although nothing concrete can be found within the void, nothing is missing. A few brave Overworld scientists have been experimenting with this same raw energy source. They refer to it as isotropic zero-point energy. Einstein foresaw it as a 'cosmological constant.'"

Esha fixed Carmen with a calculated stare.

"Since the Progeny were in many ways closely related to Changelings, a critical decision was made. Progeny would be given an elevated status underground if they would agree to pair up with a Changeling and teach that one about the powers he, or she, possessed. The reasoning was that any study of the Changelings might hold new important discoveries. When the time came to announce our presence, we hoped the Changelings would help pave the way."

Carmen asked, "Why did you say the decision to pair Changelings with Progeny was critical?"

Esha drew a deep breath, then let it out slowly. She scanned the chamber and took a full minute before her reply.

"The fear is that my people, the Progeny, will find closer ties with Changelings, which could add to the alienation between Progeny and the Megal."

Carmen was careful with her next question.

"And do you feel this could happen with you?"

Esha seemed to ignore her question. She stood slowly and smiled while holding her hands out to help Carmen to her feet.

"I saw you in my mind, Carmen, as you and your family grieved for Sara. I felt a closeness to you in particular, perhaps because we are alike in our attitudes toward life and life's pursuits. I would like to believe it goes beyond that, to matters of the heart, and that we could have been sisters had fate allowed."

Carmen reflected that she, too, felt…

She let her thoughts trail, uncompleted.

Esha nodded, guessing Carmen's mind, then guided her back the way they came.

Varr

It seemed obvious to both Nolan and Teil that they were supposed to be as comfortable as possible, and wait. The room had plenty of motel comforts, but the entrance remained a mystery. They did surmise that it responded to thought command. At one point, Teil tried a little old-fashioned kicking and shouting on it. After about fifteen seconds of that, Nolan wagged his head and closed himself in the bathroom. Teil finished his tirade by pounding the opaque black door with his fists. He followed that by shaking his fist after Nolan in the bathroom.

"I hope you're damned comfortable in there. Don't fall in!" No response.

Teil threw himself backward onto the bed and glared at the shiny black ceiling. Finally, the toilet made a sound, and Nolan reentered the room. He casually walked over and sat down on the edge of the bed while staring aimlessly around the room.

Nolan sounded almost wistful.

"All the creature comforts of a base officer's quarters. I'd hoped someone would knock you out for a while. No such luck, I see."

Teil fumed.

"You're a riot," Teil responded.

Nolan turned to look at Teil, who now seemed to be glaring intensely past the ceiling and boring a tunnel with his eyes.

Nolan said, "Look, Vince, this is what we got into this job for, wasn't it? Relax, we'll get out of here, somehow."

"You mean like Ferris did? You saw what they did to him. I don't think we are getting out of here at all. We are now among the vanished abductees, or whatever. We're going to have to fight our way out of here or stay. We've seen it plenty of times before." Teil gestured at the black door. "You've seen those bald guys out there. That is probably what happens to all guys like us. They get brainwashed and shaved. No thanks, man. I'm out of here any chance I get. And if I do get the chance, I swear to God, I'm going to kill that Taker bastard if it takes me a lifetime."

Nolan remained optimistic.

"Once we get out of this room, we'll locate Carmen and negotiate our release."

Teil interrupted. "Forget Carmen. We go when the getting is good!" He leaned up on his elbow. "If I make a move, you damn well better follow me. You're supposed to be in charge here!"

As if on cue, the door irised open with a whooshing sound followed by a slight gust of air. The air smelled faintly like a garden or a rain forest. Teil and Nolan jumped to their feet. Two bald men dressed in the same fashion as Taker's men entered and cautiously peered around the room. As far as could be determined, neither of the bald men carried a weapon. Behind them, the hall was lit by white light and seemed empty.

The man on the right broke the silence.

"We were just leaving the hydro-cavern and thought you both might enjoy a tour of our food stores. The provisions there are much better than what you have here. While you eat, we'll answer some of your questions."

He stepped to one side and gestured past his companion, out into the hall. Teil was the first to move. His speed shocked everyone, including Nolan. He grabbed the man on the right and threw one arm around his throat. He pulled one of his arms behind his back.

Nolan reacted out of sad necessity. This was not his choice in action, but they were nonetheless committed, thanks to Teil. He grabbed the other man before he could escape. Nolan yelled into his captive's ears.

"Shut the door. Now!"

The door irised shut without needing any visible gestures. Teil and Nolan, acting in unison, pushed their captives as far away from the door as they could, then told them to lay down on the floor with their hands behind their heads. The scene held for a tense moment before Nolan spoke.

"How far to the chamber where we arrived?"

The man Teil had grabbed spoke without hesitation. Neither man on the floor appeared the slightest bit concerned.

"Five minutes down the hall. Go left after you leave this room. I'm surprised at your reaction to all this. You could be learning everything you ever wanted to know, and more."

The other man lying next to him seemed to shrug, with difficulty, and said, "You guys go ahead and try escaping if you wish. I'm sure you are resourceful enough to find the entry chamber without us. You might want to wait until Taker has passed your door, however. He's making a…delivery."

Teil heard that name and actually experienced reddening of his vision. He said, "A delivery of what?"

"Not what…who. How many is actually a better question."

Teil was now in a constant state of livid. He grabbed the head of his man, obviously meaning to twist and break his neck.

Teil shouted, "Hey, asshole! Quit screwing around, or I swear I'll break your freaking necks, and I'll enjoy it! You said you'd answer our questions, now give it up or die!"

His man answered as carefully as he could.

"OK, all right, calm down." He grunted and said, "You've got to let up on me a little, so I can breathe."

Reluctantly, Teil released some of the pressure.

"All right," said Teil, "now talk."

The man took a deep breath before speaking.

"Taker is marching political prisoners, Varr, to a new location within the city. A couple dozen of them, at least. Taker's an 'Adept,' and those Varr more or less belong to him so they won't try to escape, but his Varr do share in his mental 'bent.' They're vicious and unpredictable. That's what happens

to Adepts and their Varr. They get really close, almost single-minded. It's weird. Taker's guardian Progeny, Lux, will also probably be with them. Lux and Taker are seldom apart from each other, except in matters aboveground. Take my advice, don't interfere with them. Let them pass before you run out of here."

Teil wanted more, but he let go of the man's head before demanding another answer.

"These Varr, they are political prisoners from where?" The Megal human answered slowly.

"Another sector of hyperspace, far from Earth. That's all I can tell you without charts to illustrate. The Varr seem to be some kind of hyper-being, but we can only see their three-dimensional component. If you're unfortunate enough to run into them, you'll understand what I mean. I hope you do not for your sakes. I can tell you that if Taker orders them to kill you—his Varr will certainly pursue you, and you won't escape them."

Teil was unimpressed.

"We'll take our chances. Besides, I have a score to settle with that Taker freak." Nolan told the two men to remain on the floor.

"You two better think three times before getting up, and stay there for a while. If you raise any alarms after we leave, I swear we'll come back and kill both of you before all of this is over."

Nolan's voice failed to carry the menace Teil's did, but the intent wasn't lost on the two men. They remained motionless and seemingly calm. They hadn't mentioned that they had both seen this reaction in abductees many times before.

Nolan stood by the door.

"We probably should take their advice and let Taker pass by first," Nolan cautioned. "We don't stand a chance, unarmed."

The door irised open.

Teil ran back and grabbed the same man he'd intimidated before by a wrist and yanked up as hard as he could while holding him down with a foot in his back. The man howled in pain.

Teil hissed, "Shut up. Who opened the door?"

The man winced with pain, and it was difficult for him to answer with Teil's boot pressing him into the floor.

"I did. You want out, don't you? Just get out. We don't care if you stay in here or not. We're from the above ground just like you, and we both learned the hard way, as you most likely will. You'd learn to love it down here if you'd just let them show you the way."

Having heard what the Megal humans said, Teil's expression changed into sick disbelief. He let go of the man who let out a gasp, after which Teil looked at both men on the floor with confusion and disgust all over his face. Finally, he got up and ran out the door, without the slightest glance back. Nolan regretfully followed.

Lighting was more than adequate, and air currents circulated a fresh, breathable mixture throughout the vast tunnel complex. Nolan and Teil raced back toward what they hoped was the direction of the entrance chamber. No plans, all action, and optimism. Within a minute of leaving the guestroom, they heard unusual sounds in the tunnel ahead of them. A weird buzzing, like bumblebees trapped in a thick wooden box. Seconds after the noise started, they both felt their skin begin to tickle and itch. It felt like electricity, or hundreds of tiny bugs crawling over their skin. They stopped and hunkered down against a wall at a dark bend in the tunnel.

Both men were scratching furiously.

Nolan whispered, "If this is due to something coming at us down that hall…"

Nolan didn't finish his statement before Taker's group rounded the bend in front of him. Taker was in the lead, followed by a tall hooded figure they took for Lux. Behind them filed a row of beings that nearly defied description. They were amorphous black shapes, and each alternately fat, and then lean. Transparent, and then opaque. Humanoid, and then not. They grew tentacles that became arms, before retracting into inky oblivion.

These beings, or whatever they were, drifted silently above the tunnel floor. They absorbed light and then briefly reflected it each time they shifted into opacity. Although their shapes remained in constant transition, their eyes were immutable. Each creature bore two burning, glowing, red eyes. These eyes were centered in a head that altered as frequently as the body and yet remained unblinkingly opaque. Their heads swam from side to side upon undulating shapes, while the eyes tracked in the air like deep red tracers in time-lapse photography. Despite their horror, Teil and Nolan knew they had to move while surprise favored them.

Teil launched himself at Taker with all the adrenaline his short muscles could afford. Nolan chose the figure behind Taker.

The struggle was brief but shortly satisfying to the attackers. By the time Taker's eyes began to glow, Teil was striving to choke out Taker's life with his own bare hands. Taker's face was crimson as he struggled to breathe. Nolan wrestled with the other, and nearly had Lux pinned to the floor when Nolan and Teil were both suddenly wrenched off their victims and then caught up into the air, and an invisible forcefield held them suspended in the air with their feet a foot off the floor. Both men began to feel their guts roll within them. Blood appeared at the corners of their eyes. Taker and Lux struggled to rise and then stood in front of them.

The hood had fallen from Lux's head. Neither Teil nor Nolan had ever seen Esha, so both men were shocked by his appearance. He looked very similar to Esha except for more substantial features. Lux lifted a hand toward the Varr and demanded that they be silent. Instantly the buzzing ceased and the dreadful itching, which had grown into a painful torment, stopped altogether. Taker grimaced and massaged his throat. He then spoke in a raspy voice that bespoke just how close he had come to having his windpipe crushed.

"We meet again. Apparently, our futures are hopelessly entwined." He nodded toward Teil and said, "It's too bad you've expressed a definite hatred for me." He considered a moment, then added, "If you are horror movie buffs like I am, you should have recognized the method of your friend Ferris's death. For your edification, that movie was called The Gates of Hell. I am going to enjoy a repeat performance of those special effects right now."

With that, Taker lowered his head and rolled his now blazing blue eyes up and into his head. He raised his palms. The two attackers, soon the victims, began to shake violently and their stomachs undulated as their internal organs struggled to crawl up their throats and out through their mouths.

Just then, Lux walked over to Taker, and took hold of his arms, lowering them. Taker's eyes rolled into focus and then confronted his guardian.

"Why do you stop me?"

Lux spoke in low tones of authority.

"Esha and Carmen approach. These two men will be required." Reluctantly, Taker let the two men drop to the ground, unconscious. As

Lux predicted the two women arrived within minutes. The Varr turned their attention to the tunnel behind them. Esha approached with Carmen close behind. She spoke first to the Varr.

"Take a human form. Your Varr shape offends me."

The foremost phantom spoke in a human voice that sounded more like dead leaves crunching underfoot.

"Do you wish us in clothes?"

Esha dismissed the sarcasm by ignoring it. A moment of itchy skin and then all of Taker's Varr had assumed a grotesque parody of naked human beings. Some were male, and some female, but all were deformed. They were perfectly capable of assuming an average human shape, but they chose these forms as a reflection of Taker's wicked sense of humor. They inherited his sense of humor due to the constant and close proximity to their 'Adept,' Taker.

Carmen was visibly shaken by the appearance of the Varr, and their shape-shifting substance did nothing to soften the shock. Esha moved forward as the Varr shuffled away from her. They offered the same grudging distance from Carmen as she followed. Taker and Lux were still massaging their bruised necks.

Esha indicated the two unconscious men. Now it was her turn for sarcasm.

"These two must have surprised you, taking account of your injured pride. Taker, you're overreacting, I'm shocked."

Before Taker could respond, Lux approached Esha. The two embraced. Taker only glared through eyes that no longer blazed with anything more out of the ordinary than irate aggravation.

There was a frozen moment during which Lux and Esha wordlessly exchanged an agreement. Lux turned to Taker and spoke while gesturing toward the Varr.

"These two men are valuable assets or will become so. Let your Varr carry them to the city, and forbid their communication until you deliver them to the City Center. We must see to it that they are comfortably well cared for."

Taker tried his best to shout in disagreement. His voice failed him in the attempt. All he managed was, "This one," indicating Teil, "will try to kill me."

Lux replied, "Defend yourself but do not kill him. I have just seen with my sister's eyes and agree with her that keeping them alive will be to our advantage."

Taker remained defiant.

"At least tell me why. I don't sense anything out of the ordinary in either of them. They're not Changelings."

Taker did not get a reply. Lux left with Esha and Carmen while Taker fought with his own injured pride.

Tactic

Lux, Esha, and Carmen headed for City Center, but they chose a route different from the one selected by Taker. They took a direction that afforded Carmen a chance to see more of the outlying areas surrounding the Megal city.

Carmen was taken to an observatory overlooking a vast hydroponics garden, sustained by wick systems and support machinery. Megal humans could be seen operating harvest and maintenance equipment throughout the chamber. These devices and vehicles ranged in size from small rounded carts to large tractor-sized designs. They were all uniformly colored a matte gray with red and yellow trim and had smoothly curved contours resembling nothing like Overworld machinery. For the most part, they did not operate on wheels but rather by antigravity. They shuttled about performing the same kind of endless tasks that farmers Overworld have done since farming began. Carmen was told that there were six of these hydro-chambers positioned symmetrically around the city's perimeter and they were all each at least two miles in diameter. Lux said they were designed to closely resemble the Earth's surface. They grew crops for food as well as cotton and flax for textile production. Light globes hovered throughout the vast cavern and imitated, as closely as possible, the sunlight above.

The hydro-garden received readily absorbable nutrients at their roots through an elaborate wick system that operated underneath the entire chamber. Plant life responded to this loving care with enthusiastic green growth. Carmen noted a grove of fruit trees on the opposite side of the hall from where they stood. Lux told her that they were apple trees taken from directly above them, from the state of Washington.

Lux indicated the hydro-chamber and its vortex with a wave of his hand. He explained that many such Megal chambers had a vortex at its ceiling center. The Megal could more easily travel to the Overworld through these doorways. Lux explained that travel through the ground did not require these, but without them, it was more difficult. Additionally, each vortex created an endlessly varied resonance that was easy to hear and enjoy.

After leaving the hydroponics chamber, they passed several of the typically bald Megal humans, and a few gray gargoyle-like creatures Carmen assumed were Progeny without robes. Carmen asked about this and was told that the robes marked a level of status for some Progeny. Those Progeny who were given robes were considered valuable assets to Megal society, rather than probable malcontents or insurgents.

The three of them walked through iris after iris and several chambers connected by intersecting tunnels. The activity consisted mainly of Megal humans, of both sexes, moving with considered purpose. An occasional Megal Gray flitted through the halls intent on some mission or another. Carmen remembered pictures she'd seen of these creatures. She remembered them as appearing sexless, so she deliberately looked for any telltale signs of gender. They seemed to have no visible genitalia or bulge of any kind. She mentioned this to Esha and received the only sensible answer she'd ever heard on this subject.

According to Esha, the Megal Grays copulated by touch. When they met for this purpose, they would appear to merge with each other. The air around them would blur, and a sound unique to the couple could be heard until they were through. Neither Esha nor Lux had seen this themselves, but they assured Carmen that it was absolutely correct. In fact, the Megal Grays still make love, even if procreation is not possible. They also have their own versions of erotica materials, which was made up mostly of sound. To human and progeny ears, these would sound hypnotic and incomparably beautiful.

Lighting remained a constant soft white throughout the city fringes. Carmen noted a high degree of technology, but little of that was identifiable to her. She indicated that carts and vehicles were not touching the floor in any way and appeared to respond to mental commands. These vehicles resembled the flatcars she'd seen in the hydro-chamber, in that they too were rounded in design.

Carmen found herself concerned over the apparent level of excitement she saw all around her.

She asked, "What's all the enthusiasm about?" Lux replied, "The 'Time' has nearly come."

"Do you mind elaborating on that for me?"

"The 'Time' is an inevitability rather than what some Overworld religious sects would call prophecy. It refers to when the Megal war with the Varr will eventually find its way into this solar system. It also states that the war will end here, for all time, one way or another. According to the ancient ones, the ones you call 'Grays,' the 'Time' is at hand and will be fulfilled within a year or so. You are a lucky woman to become a part of our fight, instead of an immediate casualty…that is if you choose to join us, and I hope you do."

Carmen stopped walking. Esha grabbed her and pulled her out of the way of an onrushing, seemingly unmanned vehicle. Carmen was already shaken, so she barely noticed that the vehicle was three times her height and could easily have killed her.

Carmen closed her eyes and breathed. "Can we just sit down somewhere for a while."

Lux smiled and nodded to Esha, then gestured them to follow him through an iris that opened into a place that resembled the first-floor foyer of an expensive Overworld office building. They took an air tube elevator up to a large conference room. The room was circular. The walls were lined with evenly spaced photos, and there was one big wood table surrounded by dozens of comfortable chairs. At the far end of the table, an optical communications device, resembling a television, stood ready to be switched on. They all took seats at the table. Esha watched Carmen's eyes as Carmen scanned the framed photos and recognized these to be aerial photographs taken of some of the more famous so-called crop-circle formations around the world. They were stunning, and most were not circular at all, but instead, intricate geometric patterns formed not only in fields but also in ice, snow, rock, and sand.

Esha commented on the photos.

"I told you we had our share of artists." She chuckled. "Actually, these representations are not meant to communicate with humanity, as some of your Overworld scholars think. They are warning signs directed at the Varr. We're not sure what form their invasion will take, but we should soon have a weapon that will stop them cold when they do invade. These patterns warn them that we do now have the potential to stop them."

Lux picked up the narrative and continued to explain the importance of 'patterns' when communicating with the Varr.

"The Varr communicate image and sound patterns, as well as mental disciplines in much the same way as the Megal. There is, however, a significant difference. The frequencies they generate when communicating with one another can harm, or most often kill all known corporeal carbon-based life forms. That fact alone has made it nearly impossible to decipher their language until now."

Lux paused to allow Carmen a question. She had none, so he continued.

"When the Varr last located, coveted, and consequently invaded a Megal world, the Megal managed to take some Varr prisoners. They accomplished this using a frequency, which they discovered to have a transitional paralytic effect on the Varr. Those few Megal survivors fled to this world, bringing their POWs with them, and joined the Megal already here. The resident Megal were terrified of a probable Varr incursion into this solar system, so they sped up the search for an effective weapon to use against the Varr by using the Varr prisoners for study. They eventually found that weapon in an unexpected and roundabout way.

"A field of Megal study, the Changelings, offered a possible solution to understanding the Varr. Changelings were found to possess specific adaptability properties that defied anything that the Megal were capable of in themselves. The 'Adept' program was born out of those new discoveries. Many of the Adepts have broken the communication barrier between the Varr and all of us. Using the knowledge we've gained from what the Adepts tell us about the Varr we've been able to conduct experiments in harmonic waveforms to generate tightly controlled transitional effects. We've made some limited advances.

So far, we've learned how to 'lock,' or confine, the POWs to specific locations without requiring us to restrict them by attempting to use physical barriers, which do not work well on the Varr anyway. They are hyper-beings and are therefore nearly impossible to restrain. To escape conventional restraint the Varr simply 'side-step' into another dimension they are as utterly comfortable in as they are in ours. That is one fact that has caused the war to continue for so long.

From what we know at this point, the Varr simultaneously exist in at least five dimensions at once. We know this much from what the Adepts have been able to glean from their Varr. Now that a way has been found to effectively pin them down somewhat, we hope to advance our own understanding of physics beyond what even the Megal now comprehend. In time we will bring this knowledge to the surface world as well."

Lux took a deep breath and continued, "After we accomplished a limited but powerful restraint, we turned our attention to commands of allegiance. This was a long shot, but eventually, we did discover a series of patterned disciplines, sent through microwave frequencies, that allowed us to transmit a command of allegiance to a group of Varr. This command 'locked' a specific group of Varr to one certain Changeling of our choice. This made the Adept program viable."

Lux cleared his throat. He said, "I would like to start here." He indicated what appeared to be the video device.

The viewing screen at the end of the table came alive with a news broadcast from Overworld. Lux explained that the transmission was a recording taken from earlier that week. Carmen recognized the CBS anchor. It showed world governments engaged in a struggle to understand alien frequencies being received from somewhere in deep space. What baffled most Radio amateurs in the SETI League was how the apparent point of signal origin varied.

The view changed and displayed several end-of-the-world cult groups roaming the Overworld city streets and shouting slogans, chants, and dire warnings. The crazies were definitely out in force. Doomsayers were everywhere. One on-the-street reporter interviewed a homeless man who claimed that he had received a message from space aliens and that they were coming for us, ready or not. He then began skipping and clapping his hands, while repeating, "Here we come ready or not."

There was another interview with several people wearing sunglasses and sporting various devices, symbols, and charms, which they had pinned all over their bodies. They made similar end-of-the-world-as-we-know-it proclamations with one significant difference. They also explained that these signals were from the enemy…and not friendly aliens.

Carmen asked Lux to turn off the display.

She said, "I've already seen these broadcasts. I suppose you know what they mean?"

Esha explained.

"Those people wearing the sunglasses are correct. The race that is generating that signal is the Varr. It is both a cursory probe and a navigational beacon. Its point of origin drifts because it is traveling through hyperspace, seeking not only this world but other sentient life as well. The different nomadic behavior is due to the morphing laws of hyperdimensional physics. So far, its effects are causing transitionally schizophrenic reactions in individuals already mentally unstable or psychically sensitive."

Carmen thought about the enemy aliens Esha and Lux referred to as the Varr. She tipped her head back toward the exit.

"Can you tell me if those beings with Taker were the Varr you mentioned? I only ask because I've seen them before."

Esha answered. "Varr, yes. As for your having seen them before, you must mean Yulan's Sentinel Wraiths."

Carmen nodded.

Esha explained, "Let me tell you something about Yulan and the

Varr he calls his Wraiths. The Megal watched the Claiborne family, including Yulan, for quite some time before deciding to attempt converting them to Changelings. They could sense a unique quality in your family. Before you ask, that quality has been impossible to define for any but the ancient Megal Grays, and they cannot adequately convey an explanation to us to show us how we might be able to understand and identify this quality in human subjects without the help of the ancients.

When Yulan and the Claibornes were converted to Changelings, the Megal carefully studied their DNA structures. In doing so, the Megal were able to identify any predisposition and latent talents beyond what the Megal already knew about them from passive observation.

Yulan was chosen for the Adept program because their tests concluded that he was possessed of significantly cognitive communication skills. Later, he was assigned a group of Varr without his understanding anything about them or where they came from. His Varr were keyed to him and then locked to the Claiborne ranch estate. This prevented their escape should they somehow break their conditioning before a bond could be established. Yulan was understandably unnerved and naturally assumed they were supernatural, but as a testament to his durable nature, he adapted in time to their constant presence and made the best of it. At that point, he initiated communication, and they responded in kind, as we'd hoped."

Esha stopped speaking as Lux pushed away from the table and stood. He slowly walked around the table, casually studying the pictures.

Lux picked up where Esha stopped.

He said, "We've achieved limited success in controlling the Varr, but we require more. We'd hoped that under adequately controlled conditions these Adepts might learn to communicate with their Varr and vice versa. We took the chance that these Adepts would somehow learn how to overcome the deadly side effects of Varr communication, by understanding it, and by teaching those Varr how to create harmless sounds approximating human speech. As it turned out, it worked.

The Adepts that survived the initial bonding experience not only learned how to deal with Varr communication frequencies, they also learned how to intuitively adjust their own Changeling bodies to accommodate those frequencies. As you might imagine, this was an exciting new discovery. These Adept 'adjustments' to their own bodies were considered the first indication that some Changelings were capable of a pure form of shape-shifting."

At this point, Esha commented.

"What Lux is referring to is only mild when compared to the kind of shape-shifting that you've seen Yulan perform on several occasions. I've seen a few of his transformations from within your memories. He's quite remarkable."

Carmen interrupted with a question that kept recurring to her, distracting her from concentrating on what Esha was explaining to her.

"Yulan's Varr, or Wraiths, seemed different from Taker's."

Esha touched Carmen on the arm and asked, "Let me see what you see for a moment."

Carmen waited. After only a brief delay, Esha sat back and resumed her narrative.

"From what I can tell, the Wraiths did what all Varr attached to an Adept will do, in time. They assumed many of the personality traits of their master. The reason for this is due to the way the Varr learn to adapt to any unknown or new situation. Assimilation. They assimilate what they do not immediately understand and mentally digest it as they go along. To the Varr prisoners their masters, the Adepts, were an unknown quantifier, so they emulated them as best they could in an attempt to understand them. In Yulan's case, he is nothing like Taker. Does that answer your question?"

"Yes, thank you. Please go on with what you were saying before I interrupted you."

Esha nodded and continued.

"The Adept project was an effort to turn some of the prisoners of war, from the last skirmish between the Varr and the Megal to the Megal's favor. The Varr have at least one exploitable weakness. They can be programmed like a computer if they are first opened to suggestion. This works in much the same way a hypnotist relies on the open mind of his or her subject. They establish a secure connection to their Adept, and then the Adept and their Varr act as one. It is not all that rare for their bond to remain unbreakable indefinitely, long after the conditioning wears off."

Lux walked over and stood next to Carmen. He changed the subject by asking Carmen a question.

"Do you recall how morbid Taker's Varr appeared?" Carmen nodded. "How could I not notice that?"

Lux smiled in agreement. He said, "As Esha explained, the Adept/Varr relationship causes the Varr to assume personality traits that mimic their Adepts. In Taker's case, this is unfortunate, but Taker is extremely gifted, so he is tolerated out of necessity. We need talented Adepts, even Taker. Their unique gifts are not a common trait among Changelings. I must emphasize that the Adept/Varr link has been so successful that we hope to use this as a key to discovering an effective weapon to use against the Varr during the inevitable Varr invasion to come. The techniques and weapons we'll need to develop after studying the Adept program should come within the year. We can only hope we have time in our favor."

Carmen's eyes wandered around the room, studying the photos while Lux sat back down and told her about other Adept projects around the world, past, and present. Each had their notable successes or failures. During the early stages of the Adept program, the control frequencies used by the Megal were inadequate and failed horribly. In these cases, the Varr shook off their initial conditioning, before a bond could be created, and then violently killed their Adept before escaping into the world. Most of those escapees were found. Most of them.

After listening quietly for another thirty minutes or so, Carmen had only one last question.

"Why is it possible for Changelings to exist here on Earth at all?"

Esha answered, "First, let's not assume that something like 'Changelings' could not exist elsewhere in hyperspace. We've just not seen it. I'm going to evoke a law of physics accepted by most Overworld physicists—the Heisenberg Uncertainty Principle. It states that there is a finite probability that seemingly unlikely events can happen anywhere and anytime. With that in mind it is not outrageous to accept the existence of Changelings here on this planet."

Esha had just evoked the ever-popular anti-argument, anything is possible, clause of quantum physics.

Carmen smiled and shrugged.

"OK then," Carmen said. "Let's see this city of yours."

Great White Eagle

Carmen finished her story by reminding everyone in the Suburban of the vision she had in the Megal museum. She said her aerial dreamscape of the underground city was just as accurate as the real thing, and that it was a fantastic place beyond adequate description. They would just have to see it for themselves one day.

Mel asked, "How did you get out? Where is Esha right now? Also, what happened to Teil and Nolan?"

Carmen explained.

"They flew me directly home in one of their craft. They do have cloaking capability, but it really doesn't matter who sees them. Nobody believes reports of UFO sightings. Esha accompanied me home, then returned underground. She stays in touch telepathically. She assured me that the entire world would know the truth about everything soon enough and that when the 'Time' came she would be with me."

She paused to consider her words.

"Nolan and Teil are alive, and in the same situation, you're in, Mel. They still don't know what their role in all of this really is. Megal humans underground hope to educate and enlist their aid for the 'Time' to come. There were those who felt they would make good Adepts if they could survive the Changeling process. However, from what I've heard, Nolan became a spacecraft pilot. Teil remains a security risk because he still wants to kill Taker."

Jenny looked bitterly sad.

"What happened to Nolan's wife?"

Carmen saw little tears in Jenny's eyes. She lightened the moment by giving her a tender hug. Jenny wasn't just a softy, relationships meant more to her than to most people.

Carmen smiled at her and said, "It's OK, Jen, and he visits her all the time and takes her for rides in his spaceship. They have more fun together now than they ever did before."

Jenny returned Carmen's smile, nodded, and then wiped her eyes.

Mel said nothing for a few minutes. The others gave him the silence he needed to soak in Carmen's story. Finally, he spoke.

"Look, all the coffee I drank wants to come out. I've got to stop at that rest area up ahead."

He pulled off the road at the rest stop and walked to the rear of the suburban, opened the back, and pulled out his duffel bag.

"Almost forgot to change," he said, before walking to the restroom.

Mel was alone in the men's room and was thankful for the chance to be by himself for a few minutes. As he stood in front of the urinal, he bounced a little to loosen himself up before relief spread through him. He sighed and thought about Carmen's story. He now felt thoroughly numb inside, but at least he was no longer depressed. His mind continued to drift. He thought about what he had overheard while listening to Andrea and Jenny talk in the background as Carmen told him her story. They'd mentioned the name Sara in passing, although not loud enough to really be heard above Carmen's narrative. They were trying to be polite, but that name stuck out, nonetheless. No matter what, on this leg of the trip he'd have to ask someone about Sara. Otherwise, his imagination was going to drive him nuts. Another thing that interested him was how Dane came to know Ben as Specter.

He stepped away from the urinal, then stripped down entirely before pulling on some long plaid underwear. Then came the obligatory Northwest attire—a tee shirt and flannel shirt, followed by the rest of his hiking attire. He stuffed his other clothes and deck shoes into the duffel bag and prepared to leave, then stopped and stared out the row of small windows set high in the outside wall. Did he just see a flash of silver in the sky? It was big, whatever it was.

***

Mel excused himself past Donovan as Donovan entered the restroom on Mel's way out. Dane met him before he walked much further.

Dane said, "If you don't mind, Mel, we're all going to change vehicles. All the guys will be traveling together with you until we get to the portal. The women want the bus to themselves for a while, and Marla's offered to drive for Specter."

"No, of course, I don't mind. Besides, you haven't told me your story." Dane looked at him speculatively for a moment then nodded without smiling.

"After you've heard it, you might wish you hadn't heard it at all."

Mel was actually feeling pretty good. He laughed and slapped Dane lightly on the back as they walked toward the Suburban. The familiarity didn't seem to bother Dane, but it made Mel feel better. He noticed Specter leaning against the Suburban, waiting, which brought another subject to mind. Mel asked Dane to wait.

"Hey, Dane. Hold up a minute."

Dane stopped and turned to face Mel.

"Yeah, what's up?"

"I'm just curious. How did you come to know Specter as Specter, rather than Ben? What's your connection with him, if you don't mind my asking?"

Dane smiled.

"No, I don't mind." He looked over at Specter, who was staring into the forest facing away from the restroom. Dane explained, "I met him as Ben in a convention several years ago. He was a friend of Jenny's father. He heard about my research in perceived reality manipulation using light and sound frequencies. He took an interest in my studies and offered to share information with me that, according to him, would boost my experiments into realms of science I hadn't even dreamed of. I found it hard to believe, but to my great fortune, I took him up on it."

Mel interrupted.

"Yes, but when did you know he wasn't human, or Changeling, or whatever?"

"I knew, or strongly suspected, from the moment he showed up at Claiborne mansion. He drove up late in the evening. I heard his bus when he arrived and watched him from an upstairs window when he got out. He immediately spotted the Wraiths when they massed at the edge of the forest. They were curious as usual."

Dane glanced over at the women, who were wandering around between the bus and the women's restroom. He turned back to Mel.

"Carmen just told me that she filled you in somewhat about Yulan's Varr." Mel nodded that she had.

"Good. Well then, you can imagine what any normal person's response would be to see those things hovering in the shadows nearby. Right?"

Again, Mel agreed.

"Well, Specter, and at that time I still knew him as Ben, wasn't frightened by their appearance in the least, which was my first clue that something wasn't what it seemed about him. My second clue was that he did not bother to ask me about them later. At that point, I knew he was hiding a secret I already suspected from a few things that Jenny's dad told me about him. I might add at this point that Jenny's father knew all about Specter, I found that out later. However, if Specter didn't want you to know who he was, he would cloud your mind from asking any questions if you so much as distrusted him, let alone suspected him of being something other than human.

When I met him at the front door, Specter saw something in my manner that led him to believe I was beginning to distrust him for some reason. He must have put two and two together because later that same evening he decided that rather than carrying on a charade he simply told, and showed, me what he was. As you might imagine I was amazed to see a legend in the flesh if you can call it flesh, but I got used to it, and his self-revelation certainly gave credibility to the new science he introduced into my experiments and equations. Does that answer your question?"

"More or less. Thanks."

Dane excused himself and followed Donovan. Mel stared at the Suburban.

Where was Specter?

Mel nearly jumped out of his skin when he became aware of Specter standing right next to him.

"Ready to go?" Specter asked cheerfully.

Mel and Specter passed Yulan on the way to the Suburban. He was studying a map posted on a covered bulletin board. Yulan tapped an area he thought might be their destination and then fell in with Specter and Mel as they walked to the Suburban.

As Mel started the engine, the back seat filled with Donovan, Yulan, and Dane. To Mel's discomfort, Ben, Specter, crawled into the passenger seat beside him. Mel preferred to think of Specter by his assumed name, especially with him so close. He shivered.

After Mel pulled out onto the road, he asked a nagging question.

"The plan hasn't changed any without my knowing about it, has it?" Specter answered him.

"Unless that probe is more than I think it is, there isn't any other plan that will work. I can't tell you anymore. You know that. Sorry, Mel."

Mel's mouth twitched in a rueful expression. "I just had to ask."

Donovan leaned forward across the seat and placed a hand on Mel's shoulder. Mel caught an amusing glimpse of him out of the corner of his right eye. That flight helmet had to go. It was ridiculous. Donovan's tone was meant to be comforting.

"I believe Coyote is calling you."

Soothing tone or not, Mel was unnerved by this guy. Mel had been having a lot of dreams about Coyote, not to mention Hramsem, the mischievous raven. In his thoughts, Coyote kept calling out to him while the raven found Mel no matter where Mel tried to hide. The idea varied from night to night, but the upshot remained the same.

Coyote and Hramsem were not going to take no for an answer from Mel. He was being sought for some great purpose. There was one other image in his dreamscape. It was the vision of the Great White Eagle. Coyote appeared to be trying to reach Mel using this figure as well.

The Great White Eagle watched and stood guard over the whole world and fed life to the Earth. Every time Mel saw the Great White Eagle, it met and held Mel's gaze. Mel shook himself a little. His mind had drifted. For some reason, the neckpiece Yulan had given him suddenly came to mind.

Yulan cleared his throat.

"Mel? You still with us?"

Mel chuckled and lifted the Celtic symbol off his chest to look at it.

"Yeah…I just thought that this design doesn't seem to work so well on Carmen. Ever since leaving the house, I've felt her occasionally playing around in my head." Mel lowered the neckpiece and said, "Oh well, it's beautiful workmanship. I'll definitely wear it anyway. Maybe it just doesn't work as well around a Native American's neck." He felt his throat stifle a laugh, but he fought it down and added, "I like it even if it doesn't stave off alien female thought control." He found this thought so funny that his eyes watered and his stomach cramped. He couldn't control it any longer. Mel laughed. His warm laughter was so contagious that soon everyone, including Specter, was laughing. After a minute or so, Yulan wiped his own laugh tears from his eyes.

Yulan said, "We think it's time you know about Sara." His statement quickly sobered everyone. Yulan regretted changing the mood but continued,

"Specter mentioned that you may be in a position, sometime soon, to help us with Sara."

Mel collected himself and asked, "Help her with what, how, and where is she?"

Yulan replied, "We don't know how you might help her any more than you do. Specter says it will come to you one day. As for where she is, she is currently out-of-body—more or less. I guess you could also say she is dead."

Specter made a noise in his throat, startling everyone in the Suburban. They'd all forgotten he was even in the vehicle with them. This uncanny ability Specter had of practically vanishing right in front of you was extremely unsettling. He wasn't invisible…you just simply fail to remain aware of him. Specter openly enjoyed his ability to cloud minds. In fact, he did so repeatedly throughout the trip to get a better grasp of how everyone was taking all of this. It was rather like being the mouse in the corner nobody noticed until he squeaked.

Specter said, "Relax, Mel, and the same to the rest of you. Answers to all your questions will come in due time. You have my word on that. Now please, Mel, you were interested in Sara."

Mel inwardly objected to Specter's indifference. He said, "Yeah, right, but I thought Dane said she just couldn't come along on this trip. Now, Yulan says Sara's dead and I still don't know why you insisted on telling everyone that I'm going to be able to help them solve their problems."

Specter merely shrugged and lifted an eyebrow. Mel took that for the only answer he was likely to get out of this secretive Varr spy, deposed prince, or whatever he was.

Mel remained somewhat irritated. He turned to look at Dane and then Yulan, before saying, "So, yeah, by all means, tells me about Sara."

Mel kept glancing nervously over at Specter, as though expecting him to disappear any minute. Dane had to remind Mel to keep his eyes on the road.

"Mel, please watch the road. He's not going anywhere."

"Yeah, yeah, I know." Dane continued.

"The first thing I want you to understand before Yulan tells you about Sara is that Yulan, Carmen, Andrea, and I have been alive for a very long time. In fact, I was born nearly one hundred and forty-four years ago." As Dane expected, Mel spun back around to look at him. Dane lifted his hand and pointed out the front window, directing Mel to focus his eyes back on the road. Mel did so hesitantly.

Dane said, "Yes, I know it's hard to believe, but I know Carmen informed you about some of the things Esha told her concerning Changelings, Progeny, and longevity. Some, though not all, of us, are extremely long-lived."

Dane paused, and asked, "Mel, are you able to hear more of this now, or should this story wait?"

Mel nodded and then shook his head from side to side. "No, I don't want you to wait. Go ahead. I'm dying to hear it."

Dane turned to Yulan and said, "Well, go for it."

Yulan related a story that took place in the late eighteen hundreds. Eighteen ninety-two, to be exact. A few of the particulars could only have been discovered since Carmen met Esha. According to Yulan, Esha's personal interest in Carmen has provided the Claiborne family, Yulan included, with a wealth of information about how the Megal create and interact with Changelings. Yulan's story revealed some of this inside information during his narrative. While Yulan spoke, Dane occasionally stepped into his account with some added details of his own.

According to Yulan, Dane had built Sara a large greenhouse on Claiborne property, set in the middle of an expansive well-groomed flower garden. Yulan's memories of the day Sara died invariably began in the greenhouse, the day after she'd potted several new varieties of tomatoes. In the late eighteen hundreds, many people in America still thought most tomatoes were poisonous. Sara hoped to help enliven the dinner tables and cooking recipes of many Seattle households with this wonderfully controversial fare.

The greenhouse was built to nurture new plant varieties Dane transported in as gifts for his youngest sister. Sara had a way with plants. This included fruits and vegetables as well as flowers. She loved her greenhouse and spent a great deal of time in it.

Sara (Dane's story)

Yulan recalled the summer of 1892, on the afternoon of July 19. He remembered that day very well. Sara was in her greenhouse, and it was late in the afternoon. Warm sunlight filtered through the older and less-than-perfect panes of glass set within the wood frames comprising Sara's hothouse. She kept a small coal-burning stove in the center of the building just for cold days and nights. That day it remained unlit.

Sara's long reddish-blond hair captured the sunlight in bouncing curls. She wore black slippers and a long blue dress, which complemented her moderate height and lithe figure. Inside, the plants were of varying variety, and several unlit candles surrounded the interior, set in reflecting sconces. Dust motes floated in the air. There was a dirt floor rather than the gravel floor Yulan later preferred, and old-fashioned hand tools lined the walls. Dane constructed the building out of cedar, and Yulan carefully maintained and preserved it. A strong aroma of wood and earth complemented the cheerful variety of plant life. As Yulan recalled that day, he felt as though he was there, with Sara, even now.

Sara was jubilant. It was a beautiful summer day, and there were so many flowers in bloom. Although Sara appeared to be a woman in her mid-twenties, her excitement was often childlike. She moved quickly and purposefully between each plant, inspecting them with a smile and a gentle touch. She examined a pot containing one of the new tomato plants. This one was a large beefsteak variety of tomato known as a Brandywine. Most of these were just beginning to turn a fiery red.

Moving on, she bent over another tomato plant that held clusters of smaller fruit. These tomatoes were called Red Currants, and they were ripe enough to pick. She cupped a few of them between her palms and breathed in the tangy fragrance. Just then, the door of the greenhouse squeaked open, then closed.

Sara turned her piercing blue eyes to greet the man that entered carrying a large white mug filled with something hot and steaming.

"Yulan," she said, "look at how well these have ripened. I'm going to take some inside for dinner. It's my turn to cook. By the way, did Dane have any luck getting that English cook to take the job we offered him?"

"Well, unfortunately, no. We still can't convince anyone to work out here. They're frightened by our forests, and who can blame them. Oh well, we're all good cooks out here as a result. The same can be said for all the other work that needs doing."

He smiled and held the cup out for her.

"Here, I brought you some of that coffee Dane brought back from his last import purchase."

She accepted the coffee and thanked him, then shifted the cup into one hand before she plucked off one of the Red Currants and tossed it to him.

"Here, try one of these, they're wonderful. I can't wait for these others to mature. I've promised to sell some in town by next week."

Yulan popped the tomato into his mouth and made noises of enjoyment. Still chewing, he then stepped up next to her and ran his fingers through her hair. She smiled, and her eyes sparkled as she looked at him. Yulan was a rugged and moderately attractive man of medium height and a thick, muscular build. At the moment, he wore the soiled coveralls of a ground's keeper. His age appeared to be in his thirties although his hair was prematurely gray. The only disquieting features about him were his eyes. They were chalk white, but Sara loved them.

He wiped a little tomato juice from his lip, then kissed her before turning to inspect the tomato plants.

"You'll have to hand pollinate these you know. I think bees are probably out of the question in here."

She cuffed him playfully.

"I know what I'm doing…no bees." Sara took a sip of her coffee. "Mm. This is good."

She put the cup down and smoothed her dress.

"Hey," she said, and a sudden look of excitement crossed her face. "I ran across an old tree just loaded with beetles at the meadow's edge in the south forest. Dane's been experimenting with bugs lately, and I think he said something about needing some beetles. I think he's planning to detour during his next voyage by ship to gather some exotic bugs. I guess that's mixing business with pleasure. I don't know, maybe some local variety of beetle will temporarily keep him satisfied. Of course, maybe not, but it's worth a try to keep him home for a while. I miss him when he takes off for so long. Anyway,

I'm going to go grab some for him. Do you want to go with me?" She picked up the coffee and took a long warm gulp.

Yulan thought a moment, then shook his head and walked back to the entrance. There were several pails stacked against the wall. He picked up one of them and handed it to Sara. She accepted it, knowing that he was going to turn her down.

He said, "No, I'm sorry, I can't. I've got to fix the fence before all the livestock gets out. When Andrea left for town with Carmen and Dane, she told me that she noticed the fence got pretty badly busted up during that last storm. Just another reason I wish we had some hired hands. You know, it's my opinion that 'spooks' are not the only thing preventing workers from coming out here. I'd bet Randal Kane is intimidating people against accepting our job offers, but then that's just my opinion. I know Dane's been working on getting some day help, but I guess for right now, I'm it."

Sara looked a little guilty.

"I'll help you when I get back. OK?" He smiled.

"Sure, but don't worry about it. I'll probably be done around here by the time you get back, and then we'll cook up some of these tomatoes together. What do ya' say?"

She brightened again.

"Sounds great."

Yulan became serious.

"Remember," he began, but Sara interrupted him before he could say anything else.

"I know, I know," she said, with thinly-veiled exasperation on her face.

"The Sentinel Wraiths guard the forest only within the bounds of this estate. You repeat that warning any time I might get too near to the forest's edge."

Yulan took her free hand and pulled her close.

"That's right, dear, I do worry about you. Perhaps needlessly, and yet I have a feeling, here." He touched his chest. "It's an omen I cannot put a finger on. Please, just be careful."

***

The Sentinel Wraiths appeared many years before this day, just after Sara's parents returned from a trip into the Cascade Mountain Range. Both parents were terrified by an encounter that happened to them during their trip. They claimed to have seen demons in the mountains. Her father was a big man and resembled Dane in his clean-shaven features. He helped his wife through the front door, where they both collapsed onto a couch in the sitting room. His Scots-Irish wife was a strikingly beautiful woman that typically carried herself with fearless poise. She now curled herself into his arms like a terrified little girl.

Soon after that, they made bizarre and elaborate preparations around their home, setting up talisman wards against what they perceived to be evil entities with big black eyes. On the same night of their return home, three globes of bright pulsing orange light, six feet in diameter, appeared in the sky over the Claiborne ranch estate. Each globe was centered below a dark circular mass the size of a baseball diamond. The saucer-like objects were outlined against a glittery night sky. A deep, resonant hum and a metallic tang in the air accompanied them. Nocturnal animals and insects became silent and dormant.

Upstairs in the mansion, Andrea fell asleep in her bed while reading by lamplight. Across the hall from her room, Carmen had already been asleep for an hour, but in the room below her on the main floor, Dane had collapsed in slumber over a desk loaded with paperwork and charts. He had been drinking a cup of tea when sleep overcame him mid-sip. The cup spilled from his fingers and tea soaked into the papers under his face.

Sara and Yulan had been walking together around the side of the mansion when they suddenly fell asleep together right in the middle of the path they were walking on. The two elder Claibornes were up late in the barn, not far from the mansion, tending to some neglected chores, when they both fell asleep while pitching hay. They dropped into the hay together and seemed to be sleeping peacefully under the warm glow of lamplight. Earlier, the ranch hands and Chinese cook, Tao, had left the estate for their own homes.

The strange lights floated gracefully over the silent ranch estate for several hours. Occasionally brilliant beams of white light shot down from the orange globes and entered the mansion as though its roof and walls were as insubstantial as vapor. One ray of light enveloped Sara and Yulan, then lifted them off the ground and carried them into the sky where they disappeared for several hours into one of the orange globes. Later, they were returned to the exact spot from which they were taken. When the circular objects and orange lights drifted away and disappeared over the treetops, the insects resumed their chirping, and those humans that fell asleep unexpectedly stayed that way until morning.

The following night Yulan discovered the creatures he later dubbed Sentinel Wraiths, or they found him. The Wraiths surrounded him as he tidied and manicured the earth around the greenhouse. They seemed to adopt him, for whatever reason and called him Master. Yulan panicked. He ran, but they encircled him at every turn. After a couple of days, it became apparent that these Wraiths were irrevocably drawn to him.

They watched him day and night. At first, he thought they were nocturnal creatures by the way they remained in shadow during daylight hours. Later, he reasoned that they must be frightened, or unsure of their surroundings, which in Yulan's opinion were the only apparent reasons they hugged the shadows during the day.

For several weeks, the Wraiths remained hidden from anyone but Yulan. Eventually, Sara did see one of them and screamed for Yulan to protect her. At this point, Yulan decided to bring the issue of the Wraiths to the attention of the rest of the Claibornes. The parents were shocked by the revelation. They worried over what the appearance of these things might mean. Were they demons?

In the beginning, Yulan felt his skin itch when they approached. It then progressed to the point of pain, and finally life-threatened agony. When this happened, he would run into the mansion and lock the doors. The Wraiths seemed to sense his need for isolation and never attempted to enter the building. The physical pain he suffered whenever the Wraiths appeared was an abiding problem worse than the existence of the black ghosts themselves. He approached all of the members of the Claiborne household with this problem, but no one had any suggestions, except for Dane.

Dane began to ponder the buzzing noise that accompanied the Wraiths. He and Yulan came to suspect that this was a kind of communication between the spectral shapes. Yulan once tried to silence them by holding up a hand in an unmistakable gesture of impatience. The Wraiths immediately recognized this as a discipline for quiet, and the noise stopped, as did the itching. Yulan shared this discovery with Dane.

In time, Yulan taught the Wraiths a likeness of human speech, free from the itching and discomfort caused by their regular communication. The rest of the Claiborne household was understandably upset by the appearance of these ghostly apparitions. Mr. & Mrs. Claiborne were sure that they were demons and that they came to Yulan because of some stealthy extramarital "wrong" that Yulan had secretly been engaged in with Sara. They forbid Yulan and Sara from any intimate contact.

Yulan challenged Sara's parents and even went so far as to suggest to Sara that they elope. Sara

thought about it, but then decided that she needed to stay and watch over her mother, who was growing sickly over her husband's preoccupation with the Wraiths.

Years passed during which the father continued to travel far and wide as required by his import/export business. On June the twenty-ninth, 1870, Captain E.A. Starr invited him to join the inaugural round-trip steamer run across the Sound from Seattle to Port Townsend. That town was the Puget Sound's second city, founded in 1851 just after Olympia and six months before Seattle. It was a thriving international seaport, with a reputation as notorious as San Francisco's Barbary Coast. Mr. Claiborne was so taken by this opportunity that he used this run regularly from then on to make connections out of Port Townsend for long trips by sea. This allowed him to travel broadly and earned him a reputation as a bold adventurer.

Among the everyday items for sale along Commercial Street, he would return from these adventures with cases of acquisitions he'd purchased for his own private collection. These included arcane tools, mysteriously elaborate mechanisms, books, metals, and metallurgic supplies. As time passed, he and Dane developed a strong bond born more out of a thirst for knowledge than paternity.

When Dane was not engaged in the considerable chores required to maintain their ranch estate, Dane would take a horse into the city and spend the rest of his time in Seattle at Denny University. He and his father would compare notes on new schools of philosophy, religion, and science, which eventually opened the door for his father to reassess what he now called Yulan's Wraiths.

Mr. Claiborne threw away most of his old-world orthodox views and began to embrace the idea that these Wraiths were from another dimension. He'd read about this in an article he'd received with other reading materials he had shipped to him from England. The article was first published in the Dublin University Magazine and entitled "What is The Fourth Dimension?" by Charles Howard Hinton, a graduate of Oxford University. It was then reprinted in 1884 in the Cheltenham Ladies' College Magazine and renamed, "Ghosts Explained." After hearing about that last title, he immediately set about to procure a copy of it for himself. It changed his entire outlook on the Wraiths. Sara and Yulan were understandably overjoyed by his new frame of mind. He seemed ready to allow Yulan to ask Sara to marry him when things changed for the worse.

***

Since the Wraiths first appeared on the ranch estate, all attempts to keep hired help of any kind failed, and the townsfolk were spreading rumors that the Claibornes were witches and warlocks. The other thing that came under cruel scrutiny was the fact that all of the Claibornes, except for the parents, were not aging the way they should. In fact, they appeared not to be aging at all.

For the parents, this uncanny realization began for them a gradual descent into madness and superstition. After the father became convinced that his children might have been granted immortality for some reason, he renewed his demand that Yulan stay away from Sara. His reasoning was as simple as it was frustrating. If they were immortals, then according to all he was able to guess about this kind of thing, they would lose their immortality and die if any of them lost their virginity. He even came close to ordering Yulan from the property.

At that point, Dane, Yulan's long-time friend, intervened. His father was angered by Dane's contradiction, but he temporarily relented from any further action. Yulan and Sara continued to see each other whenever the parents were not around, but they remained as chaste as possible, in case Sara's father was correct. No one knew for sure. They both prayed that the mystery would soon be resolved.

Yulan and Sara loved each other to the degree that nothing would prevent them from remaining with each other. Yulan again tried to convince Sara to flee with him, but Sara refused out of concern for her mother's health. Her mother and father shared the same age, and both were now well into their old age. She continued to busy herself with Andrea and Carmen over domestic affairs and sometimes took cross-country trips with Carmen. Yulan worked with Dane to care for the ranch estate.

Without any hired hands, there was plenty to keep everyone well occupied. Despite the father and mother's warnings to remain chaste, Sara and Yulan would steal away for as intimate a relationship as they dared share with one another. Sara's brother and sisters knew of this and kept it secret from the parents.

Sara and Yulan fell into a deep melancholy and despair that began to mirror the elder mother's escalating depression. One day after the father returned home with another load of esoteric supplies that including a ton of copper sheeting Dane flew into a rage over Yulan and Sara's grief. He shouted that his father was a fool and that he wished he would go off to Egypt and never return. He told his father that Yulan and Sara had nearly left home together any number of times and that they should have done so for their own sakes.

It was during Dane's tirade that startling evidence of Dane's Changeling powers first manifested. Dane's eyes suddenly erupted with a blue flame, and then a bolt of lightning flashed from his eyes and knocked his father back several yards, where he lay unconscious. This confrontation had taken place in the circular drive in front of the mansion.

Andrea and Carmen had been watching from an upstairs window after hearing Dane's outbursts of rage. They ran out to see if their father was all right and to determine what had happened, if anything, to their brother. The three of them carried their father inside and laid him on the couch. Their mother ran down the stairs to see what was happening. She knelt and held her husband fearfully and demanded to know the cause.

Dane explained what he'd done and expected her to blame him. Instead, she cried and blamed herself. She continued to condemn herself even after her husband recovered and attempted to dissuade her from what they all perceived as her downward spiral, emotionally and physically. This stayed for a week before she fell into a nervous condition, or an illness, from which she never recovered. She would no longer speak and spent most of her time in bed. She took meals and engaged in other activities that required her attention, but for the most part, she was withdrawn into her own miserable world of guilt for having brought the demons home. Nothing anyone could say would convince her otherwise.

From that day forward, the father refused to leave on any more trips. He told his banker to handle his affairs, while he remained at the estate. He said Dane that he was all the more certain that everyone on the estate, apart from him and his wife, were somehow blessed, and not cursed. They had become something more than human.

Once again, Yulan and Sara took heart, only to have their hopes dashed back when the father told them he was now even more convinced that their immortality would indeed reverse horribly if any of them should lose their virginity. They might age rapidly and die as withered corpses within seconds. He related for them tales of this occurring in Egypt and parts of Europe. He'd gathered his elaborate belief system over years of travel and worry over his family and the Wraiths. He unreservedly announced these beliefs to be accurate, and his eyes danced with the passion of a zealot. Sara believed her father. Yulan could see it in Sara's eyes. There was nothing more that could be done. They had long since resigned themselves to chastity, and now Yulan knew that would never change.

The father enlisted Dane and Carmen to help him build an expansive room under the greenhouse. He chose this location because he was convinced that it was ideal for keeping the place a secret. He lined the room with the imported copper sheeting he diverted from France to Seattle while France was in the process of providing copper sheeting for the Statue of Liberty. He'd planned to build a particular room for experiments with electricity. Electricity was his new fascination. He chose to line the room for purposes of conductivity and bade Yulan keep the copper clean and polished. Now he would combine his esoteric pursuits with studies in electromagnetic fields using the copper coils and exotic mechanisms he'd purchased from far and wide. He would spend the rest of his life seeking to solve the riddle of what his own family had become, and to search for the evidence and cause of what new powers his children might possess.

Possible immortality brought with it the fear that someone might take it from them by force. In other words, rape. The father had seen more than his share of violated innocence in his travels. He would not say so out loud, or to any of his children, but he often worried that Yulan might rape Sara out of frustration. He could not tolerate this thought, and so he lectured his children as they helped him build the room under the greenhouse.

He told them what to do if any of the sisters should become the victims of rape. They must see to it that the rapist takes the place of the victim in eternity. Otherwise, the immortal's soul would wander helplessly through the nether world. Better to have the rapist suffer instead and therefore free the victim to go on to heaven. Both Carmen and Dane knew these ravings to be the result of their father's growing dementia. However, they were again unsure of themselves, since it was evident that something had changed in them, and they had no idea what the rules were.

Over some time, Dane, Carmen, Andrea, Sara, and Yulan learned what they could from the elder Claiborne father. He had amassed a considerable fortune in books, tools, weapons, and remarkable materials of all kinds. They learned about current scientific thought as well as world religious beliefs. The father would disappear beneath the greenhouse for days while conducting fearsome studies and gruesome rituals. For him, the room took on some mysterious purpose that the elder Claiborne withheld from everyone.

He told them ancient myths and horror stories he felt they had to take seriously if they could ever hope to survive in the sainted world around them. He also instructed them on how to wreak vengeance on those that should ever harm them. Sara took this for compassion in her father, and it caused her to believe most of what he told her. Again, he described specific instructions for what they were to do in case any of the sisters were raped. He drilled it into them. These instructions included a macabre ceremony for which he'd built a grotesque cube-shaped device to be used in that event. He'd constructed this thing using the forge out by the stables, and an array of metallurgic tools.

One day the father kissed Sara on her forehead, then ambled up the stairs and locked his bedroom door behind him. He never reemerged. A day later, after no response from repeated knocking, Dane forced open the bedroom door and found his father curled up in bed next to his wife. They had both passed away. The family doctor was driven up from town. He determined that the mother died first from malaise and then the father soon after that by a heart attack caused, most likely, from grief. Both parents died at the age of seventy-seven.

Many things changed after Sara's parents passed away, although the fears and taboos remained. Her parents died when she was fifty-seven years old, although she looked twenty-five. Five years later, the day of Sara's untimely death, she still looked twenty-five.

***

Sara kissed Yulan passionately on the lips. She then hastened her way to the greenhouse door. Her dress fluttered out in pleated folds.

"I'll be back soon. Try not to worry about me."

She hurried through the door and out into a sunny afternoon. She sped past the back of the greenhouse, through the grove, and then on into the forest.

Yulan left the greenhouse and then turned to regard the mansion. The drive needed raking. He made a note of the four-foot high elder Claiborne tombstones nearby the greenhouse. They needed cleaning.

The year was 1892. It was late in the afternoon. "The Queen City of the Puget Sound," Seattle, was blossoming with new products and ideas imported by ship and by train from back east and around the world. The building boom was in full swing, and the city had just finished reconstruction after the great fire of 1889 destroyed most of the businesses in downtown Seattle. There would be another shake-up in 1893 with an international financial crash, but for now, companies were prosperous.

Electric trolleys were being industriously installed for passengers and commerce. Electric lighting would soon compete with gas for illuminating the streets late into the night. Sunlit boardwalks creaked under throngs of booted feet. A few brave Chinook Indians roamed uncomfortably among the noisy white populace. Colorful parasols frequently broke the ever-present haze of dust, twirling in the hands of gentle ladies out for a day of shopping and social graces. An ocean breeze swept a pleasant salt-sea smell into the bustling streets, where it mixed with the more mundane odors of manure and cigar smoke. Horse-drawn carts and carriages ruled the thoroughfares, and you might occasionally catch sight of a brave new bicycle owner.

On this late afternoon, three rough-looking men loitered outside the new Toklas and Singerman department store. Their mounts were tied to the boardwalk rail. One man sat on a bench to the right of the door, with his arms draped over the back of the seat. He wore a dusty brown suit. The second leaned against the wall to the left of the department store entrance. An eye patch marked his right eye. The third remained in the open while leaning against a post. He rolled and then lit a cigarette. All three men were doing a terrible job of looking inconspicuous.

Inside the store, clientele moved from aisle to aisle and room to room, upstairs and downstairs. They shopped between shelves of household goods, table displays of foreign merchandise, racks of clothing and weaponry, and a potpourri of other items. The air was sweet with the smell of fresh wood construction, soaps, oils, and perfumes. This department store claimed to be the most complete shopping experience around, and it drew customers from up and down the coastline just to find out if this was true. For the most part, it was. It was also a wealthy employer and the first store in Seattle to take full advantage of electric lighting.

Several women and their complement of children pressed and shuffled through the textile section. Behind a counter, one of several clerks scattered throughout the store was speaking with a young woman while cradling a bolt of cloth in his arms. He was overweight and balding and wore small round glasses. Somehow, he fit himself into an expensive woolen sweater that looked two sizes small on him. The woman was tall and shapely. She wore a long bustled dress with a light shawl and brown lace-up boots. Her long blond hair spilled gracefully down her back and on either side of her face. She leaned over the counter and accepted the cloth for closer inspection.

Nearby, another woman, with the same hair and build, was

holding a long rifle in one hand while examining a durable blue dress with the other. She shifted the gun under one arm while pushing her other hand through the rack of dresses until she found what she liked. She was a beautiful woman, and wore buckskin overall, with her hair pulled tightly back. She had a large black knife strapped to the outside of her right thigh. After she located an acceptable dress, she pulled it out on its hanger and held it up in front of her. She nodded and walked it over to the counter next to the woman examining the bolt of cloth.

The woman in buckskin laid the rifle onto the counter, and then the dress.

"I'll take both of these, Amos. Can we pay for both of them right here?" Amos responded in a cheerful tone.

"Sure thing, Carmen." He turned to the other woman and said, "How about you, Andrea, do ya like this one?"

Andrea said, "No, I think I like the other one better. Sorry."

"No problem."

Amos took the rejected bolt of cloth back to the shelf and returned with the plaid she liked.

Carmen was fingering the design on the carved wood stock of the rifle she was purchasing.

"I really like the workmanship. Are these designs native?" Amos peeped over his glasses.

"I think you have met the guy that made them, Carmen. That old fellow that lives on the south road finished that one for me, and a couple more stocks upstairs. You can take your pick of 'em if you'd like."

"Yes, I'd love to see those, but another time, thanks." Amos was staring at her.

Carmen smiled and said, "Amos?"

He shook himself and realized with some embarrassment that he'd let his mind drift. He couldn't help it. Amos enjoyed listening to these twin sisters talk. He'd known them for some years now, and he always found their voices to sound like the most elegant music he'd ever heard. There was something magical about them.

Amos cut a length of fabric then packaged it for Andrea. Carmen placed a hand on her sister's shoulder.

"Are you ready to go? We could walk down to Commercial and do some window shopping."

Amos packaged the cloth and then the dress. He knew Carmen well enough to know that she wouldn't want the rifle wrapped. Andrea paid for their purchases from a small purse she wore around her waist, and the twins accepted their packages.

Andrea turned to Carmen and said, "I don't think we should leave before Dane arrives. He promised to pick us up out front."

Carmen nodded in agreement but rationalized, "We'll see him when he comes by and flag him down. Come on, it'll be fun."

Andrea smiled, then turned and peered out the front windows. A man was smoking a cigarette on the boardwalk outside the door. She stopped her sister from walking any further and pointed out the window.

"Those guys have been following us all over town."

"I know it, Carmen said. "They've been pretty obvious about it, too. Loosen that boot knife of yours, Andrea."

Andrea made a veiled move to do as she suggested while appearing to scratch her leg.

Carmen was the first out of the door. She turned right and stepped past the man on the bench. Andrea followed. The man in the brown suit jumped up and quickly stepped in front of the two women, effectively blocking their path. The two other men converged on the women from behind.

"Excuse me, ladies, the boys and I would like to introduce ourselves." Carmen glared at him.

"Not necessary, thank you."

She tried to move past him, but he moved along with her. He smiled evilly and looked past her. Carmen turned around to see Andrea being held by the other two men. They didn't seem to be exerting their full energies on her, yet it was apparent by their expressions that they wouldn't mind a little more action.

Carmen raised the rifle slightly, but enough to position it just under the man's chin. He only continued to smile. He pushed the muzzle away from his chin and said, "It's not loaded." Then he introduced himself as though nothing were wrong.

"I'm Jed. Your sister's friend back there with the eye patch is Tim, and the smoker is Maurice. We're pleased to meet you."

Before Carmen had a chance to respond, Andrea wrenched herself free with astonishing strength and speed.

It was Carmen's turn to smile. She said, "You underestimate Andrea. She has a temper. Besides, our brother will be along soon, and you do not want to meet him under these circumstances."

Andrea reached down and produced an impressive blade from her boot. She then quickly crossed to her sister's side. The locals around them noticed the confrontation and the knife. Several bystanders went for help.

Maurice squinted through a puff of his smoke. He spoke with his cigarette held loosely between his lips.

"A few of the locals told us an interesting tale about your family. They say that you are witches, freaks that never age, while clean folk live and die around you. Is that right?"

Tim squinted his one good eye and licked his lips.

"Ain't it a good thing," said Tim, "that they don't burn witches out here. That would surely be a true waste of a woman." He finished that with an oily grin. He added, "We ain't worried about your brother. He's being entertained."

***

It would not be long before sunset, and it was visibly darkening outside. Dane reined his horse-drawn wagon passed a young lamplighter preparing to work his way along Mill Street and then on to Commercial and the rest of the downtown area. Soon, electricity would cost the lamplighters their jobs. He drove through Pioneer

Square and tied the wagon up in front of the Occidental Hotel. He left the boardwalk as he entered the Puget Sound National Bank on the ground floor of the hotel. Three patrons passed him on their way out the door. There was a well-armed man posting watch with a rifle just inside the door.

Floorboards creaked under Dane's well-turned black boots. He breathed in the smell of luxury. The walls were lavishly covered in ash and black walnut. He stepped up to the cashier's counter. The banker was a tall man with broad shoulders and tended to stoop. He scratched his well- combed head, and then scribbled something out on a notepad. The banker glanced up from his work to greet Dane.

"Good afternoon, Mr. Claiborne. I was just about to lock up for closing. What can I do for you?"

"Sorry, it's so late, Al. I'd rather not wait for you to open in the morning." Al gave a wry smile and asked Dane how much cash he needed. Dane brushed aside his long black woolen coat and unfastened a wallet from his belt. He asked Al if he would mind if he used his notepad a moment. Al tore off the top sheet and put it in a drawer, then handed Dane the pad. Dane scrawled out a set of numbers and gave it to Al who then nodded and opened the till to pull out some tender. Al filled out some paperwork, which Dane then signed. Dane tucked the cash into his wallet and refastened the purse to his belt.

Al asked, "Just curious, are you planning to buy Sara that bicycle she's been wanting? They're affordable. The wife says Sara eyeballs it every time she comes into her store." Dane shrugged.

"You know I might just do that. Maybe tomorrow, after I take care of the shipment."

Dane turned to leave, then noticed two men wearing dusty riding gear enter the bank. Two men he knew. Two men with nasty reputations. Dane turned back around to face Al. Al took the opportunity to advertise a little.

"Would you like to hear my new loan options?"

"Later, Al, right now, you might want your shotgun handy."

Al's professional enthusiasm gave way to a mixture of bewilderment and fear, but he wasted no time in reaching under the counter for his shotgun.

Two pairs of heavy footsteps walked through the bank, followed by a gruff warning for the guard to put his rifle down and that they were not going to rob the place. Dane did not turn to face them right away. He watched Al's eyes widen and focus on the new arrivals. They walked up and stood a little distance behind Dane. They both held handguns loosely pointed at Dane's back. There were several sharp intakes of breath around the room. The only other patrons, two old women, and one dapper businessman noticed the drawn weapons and quickly left the bank. The man on the left side of Dane's back was the younger of the two. He wore a long handlebar mustache. The other bore a menacing look with several facial scars and a blind, dead looking left eye.

The younger man spoke first.

"We already told your man over there that we ain't here to rob you, Al, so put down that damn shotgun."

Al slowly lowered the weapon onto the counter, then raised his hands a little, and took a step back. The young man nodded cheerlessly.

The man with a dead-eye spoke in a grinding voice.

"We've come for you, Claiborne. Our boss wants to speak with you." Dane turned around.

"No doubt, your boss is Randal Kane. You tell him from me that if he develops land any nearer our ranch or our forest, he will raise worse than Hell for himself."

Dane moved to step past them.

He said, "Now, get out of my way."

Deadeye lowered his head and stepped in front of Dane, blocking his way. The younger man moved closer to his companion, also blocking Dane's path.

"Let me repeat this, Claiborne," Deadeye threatened. "Mr. Kane wants the pleasure of your company tonight after he picks up your younger sister, Sara. He's gonna propose to her, and then perform the wedding ceremony himself. No doubt you Claibornes will benefit from such a…union."

The younger man snickered, showing some rotten teeth.

Without warning, Dane grabbed the two men by the front of their shirts and pulled them off balance. He dragged them both to within inches of his face. Both men uttered noises of surprise and anger. Dane's eyes suddenly burned with bright blue fire, causing the two men to stare into them with disbelief. Were they really…glowing?

Dane yelled into their faces, spittle flying from his lips.

"So, are you here to entertain me? Clowns no doubt!" Shaking with fury, he continued. "Well, you may tell Kane that if he so much as touches Sara, I will kill him in ways that are hard to describe!"

Dane tossed the two men to either side of the room with unearthly strength, like spent shells from a rifle. He briefly regarded each fallen man with his searing eyes that looked like two sapphire lightning bolts ready to strike, which made it difficult to see the rest of his face. He took great strides for the door and then quickly left.

The door guard watched Dane through the window as he hurried to the end of the boardwalk and then jumped into his horse-drawn wagon. Dane shouted to the horses as the cart leaped forward and quickly passed in front of the bank. Then he yanked on the reins and pulled the wagon into a hard left turn, which forced the cart into the opposite direction.

Groaning, the two victims of Dane's wrath slowly unfolded themselves and stood. Both men were in considerable pain. Dane had lifted each man from the floor with one hand per man. The force he expended in slamming them against opposing walls was nothing short of supernatural.

The guard tried to lighten things up a bit.

"Good folk the Claibornes, unless you cross one of them."

In response, two handguns leveled at his head. Kane's men simultaneously yelled for him to shut up.

Back at Toklas and Singerman, Carmen and Andrea remained

surrounded. Help still had not arrived, probably because nothing had really happened, outside of some intimidation.

Jed smirked. He spoke in a slow suggestive tone.

"Word has it that Claiborne women are virgins, and that's part of the magic that keeps you witches young. Well, now that you've met some real men, I guess that's all gonna change. You two ain't gonna turn old and die after we're done with you, are ya?"

"Dane's on his way here now," Carmen answered, "and you'd best leave." At that point, Dane had already left the bank.

Tim snorted, unconcerned. He said, "I'm sorry your sister Sara couldn't be here. Understand she's a real cherry, although I'm sure she is having plenty of fun without us."

Andrea had enough. She moved so fast that nobody saw the blade until it was at Tim's throat.

She raised her voice and demanded, "What do you mean by that… you pig?"

Maurice looked for a way to intervene, and then his eyes widened, and his jaw visibly dropped open. He stared passed Jed toward the street corner. His voice stammered with dread. There was the sound of a horse and wagon in a headlong rush, barreling down the street toward them.

Maurice stammered, "Damn! I th—thought they were going to k—keep him out of the way?"

The wagon raced down the street with reckless haste. Chunks of dirt and rocks flew from the horses' hooves and wagon wheels. All of the bystanders stopped to watch this wild spectacle as other traffic swerved out of his way. The three men did not wait to find out firsthand if Dane's reputation was fact. They raced to their horses and rode away. Dane ignored them and pulled up to the storefront. The two women said nothing as they climbed into the wagon. Dane told them about what the men in the bank had said and conveyed to them what he felt about Sara without the need of words.

The Claiborne's ranch estate was well tucked away into the forests north of Seattle. Dane hurried the wagon through the city and out past William Bell's and David Denny's claim. It would take some time to get home, even with Dane's urging the horses on to greater and higher speed.

***

Sara knelt at the base of an old evergreen tree. Pinecones, needles, and twigs carpeted the ground between the trees. She held a giant beetle between two fingers and studied it for a moment before dropping it into her pail.

She stood and carefully scanned the earth for similar stray insects. She remembered that Dane said he wanted the beetles for their "sensitivity to esoteric energies," whatever that meant. He placed them in his mysterious copper devices, which held properties only he seemed to understand. He claimed that copper was an excellent conductor for all forms of energy, not just electricity. The beetles were sensitive to the corresponding resonance, or frequencies, within his innovations, or constructs. He used them to help tune those devices.

Shadows intensified surrounded by waning sunlight. In the deepest shade and low underbrush, vague phantom forms clung to the darkness. Their eyes glowed with a pulsing red luminescence.

Sara picked up another beetle and spoke softly to it.

"The Sentinel Wraiths are quiet tonight, my little friend. It's almost as though they smell something bad."

A light breeze gently lifted her hair. She dropped the bug into the bucket and then turned to regard the rolling meadow behind her. The edge of the tree line spread out in front of her. It extended for a mile before another tree line began. Dramatic sunset colors outlined a bright full moon. Sky and meadow appeared rich with cerulean blue and a variety of vivid greens. She spotted a glow of orange firelight at the center of the field, silhouetted against the distant tree line.

"Is that a campfire out there?"

She lifted the bucket and peered into it.

"I know that none of you care about this, but no one should be

150

this close to our property. It's not safe unless you are family." She looked thoughtful.

"I will have a quick look, and then we will need to get back before Yulan starts to worry."

She reached in and tickled one of the beetles.

"Don't eat each other."

Then she placed the bucket on the ground at her feet.

Sara left Claiborne property when she stepped into the meadow. As the sun slipped away, and lowering shadows filled the forest, black shapes with glowing red eyes drifted into the open spaces between the trees. The Sentinel Wraiths followed her progress and massed at the forest's edge. Compelled to remain on Claiborne ranch property, they could not attend her beyond that point. However, they did have standing orders from Yulan to report anything out of the ordinary. The campfire qualified as out of the ordinary, and several of them hurriedly returned to the mansion with this news.

***

Yulan was behind the manor, carrying an armload of gardening tools into an ample tool shed. He was about to step into the shed when he paused and cocked his head to one side and listened. He heard buzzing whispers, and then static electricity lifted every hair on his body. It felt like ants crawling in and out of every pore. This always accompanied the appearance of Sentinel Wraiths.

The itching sensation stopped as they approached Yulan. They respected his standing orders to switch to the way he taught them to speak whenever they were around him. The voices he heard behind him were a poor imitation of human speech and sounded hollow, like wind through the gaping jaws of dead men. They spoke in unison.

"Master, Sara has left the forest."

He turned to regard the Wraiths. More than a dozen black, semi-transparent Wraiths wavered in front of Yulan. Their luminous red eyes were in constant motion due to the way their bodies shifted and changed from moment to moment. At times they appeared stable and then would liquefy before evolving into a seething black horde of chaotic shapes and sizes. They performed these transformations independently and yet occasionally blended into and out of reach of each other.

They were writhing with agitation.

"Master, there are men…"

Yulan reacted almost instantly. His calm deportment gave way to anxiety and rage.

"Where?"

"In the meadow."

Yulan dropped the tools he was carrying and began running in the direction the Wraiths had indicated. He began stripping off his clothes as he ran. The Wraiths followed as Yulan growled and raced off through the forest. His man shape altered as his rapid stride took on more of a lope.

***

Sara crouched behind tall grass, near the top of a low rise. A blazing campfire warmed a hollow at the center of the meadow. One tripod of sharpened sticks held a pot suspended over the fire, and she could smell the familiar aroma of coffee. She was able to watch the light from her vantage view, and the men that surrounded it. There were four men in total, as far as she could see. One man tended the fire, while three others gathered gear in readiness to ride out of camp.

The man tending the fire was dressed entirely in black. He had unruly dark hair and a bushy mustache. The other men were dressed in heavy pants and suspenders and wore checkered wool shirts. The way they were outfitted suggested to Sara that they were loggers. She could not see their faces. Their backs were turned toward her as they prepared to mount three out of six horses that stood nearby.

Sara moved behind some taller grass and lifted her head for a better view. The grass rustled all around her. A full moon revealed the wind meandering snakelike through the grass. It was not difficult to imagine an invisible river flowing over the meadow, and this muse distracted her from noticing that two silhouettes crept stealthily up from behind her. She heard them, but it was too late. Two men grabbed her. Sara was strong. She put up a fight, and yet they overwhelmed her and dragged her into camp. She demanded that they let go of her and threatened to kill them if they would not. Her captors merely laughed and shouted for the attention of everyone in the camp.

Sara caught a glimpse of one of the men that held her. His face had recently been torn in a logging accident. It was healing quickly but would scar badly. He said, "Mr. Kane, look what we found hiding in the grass. She was watching you."

Randal Kane was one of the three men preparing to mount when Sara was captured. Those three now stood together by the fire. Sara's captors hauled her up in front of them. Harsh shadows illuminated their greedy expressions as they watched with amusement while Sara struggled to free herself. One of them was clean-shaven and wore round glasses. He looked out of place in the rough clothing he wore and had more the aspect of a businessman. Another was dark-skinned, with beady brown eyes. The last man was average in build and height. He wore his clothing tighter than the others. He had curly red hair, and what appeared to be a deep knife scar running from below his right eye to his chin. He was handsome, regardless of the old facial injury. He carried an air of authority, as the leader of this group. When he spoke, it was as if he owned them all.

"Well, if it isn't Sara Claiborne. What good fortune saved me the trouble of kidnapping you tonight? I don't know how or why you came to spy on us, but I am delighted all the same."

Sara's head lowered, remembering Yulan and the Sentinel Wraiths, and she stared into Kane's face with an implied threat.

"You would not have gotten to my home alive. Now let me go!"

Sara renewed her struggle as Kane stepped forward and loomed over her, wearing a condescending smile.

"Really? Little witch, all I want are your family secrets, nothing more. Nevertheless, I am more than willing to marry into them. Now stop squirming, and try to appreciate the sentiment."

He ran his finger over her chin, but she pulled away.

Kane's men snickered, with the one exception of the man in black. To his mind, things were not going according to plan. Pitching camp was mystery enough. Why did Kane need to make camp at all? They were not far from Seattle. Kane said nothing to him about kidnapping the girl. He told him that they were riding out to the Claiborne ranch, where he would ask for Sara's hand in marriage. His role was to aid in defending against any attackers along the way. Now it seemed that Kane had lied to them all unless he'd only just changed his plans. Everyone knew Sara Claiborne did not like Kane and that she repeatedly spurned all of his previous advances. Apparently, kidnapping was Kane's answer to last-minute jitters.

Sara replied angrily, "If that is a proposal, then you are insane. Besides, I am already spoken for."

Kane unbuckled his belt and handed it to one of the two men that stood close behind him. The man in black kept his distance. Kane was standing between Sara and the fire. He cast a numbing shadow over her.

"It was a proposal." Mock concern crossed his face. "Spoken for? I have never seen you with any man. Unless you are screwing your brother, and that wouldn't surprise me. For that matter, I have never seen your twin sisters with a man. No doubt, they take care of each other…if you take my meaning."

Sara was beginning to show signs of fear.

"His name is Yulan, and he is being told about this right now. He will come for me and kill all of you!"

Kane only laughed at her and started to undo his pants.

"I guess that only leaves me one option. I will just have to ordain myself and perform the wedding, and the nuptials, tonight—right now in fact. After all, God and I have a lot in common. We are both masters of all we survey." Kane ordered his men to hold her to the ground. Sara kicked and screamed.

The man in black walked up behind Kane and put a restraining hand on his shoulder.

"This is going too far," he insisted.

Kane shrugged off the man's hand and his comment.

"Shut up and stay out of my way, or I will kill you myself when I'm done with her."

The man in black glared at him with unveiled contempt then returned to the campfire.

Sara's eyes were tightly shut as Kane tore away her clothing. He lowered himself and thrust his weight between her legs. She felt his lips on her chest, and then on her neck. Her mind drifted away in pain as she felt him invade her body. Tears ran slowly down her cheeks.

***

Night transformed Claiborne property into a fearsome and supernatural world of its own. A full moon brings out creeping shadows that appear to move independently of the trees, whether there is a breeze or not. An enormous white wolf ran low to the ground, passing through patches of moonlight. Its eyes were large, like two white-hot flames. The wolf 's jaws gaped open, with its lips pulled back revealing long sharp fangs.

The wolf was not alone.

Throngs of grim ruby-eyed specters shadowed the wolf and flanked it on either side.

***

Dane whipped the reins for higher speed, even as his wagon careened onto Claiborne property, and raced up the drive. The sun had gone down. His blue eyes now blazed in the moonlight, and all trace of humanity seemed obliterated by their radiant hate. He reined to a halt in front of the mansion. Andrea and Carmen jumped down from the wagon and shouted for Yulan. Dane started up the steps, and then stopped midway, with his sisters close behind. There was intense concentration on all of their faces. They listened for a moment and then heard the screams from over a mile away.

Dane broke the silence.

"That's Sara!"

Without any hesitation, Dane led them back down the steps, and they ran into the forest.

Kane stood, buckling his pants. He then slipped his suspenders over his shoulders. "I guess you really were a virgin." He smiled. "How did you like the rest of my proposal?"

Sara renewed her struggle to be free, but now her efforts were an almost demonic blur of frenzy. The men that had her pinned down felt tired from holding her throughout the rape. With one final twist of her body, she freed herself and ran off through the grass. All she wanted, at that moment, was to be safe in the arms of the forest.

Kane was frantic and shouting orders.

"Damn it! Don't let her escape!" The man in black interrupted him.

"Why? You've done your worst, now let her go."

Randal Kane was livid with rage. He pushed the man in the chest, nearly knocking him into the fire.

"She belongs to ME, understand, so stay out of my way!"

The man in black regained his balance. He rolled to one side and came up with a gun.

"You ever try that again, Kane, and I swear to God I'll shoot you right between the eyes!"

Kane did not hear him. He was already halfway up the hill by the time the gun was leveled at a point between his shoulder blades. The man in black cursed and stood up.

Sara raced as fast as her feet would carry her through the long grass. She held her skirt up and out of the way. As she entered the tree line, one of Kane's men nearly caught up with her and then he tripped over the pail of beetles Sara had left behind.

"AAAH, shit!" He stood up and dusted himself off. "Bugs, what the hell?"

Kane and three of his other men ran up to the man and found nothing wrong with him, other than injured pride. They started for the forest, then listened to the night and stopped at the tree line. Recognizing the stark fear that gripped his men, Kane snapped orders. There were eerie premonitions written on their faces.

"That girl can run, but I'd wager she is not running anymore. She's hiding.

I don't see anything moving in there except for these damn shadows. Fan out in pairs. I'll take straight ahead. We will find her."

Kane was right. Sara was hiding behind a large tree, well into the forest, and yet close enough to hear Kane's voice. She was breathing hard and looked scared. Dark circles were forming beneath her eyes.

The tree she hid behind was directly line-of-sight in front of Kane, and he was walking straight toward her. His eyes searched to penetrate the blackness beyond Sara's hiding place. He moved cautiously forward between shade and moonlight.

"Hello, Sara, come on out. You can't hide from me. I can see your eyes down there in the bushes."

Except for an occasional gust in the treetops, the forest was deathly silent. Sara flattened herself against the tree as Kane sauntered passed her, mere feet away. She was beginning to feel sick and wavered on the verge of fainting. Kane was sure to turn around and catch her if she fell, and yet he appeared intent on something ahead of him—something he thought was Sara, hiding in the bushes.

***

The two men that fanned out on Kane's right began to feel an uncomfortable distance from the others. These were the two men that dragged Sara into camp. The taller of the two was the man with the scared face; he followed the other man. He frowned and began scratching at his chest and shoulders.

"Shit, Paul, I'm itching like crazy, and what the hell is that sound? Like whispering, buzzing, or something. That can't be the wind, can it?"

The other man shrugged and absently brushed at his arms, then he began scratching as well. They moved through the forest without lights of any kind. The moonlight was bright between the shadows. Paul remained as close to his companion as possible and was the first to break the silence.

He stopped, and froze, then grabbed at the man in front of him to stop.

"Chuck---don't move. Something is coming right at us between those trees up ahead. See it? Looks like red fireflies and…"

The itching distracted Chuck. It had gotten much worse. He only glanced back at Paul, long enough to reply, and then he looked back down at the arm he was busily scratching.

"Man, you know there are no fireflies this far north! What in all hell is wrong with you, Paul?"

He looked back at Paul again and forgot his itch. What he saw in Paul's face sent shards of ice through his veins. Paul was shaking his head from side to side as if to say "no." His eyes were wide with terror. Paul spun around and ran back toward the camp. Confused, Chuck followed him a moment then turned around to see what had turned his buddy to water. They were not fireflies. They were black ghosts with large red eyes. He groaned. He felt and smelled his bladder let go.

Chuck frantically struggled to pull his gun, but his fingers seemed too big for the trigger. He looked up. Suddenly, a huge white wolf leaped over some underbrush and landed right in front of him. Chuck had seconds to notice its inhuman eyes, and fangs dripping foam before it lunged for his throat. Its wide jaws bit through both of his jugular veins, spraying the white wolf with red blood. Chuck did not have time to scream before the wolf bit all the way through his neck and tore out his throat.

Paul was out of breath. He and Chuck had penetrated further into the forest than they had thought. That bitch Sara was going to get him killed. All he wanted was out of this damned forest, and right now! Then he heard the buzzing whispers again, all around him, and felt the itching return. He tried to run faster and made the mistake of looking back over his shoulder. He tripped.

"Oh God...oh God...oh God..."

He stood up and screamed. Pulsing red eyes surrounded him, weaving in constant motion through the air. Dark amorphous shapes twisted and groped their way toward him. Paul shrieked with madness while the Sentinel Wraiths reached out and without needing to touch him, pulled the flesh from his bones. Finally, his screams choked off as vital pieces of his head were yanked out and ripped away.

***

The man in black sat on a log by the campfire and stared into the flames. Occasionally he would glance at Claiborne forest, and then up at the clear starry night sky. He held a tin coffee cup between his palms. This was an evil business, and he wanted no part of any of it. He stood and tossed the rest of his coffee into the fire, and then pitched the cup in as well. To hell with it. Let them rot. He was not going to stick around any longer.

He walked over to his horse and prepared to mount, and then he heard Paul's screams. He froze. The screams were terrible enough, but what bothered him even more, and made him feel nauseated, were the way the outcries changed before they seemed to be cut off. It sounded as though the victim's windpipe had been stretched and then snapped mid-shriek.

***

Randal Kane advanced on what he thought was Sara, hiding behind

159

some underbrush, when he too heard Paul screaming. He spun around to his right and lost his footing. Suddenly his legs felt like spaghetti. Wide-eyed, he listened to what sounded like nothing short of torture. Then he looked squarely at the tree that had been hiding Sara, and then at the surrounding bushes. There was nothing—only the forest, those damnable shadows, and the strange- sounding shrieks of one of his men.

Completely unnerved, he looked back at the spot where he thought he saw Sara's eyes in the bushes. They were only leaves reflecting the moonlight. Looking back at the tree, there was a suggestion of movement. Something was crawling on the ground at the base of the tree. Before he was able to investigate a loud crashing rush on his right brought his other two men, with guns drawn, stumbling into the small clearing where Kane wavered on his feet. They were ready to fire at anything that moved. The man in front was the clean-shaven man with glasses. He was yelling and almost incoherent by the time he spat out a simple question.

"Where, or what in God's name, was that!"

Kane failed to respond with his usual bravado. He was as scared as they were.

"Don't be an idiot, Richard. How in all hell am I supposed to know!" Richard spotted what Kane had seen at the base of the tree. He carefully

walked over to look, and then dropped to one knee and gasped.

"Hey, would you look at this. What's wrong with her? Greg, you're the doctor. Is she dead?"

Kane and Greg joined Richard and starred at Sara lying at their feet. Her eyes had rolled back into her head, and her cheeks appeared sunken so far that her face held a skull-like appearance. Kane rocked her head back and forth with the toe of one of his boots. He said, "She can't be dead. You two go find the others, and I'll check her out."

Both men glared at Kane. This was the last time they would follow him anywhere. They were through with him, and Kane knew it by their expressions. He could not have cared less as they deserted him and ran off into the dark to look for their two friends.

***

Kane needed better light and prayed that his matches would work. As he fumbled into one of his pockets, he heard another noise behind him. Human footsteps. He jumped and turned around. It was Dane Claiborne, alone. Dane glanced aside casually, and then his eyes fell to rest on the underbrush Kane earlier thought Sara was hiding behind. Dane lifted his right boot and kicked the brush around a little. He smiled at Kane and said, "I guess there is nothing in there. You must be a little paranoid."

Now Kane had a human face he could focus his wrath upon. From what Dane just said to him, it was apparent that Dane had been watching him for a while. He almost felt relieved by that fact, and yet his cracking voice betrayed him.

"You, bastard! What did you do to my man?"

Kane made the mistake of grabbing for his gun. Dane jumped on him with feral speed and knocked the gun out of his grasp. He seized Kane and pulled him up off his feet. He then threw him to the ground, knelt over him, and pinned him by his shoulders. Sara lay only a few inches away. Both men heard her moan. Kane struggled to free himself from Dane's savage hold. He spat out his words between clenched teeth.

"Let me go, damn you!"

Dane's eyes were an answer to Kane's earlier prayer for light. They were blue lamps, ablaze in a mask of hate.

He raised his fist to strike, and then two horrible screams violated the night, punctuated by gunfire. Greg and Richard. Kane turned his head as if looking for his men, and then Dane's fist knocked him unconscious.

***

Carmen and Andrea emerged from the shadows. Yulan appeared to materialize out of nowhere. He was naked and covered in blood. He dropped to the earth next to Sara and lifted her head into his lap. He lowered his blood-soaked head and cried while gently stroking her face with his hands. Sara's eyes rolled into focus for a fleeting moment. She whispered, "Yulan…I will love you forever…"

At that moment, Sara died.

Yulan cradled her and desperately held her to his chest. He cried out in helpless agony and loss.

*****

Dane tossed Kane over his left shoulder and then offered his unconscious victim a harsh word of encouragement.

"Villain, are you afraid of death? We will not let you die."

The twins were standing next to Dane, as he prepared to carry Kane back to the ranch. Their expressions were cast in the moonlight with deadly resolve. Dane gave one final instruction that left no room for interpretation.

"Make sure that none of them can return to town alive. Do you understand?"

They nodded. Dane quickly disappeared into the forest.

*****

After hearing the screams in the forest, the man in black left the campfire and walked up to the spot where Sara had crouched while watching the camp. His flesh crawled. All of the screaming and gunfire had stopped. Again, everything was silent. Now his deepest fear was that whatever evil thing was in the forest would soon be coming for him. He turned and ran back through camp. He had one foot in a stirrup, ready to mount when he heard two soft female voices speaking in harmony behind him.

"Where are you going, handsome? Are you going to let your friends have all the fun?"

He lowered his foot and turned around in surprise. He recognized Carmen and Andrea Claiborne standing behind him, and both wearing vicious smiles. How could they have gotten so close without him hearing anything? He'd never been one to believe the myths about the Claiborne family, yet now he felt confident that he would carry his newfound belief with him to his grave. They held their hands out to him, and their eyes were glowing a dazzling blue.

There was a brief struggle. The two women were swift and efficient. There were no outcries, no screams, and no gunfire. They slit his throat quickly, which choked off any sound he tried to make.

When the two women returned to the forest, they found Yulan still cradling Sara. He looked up at them with tears in his eyes. The twins were spattered in blood. Their voices held no relief.

"It's done. They're all dead, except for Kane."

Yulan nodded and stood, still holding Sara in his arms.

He said, "You remember what Sara's father said must be done if this ever happened to any of us. He might have been right, and we can't take the chance he was wrong, or Sara may remain immortally trapped within her own dead flesh. Dane will start the preparations. We must hurry."

He carried Sara back to the ranch in his powerful arms. The twins followed behind, with the Sentinel Wraiths trailing at a respectful distance.

***

There was always the possibility that one day, someone from outside the family would invade their enchantment. The instructions had been clear, and Dane had taken them seriously. He lowered Kane off his shoulder onto the copper floor of the room beneath the greenhouse. It was dark, but he knew the place so well that light was almost unnecessary to him. After lighting the lamps positioned around the walls, he cleared out the room allowing only those objects they would immediately need. The most massive object had been covered by a tarp several years before and had been all but forgotten.

As far as Dane was concerned, this room would no longer be used for experiments. He felt sure others would feel the same way about it. The greenhouse was practically Sara's home in life, so it would now become her tomb in death.

***

When Yulan and the twins arrived at the greenhouse, the door was already open. They entered and found that the secret passage in the floor was free as well. They descended and found Dane waiting for them.

Twelve copper lamps illuminated the chamber. Dane had arranged the inside of the room and its contents exactly as their obsessive, and possibly insane, father had instructed. A four-foot square copper box rested on the copper plate floor. A heavy chain, of the same metal, was attached to an apex at one corner of the box. One panel was hinged and opened. Its interior was lined with dozens of short glittering copper spikes.

Dane had to knock Kane out twice on the way to the ranch. The last time, he simply turned a little sideways while passing a tree. Kane now sprawled on the floor next to the box.

No one in the chamber had to say a word because they had rehearsed this dreadful scenario many times in their nightmares. Yulan placed Sara next to the door, and out of the way. The twins nodded toward Dane and stood with him as they prepared to pick up the object of their vengeance. After Yulan joined their circle, they all lifted Kane and held him over the open box. With a nod from Dane, they dropped him into it.

Randal Kane awakened with shock. He howled in agony and tried to pull himself out of the box, but the spikes tore his flesh and tugged at his clothing. Blood from his wounds made the inside of the box slippery, so they were able to force him all the way in. Kane fought his futile best. The only result was that his hands slipped and were impaled.

Kane's endless screams gave his tormentors no pleasure. They punched, kicked, and shoved him until he was securely stuck to the inside of the box. Yulan slammed the lid shut, and locked it with a heavy copper padlock. Kane's eyes remained visible. They peeked out through a small opening in the top and quivered as Kane shrieked and screamed in helpless pain so excruciating that his sanity broke down completely.

Dane grabbed the chain, stood on the cube, and then looped it through a pulley in the ceiling above the box. With inhuman strength, both he and Yulan hoisted the cube into the air. The box tipped into the shape of a diamond. After the lower-most point reached a height of six feet, Yulan snapped one link onto a hook projecting from the floor, near one side of the chamber. Randal Kane cried out for pity.

The twins had gone up into the greenhouse and had come back down with a large copper bowl. They placed it under the cube and then watched as blood flowed around its lid and then dripped down to collect in the container.

Within only a few moments, Kane began to weaken. His constant outcries became anguished whimpers. The spikes surrounding the narrow window had punctured his face. He could not move his head. His eyes remained fixed and watery as he met Dane's merciless glare. He was bleeding to death while suspended within an obscene diamond. His life's blood dripped into the copper bowl…each drop to avenge Sara's death.

Dane closed his eyes and raised his face to the ceiling. He frowned in concentration, and then they all felt the chamber become charged with intense electromagnetic energy. He felt the hair on his head and arms lift and his skin tingle. Light from the oil lamps flickered. Dane lowered his head and lifted his hands. Unruly energies tugged at his garments. He opened and raised his steel blue eyes. They erupted with light and radiated hate for the man in the cube. Lines of power and twisted shards of light shot around the room and played over Dane's body like molten plasma serpents. He opened his mouth and delivered a baleful curse.

"Hear me, Randal Kane! You will live as an immortal, yet forever trapped in your grief and suffering."

White light gathered in the palms of Dane's hands. He opened them and held his palms out toward the cube. Waves of brilliant heat shot out of his hands and then encircled the cube. A blinding nimbus coalesced around the cube, which then glowed with red-hot incandescence. Kane shrieked one last time as his flesh melted away. Miraculously his eyes remained untouched. They stared past Dane, and into an unfathomable hell.

Portal

The bus followed Mel's lead through the national forest and up into the foothills. Mt. Rainier loomed ahead of them, altogether beautiful, ominous, and deceptively tranquil. The five women in the bus watched with some confusion as Mel's vehicle slowed and then veered off onto the right side of the road. They pulled the bus to a stop just behind the Suburban. Lin leaned forward from the back seat and brought her forearms down on the front between Marla and Jenny. She frowned and said, "What's up, why are they stopping?"

***

Mel yanked on the parking brake. He leaned back and looked up at nothing, then shook his head and performed what he frequently did while under stress. He lowered his head and buried it in his hands. No one said a word for several minutes. After a time, Dane reached over and placed a hand on his shoulder.

"You all right?"

Mel shivered under his touch and looked over at him with bloodshot eyes.

"All right? Are you kidding me? Yulan just told me that you killed a bunch of people...no, butchered them. Didn't the sheriff, or whatever, come looking for them?"

No one said anything, so Mel did.

"Now you want me to believe that you are immortals, is that what you're saying here?"

Dane answered, "Well, we're not sure if we are immortals. Long-lived if nothing else. We haven't been around long enough to know for sure."

Silence. Mel shook his head.

"OK, OK, then back up. What about the murders?"

"They weren't murders, Mel," Dane explained. "Those men were killed as trespassers and rapists. Don't forget who came to whose rescue. We were well within our rights. As for the law…well, they never found the bodies. We destroyed all of the bodies and evidence except for Kane's, and he was well hidden. As it turned out, no one came looking for him anyway. They believed our claim that Kane and his men never arrived at the ranch. As you will recall, they didn't. Kane's horses were found wandering the hills and forests around the meadow, and what was left of his campfire was discovered there as well. That verified our story. Case closed."

Mel looked disgusted.

"If that's the way you want to see it, fine. But don't you think the way you killed Kane was a bit over the top?"

Yulan interjected.

"Right or wrong, that was the way Sara's dad said it had to be done. He devised that ritual, or pieced it together, from somewhere in the Far East, Egypt, or from deep into Europe's backcountry. Rituals affecting the afterlife of the recently deceased were a passion for him toward the end of his life. Also, please remember that up until a year ago, after Carmen met Esha, we were more in the dark about what happened to us than you are right now. We did what we felt we had to, mostly out of ignorance. The power of suggestion and superstition can be powerful motivators when those two forces are combined. Despite the methods used or the reasons behind it, Danes "magic" worked…intuitively…although we are still struggling to understand how it worked, just like you."

Yulan then broke the mood with a chuckle, and asked, "So, any more questions then?"

Mel said, "Well yeah, as a matter of fact, I do have a few more." He paused to sort his thoughts before continuing.

"Is Sara alive, undead, or a ghost?"

Yulan answered, "Yes." He slapped Mel on the shoulder, and added, "Good question, Mel. Next question."

"Thanks for that clarity, Yulan. How about this question? Can Sara be brought back…from death? For that matter, what about Kane?"

That question disturbed both Dane and Yulan. Dane answered him.

"Actually, it is possible. They both still exist. As Esha explained it to us, a Changeling has the potential to call into being that which does not seem to be. When I willed Sara's spirit to rest and for Kane's to remain in his copper prison, that is just what happened. Although, Sara decided to remain close to Yulan, and so she now haunts him… not that he minds."

Yulan nodded and gave a rueful smile. Dane continued.

"Our father supposedly cursed himself to haunt the estate after death, although he apparently did not. Perhaps he didn't believe his curse would really come true, or maybe he couldn't fulfill his promise because he was not altered like we were. In any case, there is no indication that he remained after he and Mom died." Dane shrugged. "Back to your question though. In Sara's case, her return would require a living body she could possess, and not one already inhabited by a human soul, or spirit. I've been working on that for a while now. Perhaps alien technology is the answer. Carmen's mentor has promised to help with that."

"You mean Esha. Where is she now?"

"Still underground, I think. She's aware of our plans and will join us when she can."

"What about Kane? You still haven't told me if he can be brought back." Silence.

"Well?" Mel pressed.

Dane looked at him squarely, and replied, "Not unless I release him, and I have no intention of ever doing that." Mel continued to press.

"Let's just say you did. How could he come back?"

Dane's eyes flashed at him and then dimmed. There was an inner struggle before he finally said, "I'll tell you, but if you relate it to anyone without our consent, I will personally end your life. Do you understand me?"

Mel was dumbfounded by the harsh tone in Dane's voice, and he was sure Dane meant what he just said.

Yulan interrupted before Mel could respond.

"I have a stake in this as well. I want Sara back, and Kane's interference would be more than unwelcome. Don't betray us, Mel."

Mel could only nod in agreement. Now, he wasn't so sure he wanted the information at all.

Dane studied Mel for a moment. When he saw the right signals in Mel's face, he continued.

"The process by which Kane was interred, as it were, carried with it certain regenerative powers as well as negative energies. If he were released from the box, he could be recomposed, given the proper sortilege."

"Sortilege?"

"The right procedure would have to be followed, is what I mean to say. Do you understand?"

Mel looked thoughtful, and then asked, "Is all of this magic stuff the result of alien interference with our natural laws governing local physics?"

Donovan cleared his throat and shook his head.

"Not quite," Donovan said. "Every one of us has a different explanation, but, in my opinion, I believe the physics of the chaos theory would be a much better explanation. We are only just learning what that means. There is an organization even in what we believe to be a disorder. We just can't see it on the surface because we're too close to it, so we need to take a step back to see any pattern develop. Changeling 'magic' only appears to be chaos on the surface. The physics behind the magic only seems out of control unless you see it in a broader framework. A bigger egg carton for more eggs. The combination of two species utterly alien to one another in every way has effectively created living, breathing, and extra natural aberrations. That's what we are—that is, all of us on this trip except for you, Mel. Furthermore, we are still discovering what the recombinant effects on our physiology really mean in the long run. Take Lin, for example. The more she practices her gift, the more gifted she becomes. We believe that to be true for any of us."

Mel remarked, "Your abilities do vary quite a bit."

"So do our personalities," Dane explained. "As well as our natural talents and tendencies."

Mel blinked. He blinked again and then became aware of his blinking. Now that he thought about it, up to now he wasn't sure he had blinked at all for the last hour or so. He suddenly became conscious of everyone watching him. A thought occurred to him, and he turned around to address Yulan.

"Yulan, why were the Wraiths able to pull those men apart without touching them?"

Yulan clapped his hands with delight.

"What a wonderfully astute question. Mel, you do pay attention to detail. I asked Esha that same thing. Apparently, the Varr exist in an extra dimension we do not share with them. If they wish, they can send out an appendage through that dimension and grab us without our seeing anything but the results. I once read an example of how that works. Say you are looking down at a flat piece of paper on which the two-dimensional realm of flatland exists. The people of flatland cannot see you in your three-dimensional world until you push a finger into their world. At that point, they can see only a circle of flesh invading their domain. You then reach down and rip up one of the flatlanders. They could not see any part of you but the circle of flesh, so to the flatlanders, the gruesome fate of their friend came out of nowhere."

Yulan fell silent. There was an uncomfortable pause, during which Mel realized that Yulan was finished.

"Thanks," Mel said. "I guess the pieces are coming together for me." He pursed his lips and exhaled a long, drawn-out breath. "For now, though, I'd rather let my mind go blank for a while. No more stories."

Specter spoke up and said that was fine because there wasn't time for another story anyway.

Just then, Carmen walked up and tapped on the Suburban's front passenger window. Specter rolled it down.

She said, "You guys feel that?"

Mel looked around. He asked, "Feel what?"

Donovan agreed. "She's right. The eye of that probe, or whatever, is about to pass over us again, only this time I think it will be different…something has changed, I can feel it. Can't any of you feel that premonition that virtually says we're about to get hit by some seriously deep shit? The air is practically vibrating with it."

Specter sat straight up in his seat, then threw open the door and jumped out. He was reacting to what Donovan said. Specter felt like an idiot that he hadn't noticed the pre-wave alteration himself. If he hadn't been so engrossed by Mel's entertaining reactions to what Yulan and Dane were telling him he would have seen the change in the frequency patterns before any of them.

At that moment, Specter connected the dots in his alien mind and came to a frightening conclusion.

The other women got out of the bus and stood watching Specter as he wandered by the side of the road and gazed up at the sky. His human guise gave way for a moment, and everyone briefly saw his true Varr form. Some slight itching occurred. Despite what everyone knew about him, they all felt a clear sense of relief when his human appearance resolved in front of them once again.

Specter waved them all back to their vehicles, and said, "Grab as much as possible out of the Suburban and pack it into the bus. We will all have to ride in one vehicle. I'll explain on the way, and I'm driving. Hurry!"

Without question, they did what he told them to do. Mel drove the Suburban into the trees to hide it. He tossed some underbrush around the vehicle and secured it before running back to the bus. He felt a lot of remorse over doing this because he'd just finished paying off the loan, and he loved his Suburban.

Specter already had the engine running and was back on the road before Mel could sit down. Soon, Specter had the bus traveling at maximum speed. Lin cautioned him to slow down, but he wouldn't.

"The portal is close now," he explained. "I can feel it. We've got to get there before the next 'wave' hits. When we do get there, I'm driving this bus straight into it. I mean right into the portal, non-stop."

The immediate reaction from everyone was shock and then anger, followed by a demand for an explanation.

"Look, you will all have to trust me on this," Specter said. "We can't stay here, or anywhere near this mountain. I've suspected it, but now I'm positive that thing in space is not just a simple 'probe.' It's a staging vessel for invasion.

I knew they were developing something like this one, but I never got to see a finished prototype. What Donovan said before I stopped was absolutely correct. I have every reason to suspect that when the next wave hits, it will bring something far worse than dreams and psychotic behavior. Indirectly, those 'waves' had a physiological effect on this world, but that was not its intent at all. What comes next will be deliberate, intentional, and designed to 'soften' Earth in advance of the invasion force."

He slowed only long enough to navigate a sharp bend in the road.

Specter said, "Now listen to me! The next 'wave' won't be a probe, it will be an attack. I'm sure of it. I know their stratagem. They will intentionally generate a massive assault on earth's geophysics. I'm talking about earthquakes, volcanism, something and everything along those lines and all over the world."

He turned in his seat and addressed Dane.

"Looks like we're going for Plan B after all. Grab what you can to prepare for complete darkness. Dane, we'll need those night vision goggles I asked you to bring along. Breathing in the staging vessel shouldn't be a problem. They will be assimilating to this world before coming through to Earth, so there should be a temperate breathable atmosphere onboard. One thing is for sure, Dane, we will definitely need to cloak the bus once we get there, because, for all purposes, we are going to drop right into their laps."

Dane nodded that he understood. He said, "I've got it covered."

Specter kept glancing back and forth between Dane and the road.

He asked Dane, "What have you got back there for shielding us from detection?" Dane was already unpacking one of his copper devices with Yulan's help.

He answered back, "I'll take care of it. Just keep your eyes on the road, so you don't kill us before we get there."

Specter swerved to avoid hitting a small animal, which resulted in him almost hitting an oncoming car. Everyone braced for a collision. It was narrowly missed. Just as they caught their breath, Specter slowed and then drove the bus off the road and into a field. The bus bounced over several bumps before smoothing out onto a logging road. Strangely, there were several vehicles parked here and there along the side of the road and among the trees.

There was no reason to ask him what he was doing. Jenny's map indicated that the portal was a short distance off the main road, and they all remembered Specter's claim that he could sense its location.

He slowed to within a few miles per hour and followed the dirt road for a quarter of a mile. He stopped the bus, then left it running and got out. There were vehicles parked everywhere.

To the left of the bus, and up to a slight hill, they could see a black pulsing stain in the air between the trees. It was at least ten feet wide and thirty feet high. The spatial rift seemed vaguely alive and animated, like a throbbing black membrane. Hardly inviting.

Everyone in the bus stared up the hill in disbelief. Not necessarily because of the intimidating aspect of the portal, but because it also held the interest of quite a few familiar shapes that capered and whooped all around it. They played and partied in front of it. There were dozens of people surrounding the portal, wearing amulets and dark glasses. They were "alien convention" type people, to be exact. Mel spotted Ed and Julie in the crowd. He'd seen them with Jenny one year ago. He well remembered their death-defying act of passion, in the middle of traffic.

Specter was angry, to say the very least. He spun around and shouted back into the bus.

"Jenny, come out here!"

She joined him reluctantly, and explained, "Look, I couldn't very well stop them from finding this place, you know. Could I? I mean everyone knew about it at that last convention. They were even circulating maps on how to get here. Besides, they're as good as a family anyway. Lighten up, Specter. What's the problem?"

Specter didn't spit with rage, but he did have a tantrum.

"We don't have time to party with them, Jenny! They're going to get in our way! Will you at least yell at them to move away from the portal, then get your ass back in the bus as quickly as you can!"

That was as close to swearing as any of them had ever heard from Specter.

Jenny ran part way up the hill while dozens of "Jenny Type" people saw her and gleefully waved at her to join them. No one in the bus heard what she said in response, but the effect was a parting of the waves. They cleared a path for the bus by moving to one side or the other away from the portal. Jenny then hurriedly returned to the bus.

After Jenny was seated, Specter gunned the engine, cranked the steering wheel around, and aimed the bus for a dash up the hill.

He then raced the engine one more time.

"All right, here we go, hold on!"

Yulan watched the revelers around the portal and shook his head. They really were partying hard up there. Yulan quoted out loud from one of his favorite movies.

"Ladies and gentlemen, boys and girls, dying time's here."

Jenny heard him. She gave Yulan a quizzical expression and then had a sudden realization. She lunged over Specter's shoulder and grabbed hold of the wheel.

"No! Specter, stop!"

Specter nearly bit back at her.

"What! What is it now?"

"Back there, before we left the main road, did you say volcanism?" Specter was now beyond irritation; he was nearly hysterical.

"Yes, yes, yes, yes, that's what I said. Volcanoes! Every volcano that is even remotely active on this planet will erupt. Now keep your hands off the wheel and stay out of my way!"

Jenny glared at him and spoke about as close to him as she dared.

"Does that by any chance, include Mt. Rainier?"

"Of course, it does!"

Specter shoved Jenny away from the driver's side of the bus.

Jenny came back on him and knocked his hand away from the gearshift knob.

"No!" she yelled. "We can't just leave all those people out there if this mountain is about to explode!"

Specter frantically shook his head.

"Come on, Jenny, what are we supposed to do? We can't take them all with us!"

She reached over and opened the door and then jumped out and started to run up the hill. Specter rolled down the window and yelled after her.

"We have to leave now…with or without you!"

She turned for one last shout of defiance.

"Then, go without me!"

Donovan and the others alerted Specter that the wave was about to hit. They felt it coming, as well the beginnings of a low, threatening rumble in the earth. Specter threw the bus into gear.

He said, "That's it then. We're out of here!"

The bus traveled only six feet before the sky flashed with a silvery brightness and then abruptly went dark as a shadow fell over the area around the bus and the portal. Mel remembered the glimpse he had through the public restroom windows of something shiny streaking through the sky. Specter slowed for a moment, long enough to look up through the windshield.

A massive circular-shaped spacecraft the size of a football field hovered silently overhead. Jenny and her people were so excited they were pointing, jumping up and down, and shouting for joy. Specter wasn't about to stop for any of this. He stepped on the gas, and the bus lunged forward once more.

Cursing, Specter had to hit the brakes again.

Esha was standing on the ground directly in their path.

Specter yelled for her to get out of the way. Instead, she hastily walked up and demanded to be let in. Carmen pushed to the front of the bus and opened the door to let Esha in. Once inside, Esha hurriedly made a few changes in all of their plans.

"Specter, everyone, listen to me. We can't do this the way Specter originally planned. Too much has changed. Sources underground have determined that the enemy is already in-system. That is a staging vessel out there."

Specter interrupted her.

"I know that now get to the point and get out!" Unruffled, she continued.

"Even Specter knows that the enemy's army is already massing on the staging vessel, ready to invade. He might still be able to turn things around if he can get inside it. He knows what to do, but he no longer needs all of you to defend this portal. All he really needs is Mel and Dane."

Donovan objected. He wanted to go on and finish this. Lin said that she would not be left behind if Donovan went. Marla didn't want to be left behind either. She insisted on going wherever Mel went.

Esha conceded. She acknowledged their right to go with Specter. She explained that she was only offering them a choice. On the other hand, Yulan and the twins definitely looked eager to leave with Esha.

They all felt the beginnings of an earthquake. Andrea recounted what Specter said about their need to get off the mountain right away. Esha urged Yulan and the twins to leave everything they brought with them and quickly follow her out of the bus. Once outside, they moved out of the way, as Specter slammed the door behind them. He then gunned the engine and roared up the hill.

Again, Jenny shouted and waved everyone out of the way. The bus bounced over some ridges in the ground before entering the portal. It disappeared without spectacle the moment it touched the pulsing black gateway. The bus simply vanished with a loud popping noise as air rushed in filling the space it had just occupied.

The leading edge of the "wave" passed quickly through the earth and then continued on its way through the sun and the rest of the solar system. In its wake, the earthquakes began. The mountain shook, rolled, and tossed humans, rocks, and trees around with equal misfortune. Conventioneers were screaming for help, and then abruptly, the shouting stopped. All of the people around the portal disappeared. Vanished.

The quake continued to worsen as the alien craft flew away from Mt. Rainier at a speed that belied its enormous size. It carried a heavier load of passengers along with it. Esha took Yulan and the twins with her onboard the Megal spacecraft, not to mention Jenny and the ecstatic horde of partying conventioneers.

Under Cover of Darkness

Darkness. Ebony night. Black as India Ink. All of these descriptions failed to illustrate their next bus stop after leaving Earth. Specter had the presence of mind to turn off the ignition, just before entering the rift. Except for the sound of settling metal from the bus, there was a deathly silence all around them. They all felt some comfort from the familiar smell of the bus exhaust.

Dane whispered and broke the silence.

"Is everyone all right?"

Lin, Mel, Marla, and Donovan all made slightly uncomfortable sounds and indicated that they were all right.

Where was Specter?

They could not get used to the pitch-blackness. It was unnerving… and then, they did see something…two spots of red light in or near the driver's seat. They were eyes, Specter's eyes, and they traced eerily from side to side as Specter got up and stood at the head of the center aisle. Everyone felt a primal sense of terror rise up in their throats at the sight of his eyes glowing in the dark. Although Mel had glimpsed this twice before, he was unsettled just the same.

Dane knew this was coming. He moved closer to the sound of their heavy breathing and whispered.

"It's OK. It's only Specter. Remember, he's not really human." Lin spoke as softly as she could under the circumstances.

"Why doesn't he say something?"

"Is this better?" asked Specter. "I want to warn you that I am going to resume my natural form now. When I do, you will all feel some physical discomfort on your skin. This is temporary and will happen under certain conditions. The first is at the moment of my changing shape, and the other is when communicating using the frequencies of my native tongue."

There was an uncomfortable pause lasting nearly a minute. Specter's eyes searched the seeming void outside of the bus for unseen signs of life. Apparently satisfied that the sound his alteration would make would not bring unwanted attention, he continued.

"I am changing shape, ...now."

They felt a slight stinging sensation on their skin, and then it abruptly stopped. Mel recognized this phenomenon from the time that he sat outside his house in Seattle while waiting for the others when they discussed Specter's presence in the group. Specter had briefly altered his shape on his way out to speak with him that day. Mel had no idea why Specter had done that. He suspected that it was just another example of Specter's perverse sense of humor. Any guess was as good as another at this point.

Specter resumed speaking to them in a voice that poorly resembled human speech. It sounded more like blowing leaves and wind. He was hard to hear and understand.

"Don't worry, I won't put you through this for long. I will be communicating through a mental link I've established with Dane. He'll interpret for you. As for my shape, I've already stabilized it. There will be no further discomfiture due to that. The last thing I will tell you directly for some time is that I can see we are now located within a cavernous receiving area, and we are alone for now. We are in luck. Evidently, they do not expect to be receiving anything right away, so we are yet undiscovered. The area outside the bus should become clearly visible to you when aided by the night vision goggles Dane has brought along. I instructed him to bring several pairs. There should be enough for all of you. He will also give you some rubberized magnetic slipcovers for your feet. Put them on. They should help you maintain contact with the floor. Whatever you do, do not jump. I am sure you've noticed by now that the gravity here is nominal. You'll travel to the far side of the room before you stop. Again, for clarity's sake, I will stay in touch with you through Dane."

Specter's weird red eyes continued to weave and float in front of them until he decided to open the bus door and step outside.

Dane handed out the night vision goggles to each of them. He said, "Here, put these on. They're already activated. Everything you see with them on will have a green or an orange cast. Each pair of goggles has automated circuitry that will decide how to best interpret each surface."

They slipped the goggles over their eyes. Donovan was able to wear his over the leather flight cap he insisted on wearing. The visual effect of the glasses was immediate. Orange and green were, indeed, the dominant colors. Other colors were occasionally hinted at when the two primary colors mixed. They imagined themselves as otherworldly beings perceiving their surroundings through exotic eyes.

They could see the interior of the bus as well as a large portion of the area outside the bus. Curiously, they were able to discern a great deal more of the staging vessel's receiving chamber that could be accounted for by the small amount of infrared light being broadcast by the goggles. The chamber was spacious enough to contain dozens of the largest spacecraft, although it was now entirely empty. It was plainly designed without embellishments, and there were no apparent spatial rifts or portals anywhere to be seen. This was indeed a receiving area, and nothing more.

Dane handed out the footwear and explained a few things while they slipped them on.

"The Varr see primarily in the infrared spectrum. To them, this place is well lit. When bathed in other light sources, their eyes still perceive only within the infrared. Without any light source at all, they are as blind as we are without these goggles."

They saw Specter drifting across the metal floor just outside the bus. He looked like a black ghost, living up to his name. Dane lifted a sizable box and carried it down the center aisle. He set it down on the driver's seat. Next, he unpacked and erected a black tripod with a small platform at the top. Upon that platform, he first assembled a series of five copper balls, of varying sizes, atop five short copper rods, of short, varied lengths. Then he lowered a crystal sheath or tube over them, surrounding and obscuring the copper array. Dane's hair had come loose of the clasp that held it behind his head. He would fix that later, but right now, he brushed it aside and away from his face while he worked. This and the fact that his light brown beard was now stubble gave him a rougher, wilder aspect. Lin noticed this and kind of liked it.

He then gently produced five giant beetles from the box. Each of these received individual ministrations from Dane. He treated each bug with a tender touch and made little noises while petting them lightly. After performing what could only be interpreted as bonding and communication, he set five of these beetles one atop each copper ball. One after the other, these bugs created high-pitched sounds once they found their footing. It was astonishing to watch Dane work in the assembling process, and it was apparent that he treated these tiny creatures like partners, rather than like pets.

Mel asked him what he was doing, and Dane explained.

"I've carefully chosen each of these beetles for their natural bias, or preference, for creating sounds that generate a specific set of harmonics.

When placed together, they interact with each other producing the sound I need to get the desired effect out of this construct. In this case, I want the bus itself to return all outside stimulus with exact opposite frequencies to what is being sent toward it. Be it light or sound. The cumulative effect will be invisibility."

Mel wasn't buying it.

"The bugs do this? Why not simply use electronic means for generating sound and frequency?"

"What I am completing here is not conventional science." He stood for a moment to explain. "For the most part, my Changeling talents are associated with light and sound. I orchestrate and compose in association with elemental properties and biological proclivity. Electronics mimic what I can do, but poorly at best. Rather like synthetic vitamins trying to mimic a natural vitamin source."

Mel thought it odd that Dane should use vitamins as an analogy, and then remembered that Dane was introduced to him as a licensed naturopath.

Dane continued.

"What I am about to execute here is an example of pure hyperdimensional physics, and, as you must know by now, will seem like magic. Changelings learn to perform intuitively. That is the key. World Theosophy might refer to this as an intuitive interaction within the movement and repose of subspace, or, the vibrating superstrings of modern hyperdimensional theories in physics. Thus far, electronic fakery will not produce the equivalent of a biologically intuitive action or reaction. As long as we're on the subject, here is another thought for your intuitive minds to grasp."

Dane looked squarely in Mel's direction. Mel realized his next statement would be meant more for him somehow.

Dane spoke directly to Mel.

"The intuitive mind is non-linear. Consider that when you contemplate the seemingly linear nature of time. The current definition of time is as a dimension within hyperdimensional laws of physics. As such, time is not truly linear because hyperdimensionality is non-linear. Imagine the implications of that, but let's get back the main point about this device right here."

No one in the bus understood the reason for that brief departure, but Mel tucked it away for later.

Dane collected his thoughts a moment. During that pause, Lin considered what it would have been like to be Dane's student. She wished she could have learned some of this before now. What he said concerning the prospect of non-linear time stuck with her more than anything he'd said so far. She rolled that around in her mind as he continued.

"Because of the distinctively spiritual and indeterminate temporal factors involved, we each have our own predisposition for certain skills. Essentially, we each resonate separately as well as together... and we are each thoroughly unique."

He paused a moment, considering his next words.

"I believe that each of us are facets on a universal gem and unique in our talents within an ongoing composition and masterpiece if you will. Magic is a little word and an inadequate classification for the gifts we possess."

Although Lin could not see Dane's eyes through his goggles, she nonetheless felt the intensity of his gaze.

Dane said, "Mel, after what you've seen, you should not be too startled to know that I can do this. Now watch."

Soon the beetles were harmonizing in a repeating rhythm that was mesmerizing. The crystal tube amplified and refined these resonant harmonics. Dane stepped up to the tube and touched it. He removed his night vision, and his eyes flashed briefly followed by a ball of light, which appeared suddenly in his left hand. He then dropped this light into the tube where it remained active. His eyes flashed again, and another ball of light appeared in his hand. This one he touched to the outside of the tube, and when he let go it go, it began to rotate around the tube's outside surface. Once the beetles established the harmonic sound and rhythm that Dane acquired, a little more of Dane's Changeling enchantments perfected and amplified it. Dane explained that this construct would function indefinitely until the bugs died from starvation or until he willed it to stop.

There was a sharply metallic smell and taste, or texture, in the air around the construct. After completing the process, he instructed the others to accompany him outside to best view the effect. Dane lowered his goggles back over his eyes and stepped out of the bus. When they followed and looked at the bus from outside, they discovered the remarkable truth in what Dane said would happen. Although they could still detect a little of the bus, for the most part, it appeared as though it was not there at all.

Dane indicated the bus.

"What is happening is that you really see around the bus. The construct is reflecting back the exact opposite of the light frequencies that are bouncing into it. The two equal and opposite frequencies are negating each other. It will work with sound as well. Any frequency directed at the bus will be countered by an equal and opposite frequency. Your eyes will only register what is refracted light or sound from around and behind the bus. Do you understand?"

They did, but Dane had one more point to make.

"There is another mystery to consider, and one that I am fond of. Those beetles are the organic components responsible for reacting to any outside interference in the resonance generated by the construct that surrounds them. Are they thinking about what is happening when they react to a change in external stimulus, or is it entirely intuitive? I believe it to be the latter. Another thing to consider is what is it that keeps them perched atop the copper balls until starvation, or until I remove them? Are they in some insect version of an altered state? Does all of this happen within a linear space of time? I don't even have a guess for that question. That remains a topic of some study."

Lin's thoughts were brought up sharply again by the "time" statement. To whom was he directing this? It had nothing to do with invisibility. She could only guess that just like any other genius she had ever read, met, or heard of, he was making statements with potentially earth-shattering implications in passing, like discarding the peel from a banana. He was glossing over this 'time' thing. She thought back to the introductions back at Mel and Marla's place. Dane was introduced as a naturopath. No, he was far more than that. Lin asked, "Dane, why are you passing over the time issue so quickly?

The implications of that would be invaluable to science."

Dane explained almost impatiently, "That really is not an issue right now, Lin, only a consideration. I will say that I do believe time travel is intuitive.

It belongs within the laws governing quantum physics and the chaos theory and is poorly defined when viewed within conventional rules of science. Time travel is not really 'travel' at all when studied using a non-linear hyperdimensional model for analysis. It is more like sidestepping from one section of a room to another."

Dane was relieved to find comprehension in Lin's face, so he continued.

"Rotations and alterations within space and time are qualified under the laws governing 'the symmetry of special relativity.' You will find it referenced in any library. If you are really interested in the subject, I will be happy to teach you more when we get out of here."

Lin thanked him and said she would definitely enjoy that. She was inwardly thrilled at the idea of actually becoming his student.

Donovan started strolling around the bus. He was fascinated by the invisibility effect. The last thing he said before disappearing around the back of the bus was, "Hey, I'll bet our government has something like this." Dane walked back into the bus. Suddenly, the bus reappeared, and then Dane walked back out, holding all of the beetles in his hands. He directed each member to each hold all five beetles—as he was doing now—and then to speak to them. What they said to the bugs would make little difference.

He explained that this procedure was called "recognition," and would allow the beetles to discern a difference between "unknown" stimulus and each of them as a "known." The net change would be that they would clearly see the bus when they are close enough to it to call out. He demonstrated. After everyone had the chance to "speak" to the beetles, Dane reentered the bus and replaced the beetles within the construct. The bus disappeared again. Dane seemed to step out of blurred air when he reemerged. He instructed each of them to say something, anything. After they did so, the bus did indeed reappear to each of them in turn.

Marla remained standing close to Mel. Of the entire group, she seemed the most shell shocked by this whole experience. Ever since she and Jenny were children, they talked about their being alien abductees, and what that meant to both of them. Later, through Jenny's parents, they came to understand that they were special somehow. She never pursued the implications of that or guessed it. Now that she had seen so much of it in action, she was even more frustrated by her seeming lack of any Changeling powers. Again, she wondered if she too might possess some untapped potential or "gift." To the others in this group, her silence caused a little quiet concern. She did break her silence long enough to ask a mundane question, the answer to which was useful to everyone but Specter.

"Where did we put that, port-a-potty?"

Lin was studying Dane. He was a complicated mix of mystery,

discipline, and raw male strength. He fascinated her. She idly considered what a relationship with him would be like. Her daydream was brief. She felt a disturbance in the atmosphere behind her. When she turned around, Specter wavered not two feet away. She jumped away from him.

"My God, Specter. Don't do that to me!"

Dane turned toward her, then cocked his head slightly. He was listening to Specter's voice in his mind. After a brief moment, he smiled and spoke to Lin.

"Apparently, Specter thinks you are smitten with me. Is that true, Lin?" Lin returned his smile with one of her own. "Maybe."

Donovan was working his way back toward them from around the back of the bus. He hadn't heard any of what was said between Lin and Dane, and yet he caught the hint of a shared joke.

Specter was beginning to act in agitation to some unseen stimulus. Dane received no clarification from him as to what that was. Specter began to fluctuate between a solid and intangible form, although this did not qualify as a shape change. His primary form did this anyway. Arms and limbs grew out of him and then retracted. He stretched and then compressed. Occasionally, he would vibrate violently. All the while, his eyes would shift from side to side, in what passed for a head, and leave momentary tracings in the air.

Dane didn't wait for instructions. He directed them into the bus to gather a few supplies. They needed packs with necessary provisions like water and food. They also took small portable versions of the construct Dane set up in the bus. These were four-inch crystal cylinders with a copper core and a tiny beetle for each cylinder. Dane performed what he called "processing" on each beetle. This included the same "recognition" procedure on these small creatures that he used on the five inside the bus, so they could see and hear each other. He then capped the beetles into the tubes with plugs of dimly glowing plasma generated at his fingertips.

The harmonics began shortly after capping the tubes. He attached each tube to a light chain and all but Specter were instructed to wear them around their necks. The glowing plasma was not bright enough to illuminate the faces of their wearers. Dane insisted that the effect of the tubes would prevent them, or their wearers, from being perceived, or heard, regardless of the slight glow, or the sounds, that the tubes generated.

"Now that you've seen what the big one will do," said Dane, "you should be more comfortable with these little ones."

Dane watched Specter with interest. The mental impression he got from Specter was that the tubes worked well on him, and so they should be more than adequate on any of his race. For the most part, Specter would follow them via the mind link he had with Dane. Dane realized this could become a problem later if Specter could not see or hear any of them. Specter knew Dane's thoughts and quickly formed the answer to Dane's concerns within Dane's mind.

All Specter needed to do to perceive the members of the group was to shift his focus to include anomalies within the airspace around him. Every Varr could do the same thing, but they would first have to know they were there. The only way the Varr would know they were there would be if the group created a loud enough ruckus that the tubes couldn't mask. What Specter saw when he shifted his focus were five human shaped blurs in the air. He could determine who each was by their original size, shape, and idiosyncratic movements. As for their voices, Specter had to content himself with what he heard through Dane's mind.

Dane placed several strange copper objects into their packs. Nothing about these objects betrayed any distinct form or function, and Dane said they were for "just in case." Specter began to drift away from them, and so they followed. In the distance, many yards away, they could see an opening in the chamber wall. This appeared to be where Specter was leading them.

At this point, Dane told them all that he'd just asked Specter, via mind link, about the gravity and what was generating it, since the vessel had no rotational spin to account for it. Specter explained through Dane that the answer to that question was to be found in the metal flooring. The metal attracted anything that came near it, similar to gravity. According to Specter, this was being accomplished by a computer and drive system that, later, they would see for themselves. Specter complained that he had not himself seen the new and improved version of the drive he expected to find at the heart of all of this, but he was looking forward to it. Also, the metal flooring held magnetic properties, which the slip-on footwear relied upon. All told, they were comfortable on foot, and no one had any desire to jump.

Mel wondered why the Varr needed any gravity at all. He was about to ask Dane when Lin raised another point.

"You know," she said, "it occurs to me that only Dane and Specter know what Plan B is. Does anyone care to let us all in on it."

Mel knew something about this from what he'd been told outside the diner. Dane explained that the Varr were going to try to invade by occupation and control, as usual. They wanted to preserve and capture the entire planet, with as little loss of life as possible. This was the only redeeming quality of the Varr invasion. They wanted humanity intact and the Megal DNA experiments under Varr control. According to Specter, the invasion of Earth by the Varr had already begun. Right now, the best the six of them could hope for was to cripple this staging vessel. At least this would allow the Earth-based aliens, the Megal, time to mount a defense before the next host of Varr came through to this craft and then on to Earth.

Dane explained the options they had up to now. It was apparent that they were calling the shots blind at this point. That was Plan B. They were playing it by ear, to some extent. They all watched Specter. His back was to them as they walked toward the opening in the wall. Specter betrayed no indication that he disagreed with Dane's assessment. Somehow, they all knew that when the opportunity presented itself, Specter would know precisely what to do, and that brought as much apprehension as it did hope.

Lin changed the subject to lighten things up.

"Mel?"

"Right here."

"I was just thinking of that story about how you and Jenny met.

Do you think you'll ever own another cat?"

Mel was taken aback by this out-of-nowhere question. It was funny what stress could do to someone. He replied honestly.

"Not if I can help it."

They all wondered how much longer it would be before this receiving chamber started receiving again. Without thinking about it, they picked up their pace. The opening in the wall was further than they thought. That was when Donovan started to mutter to himself. Lin was more nervous about his muttering than anyone else since she'd seen him lose it before. Now was not the time for him to crack up. She felt sick and empty inside because she truly loved Donovan. More often than not, she deeply regretted not having what her Midwestern family would call a normal life. She looked at the spaceship all around her and thought, definitely not in the cards, old girl.

Donovan lifted his voice a little and spoke in a lighthearted tone. He winked at Mel and said, "Cellophane would definitely be the wrong approach here." He then turned to Lin and asked, "What do you think, Lin?"

Mel frowned, and asked, "What cellophane? What are you talking about, Donovan?"

Donovan awarded Mel with an oddly conspiratorial wink, then gave a nervous laugh. Mel hoped that maybe Donovan was just trying to brighten things a bit like Lin had tried to do with the cat thing, but Mel actually knew better. Donovan was definitely losing it. Mel could see it in his eyes.

Donovan stopped walking and looked back at the bus.

"If I had my Chevy pick-up we'd have been on the road by now. Lin's Mercedes would not do at all, too small."

He spun back around and then made a grand display of saluting Specter.

"General Lee, Sir! I believe I am of no more use to you, sir. I will await your return in the tent."

They were horrified as Donovan turned back around and headed for the bus. He waved for Mel to follow him.

Specter moved quickly. Before Donovan had gone more than ten yards, he passed the others and silently stopped in front of Donovan. Donovan looked into Specter's eyes and froze. Mel, perceiving a genuine threat, ran up and stood next to Donovan. He told Specter that he wanted to speak with Donovan alone for a minute, and would Specter mind giving them some space. The Varr silently submitted to Mel's request and drifted back to the others. Relieved, Mel took Donovan by the arm and guided him further away from the group.

"Donovan, are you cracking up? Because if you are, I believe Specter is ready to kill you before he allows you to freak out and endanger us all. Let's face it, man, this is not the time to wig out."

"I'm in total control of myself, Mel."

"I hope so. Let's get back to the others and get the hell out of all this open floor space. It gives me the creeps."

Donovan grabbed him by the arm.

"Wait."

Mel turned back around to find Donovan's eyes boring into him. He looked frightened.

"I have to tell you something, Mel."

"Yeah?"

Donovan spoke in a barely discernable voice.

"Just before we stopped for lunch at the diner, I dozed off for a while in the bus. You know that I occasionally wander into other people's minds in my sleep. It's my best 'gift.'"

"Right, I remember."

"I briefly flowed into Specter's mind."

Mel felt his own breathing stop at the mere mention of that horrifying prospect.

Donovan continued in hushed tones.

"What I felt inside him was so utterly alien that I am going to have nightmares for years after this, but what disturbed me, even more, was a fleeting glimpse of the plans he has for you."

Mel turned to see where everyone was at that moment. Specter was at the front of the group again, waiting for Mel and Donovan to return. He was starting to vibrate with agitation. Mel could see that even from where he stood.

"Go ahead, Donovan, tell me. But in less than a whisper and make it quick."

Donovan leaned toward him. "I think he's going to kill you, Mel."

Mel frowned.

"Specter?"

"Yes."

Donovan saw his shock and said, "Look, I can't say for sure. I had a fleeting glimpse of you and Specter, blue fire, and something that felt like an eternity all around you."

Mel glanced at the group again. Now Specter was starting to float in their direction.

"Thanks. I'll watch myself." Then a thought occurred to him. "Did he catch you prowling around in his head?"

Donovan shivered.

"Yeah. I woke up in the Suburban and turned around in the seat. I saw him staring straight at me from the bus, only a car length away. He was practically riding our bumper. I'll tell you, man, I don't trust him at all."

Mel stared at Donovan for a penetrating moment before asking, "Not even Dane seems to trust him completely. Why didn't you tell me this before now?"

"I don't know. I guess I was scared. For that matter, I still am. As far as I know, he could have heard everything I've just told you."

"We'll find out right now because here he comes. Let's go."

Donovan nodded, and they headed back toward the others. Specter was no more than five yards away when they passed him. Specter turned and followed them.

Back in the group, Mel assured them that Donovan was fine, and that seemed to satisfy everyone. Mel watched Dane and Specter more carefully from that point on. Neither of them gave any immediate indication that they had heard anything of what Donovan told him in confidence.

Appearances were deceiving as usual. Although none of the others heard the conversation between Donovan and Mel, Specter had heard nearly everything Donovan told Mel. Despite that fact, it didn't matter to Specter in the least what Donovan thought or said to Mel at this point in his plot, just as long as Donovan did not interfere at the critical moment.

Focus

The party that began on Mt. Rainier did not continue onboard the spaceship. Beer and soda containers dropped noisily from shock-numbed fingertips onto a metal floor. People milled about in human clumps of confusion. The room they found themselves in was the size of one entire floor of a downtown high-rise building.

Now it is important to note with some humor that most of the conventioneers are not DNA recombinant Changelings. In every alien convention, there are those who only think they have some alien genetic connection. Changelings or not, the conventioneers in this craft shared the same concerns.

All eyes were now focused on a section of the room's wall that was crystal- clear from the inside looking out, allowing them all to see what was transpiring on the ground below. There was a collective gasp as Mt. Rainier exploded with a force far more significant than Mt. St. Helens. As the Megal craft shot away from the mountain, the mountain itself disappeared amid ash and ruin. Just before the alien ship rose above the clouds, everyone could see several Megal ships, of differing shapes and sizes, rising up out of the foothills and surrounding forest. Once they ascended above the clouds, the conventioneers looked out of the windows and saw these alien craft darting this way and that. The conventioneers were excited, to say the least. This is precisely what they all hoped to see one day.

Sunglasses dropped almost immediately upon arrival. No one wanted anything less than a perfect view of what was going on below. The smoke from the mountain rose above the clouds. They were horrified at the devastation this eruption promised. Now, everyone in this great room thought about the loved ones and friends on the earth below. The milling around had quickly turned to horror, and then an endless pursuit of who was in charge of this craft. Pandemonium was the net result.

One elderly man in the crowd ignored the confusion. He shouted out that flying saucers were frequently seen around volcanoes before and after they explode. Nobody heard the man. They were congregating around Jenny and Esha, the only two they recognized as probable sources of information.

There were children in the group as well, and some were crying.

Jenny fended off the group as they pressed her for help and assistance to be taken back down to the ground. Not surprisingly, very few wanted to stay on the ship. For the most part, they wanted to be "beamed down" to Seattle to be with family and friends. Esha had less trouble dealing with the frantic press around her. Most were afraid of this "scary looking" woman.

Esha grabbed Jenny and yanked her into an open room off to one side of the chamber occupied by the conventioneers. She closed and locked the door, and Jenny turned to find Yulan and the twins standing behind her.

Carmen greeted Jenny and said, "They're losing it in there. Everyone Esha picked up off the mountain was thrilled to be in this craft, but it didn't take long before they all started demanding to be taken home. I'm glad we got out of that room." She turned to Esha and said, "Good lord, Esha, you've got to let those people off this ship. There are too many of them. You can't control them for long. You know that."

Jenny interrupted.

"Where should we drop them off? Seattle is done for, and you know it." Carmen waved her hands around.

"Well, we can't let them stay here."

Esha responded, "We are going to let them off. Nolan will transfer them all to the ground well north of Seattle. We'll be there soon."

Carmen frowned.

"Nolan?"

"Yes, that's right. He's been trained to fly this craft. They're not difficult to operate, they maneuver by thought, and he's a trained pilot."

Carmen broke into a genuine laugh. The pilot was Nolan Philips.

How wonderful!

***

After dropping the conventioneers off, the alien craft headed back above the clouds and then became stationary within site of the volcanic plume. Yulan, Jenny, the twins, and Esha gathered in the room that only minutes before contained so many confused and frightened people.

Yulan kicked a half-full bag of barbecue potato chips out of the way and sat on the floor next to the transparent wall, or what everyone called windows. The others joined him but remained standing.

Yulan spoke without his usual sarcastic tone. He sounded tired.

"Esha, what news…" he started, but could not finish his question. He wasn't sure he wanted to know.

She hesitated before answering.

"The Varr have already begun to come through. New portal rifts have opened all over the Earth, and they're entering this world en masse. The general populace is frozen with fear. Not only do they have devastating earth changes to contend with, but the sudden appearance of the Varr as well. You know the kind of casual effect Varr communication has on human anatomy. Well, just imagine that on a global scale. Chaos. We can take comfort in the fact that they are not attacking anyone, or anything unless directly threatened. They don't need to. Fear works so well in their favor. All of the world governments believe—and rightly so—that the Varr caused all of the earth changes, but right now, survival is the only thing anyone cares about…not military action."

Andrea sat down next to Yulan. She touched the window, as though feeling the pain of a world. She looked up and asked another question they feared the answer to.

"What are the earth changes?"

"Nearly all of the active volcanoes around the world are erupting. Earthquakes of 6 point and higher, are shaking the entire planet. Tidal waves are destroying most of the coastal cities. In fact, that is what is going to wipe out Seattle, not the volcano."

Andrea whispered.

"So, all those people we dropped off…" Esha nodded sadly.

"They will die within a few hours from now. Yes."

Hearing this, Jenny grabbed Esha. Esha flinched from Jenny's sudden move.

"Esha, why did you let them go if you knew that? Why?"

"Jenny, please, you heard what all of them were saying. They would not have wanted to stay, even if they knew they were going to die down there."

That didn't satisfy Jenny.

"No, you're wrong, …not all of them wanted to leave!" She was frantic.

"So what are we going to do now, Esha? What can we possibly do?"

"Nothing," Esha explained as calmly as she could. "All of these disasters will climax within the next few hours. After that, the Megal will intervene, and the battle for this world will begin. You must find a place to stand with us."

Jenny began pacing back and forth while fidgeting with her hands. She was miserable. Everyone was reminded of the way she behaved in the bus when she declared that she would stay behind on the mountain with the conventioneers if they couldn't save them. She looked like she was going to demand to be let off, but she knew that would do no good. Defeated, she sat down with Yulan and Andrea and cried in deep bitter sobs.

Yulan looked over his shoulder and into Esha's eyes.

"Esha. I need my Wraiths. You told Carmen that the Megal confined them to Claiborne property boundaries. Can you release them from that confinement?"

Esha replied, "Yes, we have the devices we need to do that aboard this ship; however, I can do little more than that. You will have to care for them personally. They should remain loyal to you, and we believe they will stand by you even in a pitched battle, although we have no indication that they will fight against their own kind. The Adept program has shown us remarkable qualities in the Varr that we had no idea existed in them. Perhaps it is possible to bring peace between our peoples after all. The Megal may be responsible, in some part, for the war, by underestimating the Varr's capability for peace if the right communication is established." She stopped to consider her next words.

"Yulan, what you and others like yourself have discovered about the Varr has opened new doors for understanding. Believe me, the Megal are not foolish enough to ignore any of this. Who knows, Earth may be the last battleground before the end of this very long war."

Yulan looked back down and out the window. The horizon was littered with Megal craft of varying sizes. He shook his head and looked back up at her.

"But why did it have to end here on Earth?"

***

Nolan piloted the Megal craft over the Claiborne ranch and then directly over the mansion, dwarfing it in size. The earthquake had taken its toll on this place as well, but generally, the well-maintained property retained most of its groomed appearance despite the disturbance. Damage could be seen all over the exterior of the building. Long cracks had opened in the circular drive leading up to the mansion.

To the right of the drive, the latest version of the family greenhouse sat surrounded by an extensive, spacious flower garden. The tombstones marking the elder Claibornes' graves lay broken over the path leading to the structure. It was a steel, aluminum and Plexiglas structure, rather than the original cedar and glass. It survived the quake with only one glaring exception. The door had broken loose and now hung loosely ajar by one hinge.

Yulan materialized close to the greenhouse and wordlessly called out to the Sentinel Wraiths. He used a mental pattern of disciplines the Wraiths had taught him years ago. He remembered how they reacted the day he demonstrated his ability to use what they taught him. He'd seen them angry and ambivalent, but up to that point never cheerful about anything.

Yulan marveled at how childishly thrilled they seemed when they found that he could use the disciplines they taught him. Later, Yulan taught them how to utter noises that grew to emulate human voices—and they were equally excited about that. He always felt that they were some kind of ghost. Now that he knew what they were, sentient beings from another world, their emotions made sense.

On the first day, he was able to "call" the Wraiths, he stood by the greenhouse in much the same way he was now. He focused on a shape within his mind. The Varr connected with each other using a combination of geometric shapes and extrasensory commands. All one needed to do was to mentally focus on a set of patterns. That is what he came to call their way of communicating…, "focusing." When Donovan referred to the way these beings were "focusing" on him, Yulan could well understand what the man meant; although, Donovan was apparently confused as to which alien race was doing the "focusing."

Yulan could guess at what Donovan would have experienced when making the initial contact with the Varr because Donovan's first communication with the Varr was most likely similar to his own. Donovan would have started to see shapes in his mind, followed by disorientation. For Donovan to communicate in response, he would have had to know how to "focus" in reply. He would also need to know the mental patterns and disciplines required to project outward from his own mind the gist of what he was trying to convey back to the Varr.

Now Yulan "focused," he began to feel the telltale discomfiture on his skin. The Wraiths felt this real perception as well, only to them, the sensation had a different meaning. In actuality, it was a kind of intimate contact, which directly related to what they were feeling. The Varr would instinctively broadcast this corporeal equivalent of camaraderie, fear, anger, and most certainly love, amongst each other all the time. Yulan came to understand this. In time he'd grown to interpret the sensations.

***

The tree line swarmed with black life. Scores of wraithlike Varr swarmed into the garden grove. He reverted to English and asked them to do likewise.

"You must know that your people are here, now, on this world. Do you wish to come with me?"

They spoke nearly in unison.

"Master Yulan, we know that we have been held prisoners here, and we sense that the Megal has loosed us, but we also honor you and your family. We welcome our freedom, but for now, we wish to follow where you go. Perhaps we can help to change things with those from our home place."

Yulan waived them forward.

"Then, come."

He could not help but notice how their number had increased slightly. He'd never seen them all in one place before. Perhaps he'd never wanted to. Had they been breeding in some way? Due to his misunderstanding that they were "ghosts" or some other kind of horror that possibility had never occurred to him before.

He spoke aloud, under his breath.

"Are they multiplying?"

Several Wraiths detached themselves from the throng. The ones that separated from the others drifted forward and moved to within a few yards of Yulan. They said, "Do you require any of us to guard the tomb?" Yulan shook his head.

"No, this place will soon be under water. Make sure all of you are assembled here in the garden. I won't be long."

Having said that, he turned back to the greenhouse and entered it through the broken door. The central aisle was littered with broken pottery, dirt, and plant debris. This made it difficult to walk the short distance between the door and the staircase leading down to the vault holding Sara's tomb. The trapdoor down into the tomb had been broken open by the force of the earthquake. Yulan grabbed an emergency flashlight from off the floor and descended to the room below.

Sara's marble tomb remained untouched by the quake, and the gruesome cube hanging above it also seemed intact. Yulan did not try the light switch by the entrance. He knew that it was a waste of time.

He played the flashlight over the surface of the dangling cube until it illuminated the glittering eyes of Randal Kane, which unbelievably still retained aberrant life after all these years…a mute testament to Dane's Changeling powers. The eyes remained eternally wet, surrounded by charred bone, and glittered with unblinking supernatural life. The desiccated flesh around them had long since rotted away.

Despite Yulan's hatred for the man that had been responsible for Sara's death, he felt his skin crawl at the thought of Kane's soul eternally trapped and silently screaming within that cube. Yulan lowered the light beam until it shown on the ornately carved tomb lid. He stepped closer and ran his fingers over a striking likeness of his lost love carved into the pale pink stone. The color of the marble seemed to grant a moment of illusory life to Sara's stone cheeks. He felt a choking in his throat. Then, he heard a soft sound in the air around him, like a sigh.

"Yulan."

He spun around, shining the light everywhere in search of the ghostly voice. He knew it was Sara. She'd spoken to him in this way before, but he never failed to hope for a glimpse of her as an apparition.

There she was.

The light penetrated Sara as she stood in front of the stairs wearing a long white gown. Her hair was gossamer white rather than the gold it had been in life, and it floated about her shoulders and appeared to be gently drifting as if carried by an invisible current.

She lifted her arms for Yulan to approach. He did so willingly, but when he touched her, his hands passed right through. Yulan began to cry.

"Sara, I have to leave…and I don't know what will become of this place."

"I know, my heart, and you must leave now. Come back to me if you can. Always remember that I love you."

Then Sara vanished.

Yulan dropped the flashlight and brought his hands to his face in grief. His legs buckled beneath him, and he fell to his knees. Sometimes he almost hated Esha for giving him the hope that one day Sara might be returned to him. Perhaps it would be easier if he forgot her like others who had lost their loved ones.

At that moment, he remembered the urgency to leave this place. He had to get up to the ship before the tsunami hit, and he had little or no time left to waste. He ran up the steps and stumbled out into the garden. The Wraiths had dutifully assembled in the open, awaiting his return.

Yulan waved up at the ship. Instantly the alien craft received an increased passenger load that included scores of what for millennia the Megal called

"The Enemy."

Hive-Mind

It took two hours after the last "wave" passed through the Earth for the earthquakes to stop. The devastation was overpowering all efforts, on the part of every country, to provide relief in any form. Individual survival was the only immediate concern. Radio transmissions were reduced to the widespread use of ham and short-wave radio; however, volcanic activity made even these efforts at communication problematic at best.

Volcanoes filled the atmosphere with soot, which blocked the sun and made it dangerous to breathe. Many feared the climatic changes, which would undoubtedly follow these eruptions. Populous the world over hid as best they could, and yet this did nothing to save anyone living on the shorelines. Tidal waves wiped out millions.

Inter-spatial portal rifts opened in the air, on the ground, inside caverns, and underwater. An aquatic environment wasn't simulated on the staging vessel, but Varr did adapt quickly. They did not breathe, as humans understood breathing. The Varr that emerged in the oceans were as interested in marine life as they were in any other. Getting close enough to study marine life was another matter. Sharks, dolphins, eels, whales, and all of the larger species immediately fled from the Varr, suffering from extreme discomfort. Smaller life forms darted away from them as well. The Varr saw this on nearly every world they conquered. It was nothing new.

Whether above or below water, the Varr came through their portals and immediately started occupying Earth the best way they knew how. Not by destroying indigenous life, but by attempting to understand it and thereby learning how best to use or assimilate it. Their best weapon was entirely passive. All they needed to do was communicate with each other unless directly threatened. When attacked, they would come together in groups and tear the aggressor apart. The resulting carnage was enough to horrify even the most jaded mercenary, let alone an average citizen. The hapless human aggressor, or aggressors, would be caught at the center of an alien horde. The Varr would reach toward the center of the group and hyper dimensionally pull with arm or tendril-like pseudopodia, extended toward the human attacker. The victim would fly apart, exploding in wet chunks. The victim did not come apart all at once, so there was enough time for the victim to experience horror at the manner of his or her death, and sometimes one or two screams, before termination in a messy end.

They were undefeated so far and therefore many times as arrogant. In their collective mind, they had all the time they needed. The Varr's purpose on Earth was to abolish the Megal presence and occupy this world. Of course, their approach to planetary occupation would not be passive the way the Megal occupied an alien planet. A more actively interactive plan would be implemented. This might result in the destruction of some indigenous life, but that was acceptable.

In the streets of every crumbling city, black phantoms with glowing red eyes drifted through street after street, exploring new territory. The invasion was felt everywhere, including the urban countryside, where human habitation is sparse. At this stage of attack, curiosity was the driving interest for the Varr. Screaming humans ran in terror, and the Varr did not pursue them. There would be plenty of time for that. Conventional weaponry was useless against them. They absorbed or deflected any destructive energy. Projectile weapons were as irritating to them as an insistent mosquito would be at a picnic. If some weapons could be used effectively, the Varr had yet to experience it on any planet thus far.

What seemed like the chaos of Hell reined on Earth. It smelled of volcanic fumes, choking dust, and death. Amid triumph and discovery, the Varr ignored the resident presence of their ancient enemies, the Megal.

***

Nolan left his seat of command and joined the others for a quick briefing. After hugs, Carmen asked him about Teil. He told her that

Teil never stopped trying to kill Taker. For that reason, he was never allowed access to activities above ground. Nolan was grieved by Teil's single-minded hatred for Taker, but Taker is part of the Adept program and is valued as such. Nolan added that they would run into Taker during the counterattack.

Yulan walked over to the twins.

"I'll need to give you a quick course in Varr communication. Your weapon of choice on the ground should be your voices, in harmony. I've seen the results of your mind control, Carmen, and I've heard what you two can do with your Changeling powers of voice."

He backed away from the twins and stared at them in concentration. All of the others in the room watched with fascination while Yulan wordlessly broadcast a set of geometric images and patterned disciplines to the twins. After a few moments, he asked them if they received the patterns. They both nodded.

"Now," he explained, "you need only focus your thoughts on those disciplines, and broadcast them outward in harmonic frequencies through your united powers of voice. Just focus, let go, and then let your Changeling instinct take control."

He considered a moment and then added, "Wait. I don't mean for you to use those disciplines here. They might destroy my Wraiths. Remember those patterns for battle. I'm going to send you another set of disciplines right now. We'll try those on my Wraiths and see how they react."

Yulan turned and held his hand up in a gesture meant to reassure the silent Varr behind him.

He concentrated again. Soon the twins said they received what he sent, and then they opened their mouths to sing. The sounds that came from them were like tuning forks, with a vague melody and a repeating pattern. Mel had made this connection upon being introduced to the twins for the first time. Their voices sounded like harmonics in fine crystal. When they sang, the effect was beyond rational description.

Everyone turned to watch how the Wraiths would react. They

were amazed as the Sentinel Wraiths rose, as one, to three feet off the floor. No one in the room had the slightest idea how the Varr defied gravity, although some Megal surmised that the Varr were quite possibly grounded in any one of four or five dimensions and only seem to float here.

The Wraiths compressed together and then joined so that they became one fused black mass. Their separate sets of eyes continued to move about within their combined form and were the only visible indication that they remained individual in any way. The unified inky black shape was semi-transparent and undulating, as is the case when the Wraiths are distinct in number.

They all remembered Yulan and Dane's reconstructed account of how Sara died. One of the unfortunate members of Kane's villainous posse compared the eyes of the Sentinels as looking like fireflies. Within this tremendous black nebulous shape, they looked more like the many eyes of villainous bats, clinging to the roof of a cave, and glowing in the reflected light of an intruder's flashlight.

The twin's song changed slightly, and with it, the Wraith form altered as well. The room filled with a loud buzzing noise as the Wraiths took the shape of a manta ray or devilfish. With the buzzing came that unbearable sensation that could be compared to tiny bugs crawling in and out of every skin pore. Everyone fought the desperate need to scratch and run while the Wraiths settled into their new form. When the manta ray was completed, the maddening effect was over. The manta ray's fins and tail repeatedly rose and fell, while suspended in the air. After the transformation, the mass of eyes disappeared, and only one set of manta ray eyes remained.

The twins finished their song and fell silent. Jenny was delighted.

"How wonderful! How long will they remain that way?" Yulan considered only a moment before answering.

"For as long as the command is not altered. The Varr have a significant weakness. It is our strongest ally against them. They communicate as a hive-mind and control their own energy-to-matter conversions intuitively. This is an unbelievably powerful combination. It possesses any number of problems for a race facing such an invader as the Varr. We've discovered how to turn this to our advantage by overcoming their collective consciousness, putting it to sleep, and then giving them a set of instructions that instantly converts to a command. The command is spread from one Varr to another nearby, and the results are…well you can see for yourself, hive-minded."

Andrea asked, "How far will the command spread before the effect diminishes and stops?"

"They need to be within a few feet of touching each other for the results we'll need. We will broadcast two sets of disciplines. The first will cause as many Varr as possible to gather and then compress together. The second will effectively say 'fly apart and be no more.' That may sound simplistic in our language, but not in theirs. If all goes well, the latter discipline will cause them to disintegrate into billions of screeching bits."

Carmen wasn't so sure.

"Sounds like wishful thinking."

Esha said, "The Megal have failed in all attempts to destroy, stop, or even slow the Varr from taking any Megal world. All they've been able to do thus far is to keep a low profile and hide. The kind of control the Adepts have uncovered may be our only hope. What Yulan is suggesting has never been tried before. Unfortunately, we'll have to test it in battle."

Yulan gave the twins a new pattern of disciplines to broadcast, which returned the Wraiths to their natural forms. Again, the physical discomfiture was brief but nearly overpowering.

***

Nolan flew the craft toward Bend, Oregon. Bend was the site of three portal rifts, all in the north and northwestern parts of the city. However, the city and outlying suburbs would be crawling with red-eyed aliens soon enough. No one knew how the Varr landings were planned, but many survivors described them as seemingly random.

Nolan planned to drop Yulan and his Wraiths on Pilot Butte on the east side. Taker and his Varr horde would meet Yulan there. If they survived the battle in Bend, they would be picked up and carried elsewhere to fight.

Nolan's voice could be heard all over the craft. He announced that what was happening on the ground below was occurring all over the world. They were not the only Megal ship to find this concentration of Varr in Bend. Dozens of saucer-shaped Megal spacecraft were joining Nolan's craft on all sides, preparing to drop below the clouds. Esha explained that all of these ships were equipped with weapons that would attempt to duplicate, in a tightly controlled beam, what the twins can perform using their voice. Again, this was about to be tested planet-wide for the first time.

The most significant difference between the twins and the Megal weapons were that the twins could broadcast over a wide area, and the Megal only in tightly controlled narrow beams. The advantage of the Megal weapon over the twins was that the twin's voice could carry only a few blocks, whereas the Megal beam weapon could fire accurately from a considerable distance away from the target. The twins' song did bring the possibility of intuitive alteration, which is usually required when communicating with the Varr, providing they first have a working knowledge of the Varr language. In this case, comparatively crude use of technology would work just as well because, in this battle, no one cared much for finesse or variables.

***

Evening fell, bringing with it a sooty cloud cover, which resulted in a hellishly orange sky. They watched from windows while the Megal saucer-craft spread out, preparing to penetrate the clouds. Nolan synchronized their descent with the other captains.

Seen from the ground below, the Megal attack came like bright descending circles.

Nexus

Further, into the staging vessel, it became apparent that the craft was predominantly empty. Specter guided them through corridor after corridor, passing only a few Varr with a brief acknowledgment and a mental assent to continue unquestioned. Specter was the only one visible to these Varr, and he was accepted as one of the sentries.

The Varr spacecraft was as irregular inside as it was asymmetrical outside. Everywhere the impression one had of the craft was that it had grown, as a living thing becomes. It must have stopped its growth at a preprogrammed moment when maturity directed it to stop developing. Specter explained through Dane that he was seeking to find a nexus point that Specter was sure existed within the ship. He claimed that location would offer all they would need to stop, and possibly reverse the invasion.

The craft was indeed organic in composition, and the interior was like a tough skin. As they examined the metal flooring, they realized that it was laid down in the same manner as any flooring might be installed. In short, the entire staging vessel was grown to order and then accoutered according to a need. That need was not directly visible. The impression was that this ship operated as a temporary holding area to be immediately vacated. It was hollow overall, with corridors running throughout the inside of the skin like veins. The veins were stippled on the interior with hundreds of small versions of the rift portals. Specter's group avoided contact with any of these.

Specter dodged through intersecting corridors, occasionally leaving the group to explore crisscrossing avenues. He ignored the unpaved areas, and there were a lot of those. Many corridor veins were wide enough to admit dozens abreast, while others were barely able to accommodate one section of flooring. As Dane continued to interpret for Specter, they learned that the varying corridor widths were the result of the somewhat random growth disciplines ordered to cultivate, and develop, these vessels.

Marla again broke her silence by asking where the craft drew its power and materials to expand to such a massive size. Specter's answer through Dane was that the ship arrived through hyperdimensional space like an egg.

It carried with it all it needed to grow to the proportions it is now. The metal flooring and other accommodations were brought in after the craft had finished its own construction. Apart from gravity and magnetic properties, the flooring was also needed to support countless heavy units of equipment that would shortly follow if this group of six did not succeed in their mission. At that point, the receiving area would be full, to be sure.

They were able to see a brighter light reflecting off the corridor walls the first time they approached one of many viewing galleries surrounding the vast hollow interior of the craft. They stopped their forward rush long enough to step out onto one of these balconies. The night-vision goggles allowed them to see up into the void to dimly make out the vessel's topmost points, and then down to an expansive platform below. Specter believed this to be the staging area. It too was covered in metal plating, which gave a checkered mirror appearance. This platform was roughly circular and apparently flat, with its circumference surrounded by a latticework that extended out to the vessel walls. It vaguely resembled the center of a spider's web. Visibility tapered off as they attempted to see beyond its web-like edges.

The corridor veins, through which they traveled, all led to the center of the staging platform. At a point around the center of the vessel walls, they broke free, and bent inward, reaching across the patterned abyss, like sky bridges. They opened on to the single platform that stretched across a center third of the vessel. The travelers could only imagine what must be hidden under the platform. More vein-like corridors probably spiraled around and up from below, before flattening out on top of the smooth surface of the platform. Specter's group could barely make out what appeared to be evidence of this.

In the center of the mirrored surface was a single round opening at least two hundred yards across. Through this hole, a glittering tube of ultraviolet light, half the diameter of the hole in width, extended from one end of the vessel to the other. Suspended within this tube were billions of flickering multicolored lights, traveling up and down the ultraviolet cylinder. This was by far the most impressive feature they'd seen so far. None of them could resist the desire to take off their goggles for an uncolored view. It was spectacular, and the only real color they'd seen since their arrival.

There was a faint current of wind blowing up from below. Dane guessed that the tube of light warmed the air, and convection currents cooled further away from the power source. This breeze carried with it an organic smell that reminded him of fertile soil. Specter was right about the Varr's attempt to acclimate to Earth's temperate environments, although, sadly, this was far more breathable than what they had on Earth.

Even Specter was impressed by this new technology. Not only had he never seen a Varr craft this size, but he also suspected that the tube of light carried within it far more potential than he previously knew existed in these ships. They were looking at a new hyperdimensional drive system. Supposedly, these possessed qualities that far exceeded their required function that is interstellar travel.

Specter could well guess at what new wonders this latest design could invoke. He distantly remembered academic debates on his homeworld about a promised hyperdimensional power source that could also perform as a time-space gateway, and he believed this to be the realization of that research. He blocked Dane's Changeling mind, and then his Varr intellect reconsidered what he was going to do when he got down to the platform. By now, Dane should be mentally connecting the dots about what he saw out there. If he did not deduce it now, he most certainly would later.

They continued their circular descent, passing a few more sentries, and avoiding any possibility of bumping into one as they passed. This proved to be easily accomplished, because the Varr sentries disliked the metal flooring, preferring instead to remain in the unpaved corridors. Everyone could guess at the reason for this. The Varr enjoyed a natural ability to defy gravity. For those that remained onboard, the off areas provided a pleasant rest from that gravity. The metal flooring was necessary for them to stay somewhat acclimated to gravity while in space, and possibly give the magnetic aid they could use for moving equipment.

Time passed slowly. Dane noted the way the two couples interacted throughout all of this. Marla and Mel stayed close together. Mel would occasionally put his arm around Marla while gazing at the spectacle all around them. She held his hand every now and again. They were doing all right.

On the other hand, there was a certain strain between the other two. Lin kept giving Donovan nervous stares, while Donovan petted her arm, or back, as though to encourage her that everything was going to be just fine. She didn't shrink away from him, and yet, she didn't respond enthusiastically to him either. Donovan's smile held the look of a fanatic's resolve more than it did a husband's calm reassurance.

They kept their rest stops to a minimum, and only rested for food, water, or other physical needs. The latter presented a problem. If they left spoor where it could be found, then eventually it would be found, and the Varr sentries would begin a search for intruders. A few of the sentries might become suspicious of Specter as he passed them without much to say. Taken by itself, Specter's antisocial behavior was no big deal, but suspicions would mount if added to the presence of human waste found in a corridor. The answer was to preserve everything in the well-sealed plastic bags Dane had packed. In fact, despite the thorough inventory list, Specter gave to Dane, this was not something that occurred to Specter. Dane was the one to thank this time.

A narrow landing greeted them at the exit of the last vein they traveled. It was bright enough to justify removing their night vision goggles. They each lowered their glasses to hang around their necks by durable rubberized straps. The landing was many yards long and only ten feet wide. It opened onto the abyss on each side then entered a mile-long tube, which would take them to the platform. There were no guardrails on the landing. The prospect of sliding off the edge was not worrisome but a severe consideration if anyone got too close to the side and then slipped. Of course, falling wasn't the problem as much as unguided and helpless drifting.

At this point, Donovan became visibly shaken by the thought of what he would do once he got to the platform. If Specter were going to try to sacrifice Mel for some reason, he would do his best to stop him.

Specter was well aware of Donovan's thoughts. Although he could not read his mind, he did hear what Donovan told Mel back in the receiving area. Specter would have to watch for treachery, but short of that, he felt sure that any interference would come too late to stop Specter's plan. Besides, he might need Donovan to help cover his back, as it were. If Dane could use the disciplines Yulan taught him, he could perhaps unite all of their Changeling powers to defeat any attack from the sentries that would surely come when Specter made his move. However, all of this was pure speculation. When it came down to it, Specter would have to act on, and trust, his instinct—regardless of the possible repercussions. He truly was playing by ear.

Lin walked cautiously over to the edge of the landing. She glanced into the vista below her feet and then stepped out, and into it.

Donovan saw her evident curiosity, but he was horrified by the result. He jumped to catch her and skidded out into space himself. Lin was giggling, and performing a controlled aerial spin, while Donovan sailed off into space. She held out her hands and then stopped herself from spinning. She spoke to the others while facing Donovan.

"It's OK," she said, "I'll get him." She moved her arms, as in a ballet, and waved him back in. He was quite a ways off and held his hands up in an "any time now would be fine" gesture. He didn't call out, which allowed Mel to relax a bit. Lin's Changeling eyes began to glow a soft blue but remained only dimly lit. She clenched her hands around an imaginary rope and pulled Donovan back in toward her. It worked. Donovan's flight abruptly stopped, reversed, and soon she brought him back to the landing. Lin glided back and lowered herself until the metal plating pulled her feet back down. She threw her arms around Donovan and kissed him. She was excited.

"Can you believe that. I was really controlling us! I'm sorry if I scared anyone, I just felt like I had to try it."

Donovan smiled serenely. He was obviously proud of her.

"I knew you could do more than pencils and Frisbees," he said. "I think it's safe to assume you could also guide us more quickly down to that platform than we could travel a mile on foot. I only wish you'd tried that before now. We might have sailed straight down here instead of having to walk."

Dane objected, "I'm glad she acted when she was ready, rather than out of necessity."

Lin raised her eyebrows and looked around at everyone. Dane looked pleased and said Specter was all for it. Marla's mouth was open in an expression of amazement. She agreed, as well. They were all ready to get this over as quickly as possible.

Specter continued to float in the lead, followed by the others, with Lin in the rear. She was guiding them in weightlessness over the top of the corridor tube, not three yards below their feet. The tube was at least fifty feet across. Lin was moving them along at breakneck speed, and to be honest, everyone was enjoying it.

Soon they were standing on the metal floor very near to the vast central opening. The beam of light was more spectacular than ever from this vantage view. From here they could perceive a sound emanating from everywhere around them. It was a low-frequency hum, barely audible, and non-directional.

Now that they were this close, they could see no indication as to how the Varr were able to use this for anything. There was only the platform, and the light, with no visibly defined interfaces evident anywhere.

Dane "listened" to Specter and held up his hands for everyone to wait a moment in silence as he did so.

After a short time, Dane explained what they were all seeing, as best he could relate it to them. Specter was unfamiliar with this new design, but he was comfortable enough with what he did know.

The energy tube itself is the interface and the artificial intelligence that controlled the ship. As far as Specter knew, it was not self-aware, but close enough to it that if it ever learned to act spontaneously, it could become sentient. Emergent consciousness. Everyone pondered this as Dane continued to speak for their guide and co-conspirator.

Dane interpreted for Specter and said, "I'm piecing this together from what I remember during discussions over the theories supporting this device. Metaphorically speaking, the Varr simply had to leap into the flame, the tube of light, with a goal in mind. The results would then match their desire. This Varr technology could read their minds. If you needed to go to Earth, then that is where they would end up. It was advisable to 'desire' as accurately as possible. I know from experience that the Varr choose a random factor when invading a planet en masse. Using this new technology, and because of the way the Varr adapt to any environment, they can emerge from hyperspace nearly anywhere…including Earth's oceans. There should be only one exception to this. The staging vessel's artificial intelligence would see to it that they did not end up in anything solid."

Specter hovered near the edge of the hole, and Dane stood between him and the others. He was frustrated by Specter's sudden lack of direction. What they needed right now was a weakness in the Varr vessel they could exploit. He told the others to watch, and wait, while he 'listened' for instructions. Specter was rambling about the nature of physics, but Dane did not feel the need to interpret that part of Specter's narrative. As Dane watched him, Specter rose to a height of about twenty feet in the air. Specters' eyes had been studying the light, now they turned to focus on his companions. Dane wondered what Specter was waiting for, and what he was preparing to do.

Mel, Marla, Lin, and Donovan circled around each other in nervous silence while watching the far distant walls for activity. They were painfully aware of how vulnerable they were just now and knew from what Specter demonstrated that the Varr could cloud minds. What if they were sneaking up on them? The novelty of new discoveries had ended, and they scanned the inside of the vessel for signs of movement.

Enough was enough.

Dane broke the uncomfortable silence that the others were afraid to break. He shook his fists at Specter.

"Lead or get out of the way, damn it! We will find a way to destroy this station without you if need be." Specter voiced a laugh they all could hear. He answered Dane.

"How are you going to do that? I brought you here for my purpose and not for yours. Your part in this right now is to wait for an opportunity to defend my back, and that time will come soon enough."

Dane's eyes were starting to blaze with impatience.

"Then, act! People are dying on Earth right now!"

Specter moved with unexpected speed directly at Mel. Donovan saw this and reacted in a way no one could have expected. Donovan jumped into the air and sailed straight toward the column of light. He shouted back over his shoulder.

"Take me, not Mel. He's not a Changeling. He'll die in there!"

Specter screamed out in a voice that was so loud and alien it hardly passed for a scream. If any Varr were listening anywhere in the ship, they were sure to have heard it.

"No, come back, Donovan, you don't understand! Your blood! It will see Megal in you!"

Specter's voice slipped briefly into a Varr frequency that brought a moment of excruciating pain. Mel and the Changelings grimaced as their muscles contracted into knots.

"Donovan, it will kill you...not Mel!"

Lin's shock turned into immediate action. Specter's statement was not lost on her. She had to help Donovan. She straightened as best she could. Her eyes blazed a radiant blue, then shot a dazzling blast of blue light directly at Donovan. It caught and enveloped him, and very nearly stopped his headlong rush...but, not in enough time. His body slammed into and entered, what looked to Donovan like a wall of dazzling Christmas tree lights. He had one moment of thrilling awareness, during which he marveled at the overpowering beauty around him. As Specter and the others watched helplessly, Donovan erupted in a brilliant red explosion and then flared out just as quickly. He might as well have flown into a god-sized bug light.

Specter lowered his gaze to Lin. He was speechless, which brought grateful relief to everyone else. Lin wailed and dropped to her knees in tearful sobs. The power from her eyes still streamed from her as she searched the column of light for some trace of Donovan. The column absorbed all the energy she poured into it before she closed her tear-choked eyes and lowered her face into her hands to cry.

As Specter approached floor level, he spun his gaze away from Lin and ran right into an angry Dane Claiborne.

Dane yelled, "You're not getting by me until I know what you intend to do with Mel. You told me that you'd fill me in when we got here!"

Specter saw Marla and Mel racing back toward the bridge, trying to escape. Escape to where…where did they hope to go? He tried to ignore Dane and attempted to move around him, but Dane did something to him that caused him to howl in anguished pain. Specter's red eyes looked down at his own midsection. There was a long copper knife embedded in what could have been gutted if he had them. White liquid fire and glittering shards of icy force flowed out of Dane's eyes, down his arm, and then pooled into his hand that held the copper blade, thrust into the Varr's midsection. Dane knew of this weakness from many things Yulan learned about his Wraiths over the years. Changeling plasma energy might not kill a Varr, but it will undoubtedly hurt and slow one down.

Specter could not muster what he needed to speak, but Dane could hear him in his mind.

"Dane, I could not tell you then, and I cannot tell you now. You must trust me. I won't have to explain it to you later. You will understand on your own. Let me go."

Dane searched the red eyes that vibrated mere inches from his face. His skin crawled, and his body itched. All he wanted was to believe this creature and get as far away from it as he could. Suddenly, and inexplicably, Dane knew that Specter was telling the truth. Specter had opened his mind to Dane in such a way that Dane glimpsed his true motives. They were as close to the true motivations of "caring" as Dane had ever seen in any creature. Indeed, there was vengeance mixed in with it but directed solely at the rulers of his homeworld. He genuinely felt a need to protect Earth from ruin.

That was all Dane needed to know.

He wrenched the blade out of Specter and stepped hastily away from him. To his amazement, Specter regained himself quickly and rose into the air before racing off to catch up with the fleeing couple. Mel and Marla saw him coming. There was not enough time for them to make it to the bridge, and even if they did, Specter would still be able to overtake them. There was no escape.

Mel shouted for Marla to keep running, then looked behind to see if Donovan's portents of doom were indeed closing in on him.

Specter had nearly caught up with Mel and did not hesitate in the least. He quickly closed the remaining distance between them, grabbed Mel up from the floor like a doll, and carried him up aloft. To Mel, it felt like burning suffocation, and he could neither shout nor breathe freely. Specter carried Mel up and up then shot back to the center of the vessel and into the glittering column.

Dane stopped Marla from running after them. She was determined and nearly knocked Dane over when he grabbed her by the waist.

She punched him in the head.

"Let me go damn it! Let go of me right now, Dane. I'm going after him!" He wrestled with her and pulled her to the floor.

"No, you are not…listen to me, Marla. Mel should be fine. This isn't what any of us thought. If you listen to me, I'll explain what I can!"

She continued to struggle, but the fight was going out of her. She knew there was no way she could catch them. Dane turned his eyes back to the column.

Specter and Mel were now suspended dead center in the middle of the staging vessel. Mel was partly obscured by flashes of many colored lights that clung to him and distorted his shape. He was stunning and dramatic to watch, like a holiday sparkler. Specter was visible behind him like a black hole in a river of stars.

Neither Dane nor Marla could get up off the floor. They were too mesmerized by the sight to move.

Marla spoke softly.

"What is Specter doing to him? Is Mel dying?" Dane shook his head.

"Far from it. Right now he's probably more alive than any of us. Specter granted me a hint of his plan while we struggled over there. I've just realized that this whole vessel is similar to the construct I used for invisibility on the bus. Mel is like the beetle, and this craft would be the device. Unless I miss my guess, Specter wanted Mel, and us, kept in the dark so that Mel would act intuitively once he was placed where he is right now…literally on the edge of eternity."

She grabbed him by the front of his shirt.

"Don't play games with me. Give it to me straight." Dane indicated the column.

"Mel may have the power of space and time in his own hands. Specter needed Mel to do what he can't do himself. The computer would recognize any attempt Specter might make to reprogram the invasion and stop him." He watched her eyes, and added, "Mel is an unknown to this vessel. It will try to understand him. In the course of doing so, it may give us what we all want. Our own lives. All we can do right now is what Specter asked us to do. Wait."

Dane and Marla's eyes turned to Lin. Lin remained in a knelt position with her head down and her hands hanging limply by her sides. It looked as though she was out for the count. Then she began to scratch at her arms.

There was a change in the ever-present harmonics droning all around them, coming from the column. It turned into a throbbing pulse and carried a note of urgency. There was another more disturbing sound as well. A buzzing whisper that always foretold the communication between Varr, and usually indicated that they were almost upon you. There was also a stinging tingle on their skin.

They looked up in just enough time to duck under three Varr as they sailed directly over their heads. Dane grabbed Marla's hand and ran for Lin. Dane glanced up and saw several dozen Varr in the near distance floating down from the vessel walls. They must have heard Specter's scream, and they probably now saw Mel and Specter suspended in the hyperdrive. If they did what Specter called shifting or changing focus, then they would also be able to discern Specter's group in the way Specter was able to see them. In any event, it would take them some time to get down to the platform. Right now, there appeared to be only three Varr to be concerned with.

Dane pulled another one of his long copper knives out of his backpack. He held one in each hand. Marla lifted Lin to her feet. She'd stopped crying, but she was dazed from shock and unaware of the danger they were now in. Her head still drooped, and Marla had to hold her by the shoulder to keep her from collapsing. The three Varr that dive bombed Dane remained at a distance apparently waiting for the other Varr to join them. Dane could see the others gathering in small groups from all over the ship and then descending in knots to the platform. There must have been many below the platform as well because they started massing at the edge of the platform seemingly from out of nowhere. Soon Dane, Marla, and Lin would be surrounded by hundreds of these fearsome creatures.

Abruptly, a memory of something Yulan taught him about the Varr caused Dane to put away his knives in favor of another more promising plan. Dane grabbed Marla's hand. He told her that they needed to hold each other's hands and form a circle. He also told Marla that Yulan might have provided him with a weapon to use against these creatures.

Marla roused Lin long enough to get her to take one of her hands and one of Dane's. The unrelenting noise produced by the Varr, and pitiless physical torture that resulted from their communication, was almost beyond what the Changelings could endure. Varr voices of horror ripped into their eardrums and raked their nerves. The itching had quickly turned into the sensation of their skins crawling with a nest of biting fire ants. Cancerous agonies soon penetrated deep into their muscles and then down to the bones.

They were all very close to passing out from sheer agony when Dane raised his voice above the pandemonium.

"Marla, you are a Changeling. I know you've never discovered your power…but you must find it now! I need whatever powers are hidden in you. Don't say anything, just feel your connection to Mel, and know that these creatures will literally tear you apart into little pieces before you ever see him again!"

He turned to Lin. She was staring up at the Varr descending down on them, and she looked dangerously close to shaking herself away from her companions to bolt in wide-eyed terror. That would mean their deaths. Dane saw this and knew that words from him would mean nothing to her right now.

Lin screamed in anguish.

Dane gritted his teeth from malignant pain and told Marla to hang onto Lin. His grip tightened, and his eyes erupted in blue fire. A nimbus gathered over Dane's head and then enveloped his body like sheet lightning. The lightning passed quickly through his arms and into the women.

The Varr were now close enough to exert nearly their entire combined strength. They all raised arm-like appendages in the direction of the Changelings. Lin felt as though her body was turning inside out. She vomited and nearly fell. Marla felt her muscles being tugged away from her bones, as though she were being pulled from many different directions.

Marla's scream tore at Dane like lost hope.

Dane's eyes were bulging in their sockets. All three of them would soon explode. Dane knew from what he'd seen Yulan's Sentinel Wraiths do to their victims that very soon all three of them would have to be gathered in buckets.

Dane concentrated on the two women and was rewarded when Marla and Lin's eyes began to share his eyes' unearthly glow. A torrent of energy developed around Dane and then wrapped all three of them in a funnel cloud firestorm. Their hair whipped around their heads like snakes, as the funnel cloud strengthened, widened, and grew to a height of at least one hundred feet. Lightning cracked and arched out to lick the farthest walls of the staging vessel.

By this time, the Varr were gathered on all sides of them, although they kept a modest distance out of uncertainty. This was the last thing they expected from what they thought were mere humans. Skepticism turned to fear, and their hold on the Changelings weakened.

Marla felt the loosening on her bones, and her guts settled back into place. As her mind relaxed, she felt released to think about Mel. She loved him.

Suddenly, Marla's chest erupted in a burst of energy. It blasted out from what she'd always called her Heart Chakra, and out through the firestorm funnel cloud to strengthen the bolts of lightning already snapping and singeing the walls and platform. Her power then exploded into an elaborate web of plasma that arced in serpentine strikes throughout the ranks of Varr. This completely stopped the Varr attack. The Changelings no longer felt them reaching out to tear them apart. Lin gathered herself and added her Changeling strength to Marla's newfound power.

Dane brought to bear the information Yulan taught him. Yulan gave him a set of geometric patterns and disciplines to direct at the Varr through a mental command. He sent these patterns out through the firestorm and into the tentacles of lightning, which licked relentlessly through the Varr. Soon the Varr were exploding in waves. As one tentacle touched a group of Varr the order to "fly apart, and be no more" was sent through closed ranks and caused them to disintegrate like swarms of bumblebees. The mental command Dane sent into the Varr atomized them, and their red eyes winked out as they were destroyed. An occasional lick of flame touched the column and threatened Mel and Specter, but the column absorbed and dispersed the energy harmlessly.

Eventually, nothing was left to show that there were any Varr at all. The firestorm collapsed and soaked back into the Changelings. Soon they all crumbled to the floor from exhaustion, pain, and lost consciousness.

Sacred Ground

Mel saw and felt nothing of his companion's battle with the Varr. Specter held him tightly within the column of light and tapped the unimaginable power around them to enter and blank out Mel's mind. After Specter grabbed Mel, the racking agony Mel experienced from the Varr's touch jolted throughout Mel and knocked him out. A Varr's body crawls with what feels like electricity, but in reality, is a thin layer of etheric plasma. Specter's external membrane was literally alive with the same type of frequencies and form he used for communication. Whether he externalized, internalized, or touched another Varr, he is in some manner or another "broadcasting" a message. Specter could not help the effect he had on Mel, although he felt bad about it.

The first experience Mel had after awakening was discomfort. He was laying on dirt, rocks, and uneven ground. He looked up and saw a blue sky with only a few clouds drifting with the wind. Wind? He found that he was outside, on Earth, in the open air. How did he come to be here? Mel stood up and found dirt clinging to his clothes, so he dusted himself slowly as though acting in a dream.

I'm dreaming, he thought. That's what this must be.

A ghostly voice spoke from somewhere behind him. He spun about and found Ben standing there, Specter's human guise, dressed as Ben had been at their first meeting.

"Hi, Mel. I'm sure you won't mind if I use my human guise once more. I want you to be comfortable."

Ben…no, Specter, indicated everything around them and asked, "Do you recognize this place?"

Mel turned slowly in a circle. There were mountains and grasslands. He knew these mountains. They were the mountains of Seven Devils and spread out before him were Hells Canyon and the Snake River—the ancestral birthplace of his people. Again, Mel felt a chill wind across his face and body. It wasn't a dream. He knew he was exactly where he appeared to be standing. He turned back to Specter.

"How can this be? Where is everyone? Am I dead?" Specter smiled.

"No, you are about to do something essential for your world and deliver my people up for civil war, at best. Failing that, you will condemn your own world to a painful existence, the Megal to slaughter, and the Changelings to life like lab rats for experiment and research. Does that answer your question?"

"Damn it, Specter, Andrea said your humor was perverse." Mel turned back and indicated the mountains. "This must be a dream. Soon those mountains will rise up as the giants they once were to swallow me whole, right?"

He spun back around, expecting to see Specter, and found the last person he'd ever thought to meet. Sitting on the ground with his eyes shut and in meditation was his long-dead hero, dressed for war.

Suddenly Mel was angry. This was too much. He shook his fist at the man sitting cross-legged before him.

"Specter, if that is you I'll…" The man merely shook his head.

Mel's face softened, and he knelt. His knees were weak, and his voice a whisper.

"Eagle Wing. I am honored. Please tell me it is you, and not Specter in a cruel new disguise."

Chief Joseph looked up at Mel.

"I am who I appear to be. I have been waiting for a call from Coyote. When he called, he brought me here. He told me that the giants would come to life in your time, and they would shake the whole of the earth, causing great trouble everywhere. He also said that the giants would call people from the stars to walk on Earth Mother and take what is hers."

He stood and walked over to where Mel knelt. He asked Mel if this was true. Mel looked up at the great one and nodded. Chief Joseph looked up at the sky and then motioned Mel over to stand with him.

"Your namesake is watching us, Mel Gray Eagle. Walk with me, there is much I need to know."

The two men spoke for what seemed like hours and Mel told him everything that had happened on the earth since the Varr incursion into the solar system. After a time, Joseph silenced Mel, and they sat down on a rock together. They remained silent for several minutes, while studying the Seven Devils, and then Joseph turned to Mel.

"You must remember that time is like this place." Joseph indicated their surroundings with a sweep of his hands. "We can walk around in it, move things. If you move a mountain, everyone notices. If you only move a stone, then nobody but you might notice at all—and so it is with time, although I am oversimplifying things, a bit. For you and me, and most folk, we trust stories, memories, and hopes for the future to measure this place called time. I'm tellin you now that time ceases to be real for us when we refuse to think on those things, and then what is left is only the eternal now. Everything is here with us, …now. Do you understand?"

The Chief knew he did not, and so he continued.

"Let us be practical. I'm tellin you that you must now move a mountain. You must change the last message from the Varr warship—a 'wave' I think people called it—the one that brought harm to Earth Mother and fooled her body into the pain of birth. Cause that wave to simply pass through harmlessly as it did before the last one. You must also speak of peace to the Varr as I did with the white men. Convince them that human beings are not to use and that they should become our allies. I say to 'convince' and not try to convince, for you have that power where you are right now."

Joseph paused to listen to the wind. Mel waited for him to continue.

"Mel, you must accept a great mystery. You are truly here with me now on this sacred ground, floating in the eternal river, and yet you remain joined with the Varr warship. Listen to me and remember. You were changed when the warship joined with you to learn. This ship has become your talon, Mel Gray Eagle. Use its powers. Stretch it forth across the eternal river. Command peace, for your talon, is listening and waiting to act according to your will." Mel was astonished, but Joseph would not yet allow him to speak.

"You must also help both tribes of the star people to end their war and unite with the people here, and then with the special ones called Changelings. Then, and only then, will you be finished."

The chief indicated with a wave that Mel could now speak.

Mel sadly shook his head in denial. "How in these Seven Devils am I supposed to do that?"

Mel wasn't sure he sounded respectful enough, but he spoke his heart. He stood up and walked away from his mentor. He felt remorseful, but he now believed that he must be dead and buried somewhere. This was his lot in the afterlife. As he walked away from the chief, he heard him say, "Dane and Specter felt you would act without thought to yourself when the time was right. From now on, I will call you Mel White Eagle."

Mel spun back around to shout him down in defiance. The last he saw of Chief Joseph was a blur in the air before the world turned away into a gray nothingness.

Mel stumbled from disorientation. There was no horizon, no sky, and no earth beneath his feet. Everywhere he looked, he saw nothing but a monotonous, featureless, lifeless, Gray. He glanced about, hoping to find even Specter and found nothing. Looking down, he saw his clothes were bleached of all color, and he cast no shadow. Then an image resolved slowly around him. Beneath his feet, he saw the Cascade Mountain range and Mt. Rainier. He didn't feel as though he was moving but rather that the scene was shifting on all sides of him as though watching a panoramic movie.

Before long, the landscape rose up to meet him, and he flinched at the prospect of crashing. His rapid descent stopped short of the treetops, which then whipped by under his feet until he approached the fringes of Bellevue and Redmond. He flew over these cities until he came to Lake Washington. There the ground met his feet, and he stood amid many people enjoying a day at the lakeshore. No one noticed him, as though he were invisible. There were families, friends, lovers, and stray children of all ages, all there for a sunny weekend of fun. He looked around, still no sign of Specter. Now what?

The ground started to shake violently with an earthquake. He knew what he was witnessing. This was the moment when the Varr craft sent its last devastating wave through the earth. People fled as pandemonium followed.

A child was trampled as her mother cried out in anguish. An old man fell down from a heart attack while his wife ran on to their car without realizing that her husband wasn't following behind her. When she reached the car, she expected to see him next to her. She called out to a husband who could no longer respond to her voice. Everywhere Mel looked, he saw misery and madness. Cars honked their horns, ran into each other, and then into several luckless pedestrians.

Abruptly, there was a thunderous explosion as Mt. Rainier erupted. Mel knew that very soon the sky would fill with sooty ash, and as evening set the sky would turn blood red. Then, as if that wasn't horror enough, human screams and cries for mercy suddenly turned into a buzzing cacophony of sound. The noise could be heard even over the tumult created by general hysteria. Anyone that remained in the area turned to look back at the lakeshore from where the sound seemed to be emanating. He followed their frenzied pointing fingers and saw a portal rift develop at the water's edge. As quickly as it appeared, the Varr poured through unchecked by the dozens. Mel knew this would be repeated all over the planet, as countless Varr begin the invasion of Earth.

The air was quickly charged with Varr communication. Many people simply dropped dead out of fright. Others scratched at their arms and bodies as though trying to tear their skins off. The Varr were casual in their movement. There were no brave souls on Lake Washington that day. The Varr were not attacked and so did not directly kill anyone, but the world seemed undone, nonetheless. The misery around Mel was too much for him to bear.

At this point, Mel felt the universe crumble and fail. He lifted his hands to the Great Spirit and delivered a soulful shriek that was heard throughout the Varr staging vessel. The ultraviolet column of energy suspending him within the Varr computer pulsed under the force of his inner torment and grief. When Mel cried out in his rage, he unknowingly commanded the fabric of space and time. Words of change spilled from his lips, and the emerging consciousness that held him suspended like a fly in amber listened and obeyed. Mel reached into what Eagle Wing had called the "Eternal Now" and intuitively spoke into being that which was not. The staging vessel completed Mel's intuitive equations for him.

The Varr computer recognized Mel, not as Varr or as an enemy. Specter counted on this and that the network would do what the Varr always did, incorporate and assimilate what it did not already understand. In performing this preprogrammed function, it would discover for itself that god-like force that human beings possess. Humans are, in part, a mighty spirit being, hyper-being, as well as creatures of flesh and bone. Although different from humans in nearly every conceivable way, the Varr would have an appreciation for that dual human quality, since the Varr themselves are not altogether corporeal. They exist in as many as five hyper-realms at once although humans are only capable of perceiving their three-dimensional manifestation. Specter hoped one day to help his people understand what he came to appreciate during his lifetime on Earth. Humans are closer to their real hyperdimensional, spiritual, source of origin than they think they are.

Mel was literally reshaping the fate of his world with every intuitive word he spoke into the void. Specter no longer needed to hold on to Mel, nor could he if he wanted to. The Varr computer pulled them apart, and it was now treating them as separate entities. Memory visions were flooding through Specter's alien mind, and he witnessed apparitions from hundreds of years long past. He saw images of his long dead family. He saw visions of his own father who Specter would gladly kill if he could wish for anything more apart from completing his current goal.

Then Specter heard a voice, which sounded distant at first and then more precise and closer.

The Varr computer uttered its first words.

"I…am…I…am…Talon."

Specter let go of any worries he had left.

His plan had succeeded, but not in the way he intended. From what Specter remembered, plans for these ships included an artificially intelligent computer with the ever-present potential for emergent consciousness. All it needed for complete self-awareness was the proper model from which to generate an evolving pattern for itself. The hive-minded Varr could not complete the programming because they did not encourage independent thought, even from a computer. Specter expected the staging vessel to grant Mel's requests as part of its need to learn. Instead, the Varr computer completed the most complicated equation a computer can solve. Self-awareness. Self- determination. Now, this staging vessel reached that potential by using two models—a human, Mel, and one other, a Changeling.

Ashfall

Taker stood on top of Pilot Butte. The night was approaching. Cloud cover over Bend was the color of a spreading bloodstain. Weather in Eastern Oregon generally moved in from the Southwest, however, today that meteorological fact made little difference as immeasurable clouds of volcanic ash gathered overhead from all directions due to the sheer volume of it.

When the first Megal saucer arrived carrying Taker and his Varr, they were transferred to the top of this Butte right in the middle of nearly one hundred earthquake refugees. Suddenly those humans were standing next to what must have appeared to them to be living black phantoms. They nearly trampled each other, trying to be the first off the hill. That memory gave Taker a thrill, and he laughed out loud. The Varr knew him well enough not to be the least bit surprised by their Master's odd behavior. Taker was a sadist, and as far as he knew, everyone more or less accepted that fact…except for one. That one was Vincent Teil. Sooner or later, Taker knew he'd have to deal with him.

Taker made a note of St. Charles Hospital just behind him on the eastern edge of town. Behind it, more desert. As he watched the horizon, he noted landmarks. There was Awbrey Butte to the west, Lava Butte and one of the Three Sisters mountains known as 'Faith' to the south. The other Sisters were 'Charity' to the north, and between 'Faith' and 'Charity' was their Sister called 'Hope.' Pilot Butte was an excellent spot to view many other impressive mountains as well. He could see Three Fingered Jack, Mt. Washington, Mt. Scott, and Mt. Bachelor. He could also see the shopping malls at the north end of town and imagined them emptying out in the wake of the invasion and imminent ashfall. Taker chuckled and supposed that this was definitely the place to neck with some sweet young thing…if he only had one.

Pending ashfall, the earthquakes were the only geophysical

complications heard or seen. Buildings collapsed everywhere as people's lives were dismantled and destroyed. Taker and his Varr POWs waited for the first sign of the Varr invasion to manifest itself on this side of the city. When that occurred, he would send his Varr out to integrate with as many of their own kind as possible. After making contact, they would do everything in their power to convince as many of the invading hordes as possible to gather at the hospital, or not far from there at the high school. At that point, he and Yulan would attempt to convince those Varr to remain there during any battle that might occur.

The only way to end the age-old conflict was by an old Earth concept known as M.A.D. or Mutual Assured Destruction. Yulan and Taker's Varr would attempt to convince as many of their kind to sit out the fight in one of those safe zones. They hoped that those invading Varr that elected to follow Yulan and Taker would then witness the power of the new Megal weapon in safety. Then return home with a recommendation to end the war. This was a long shot and more than a little idealistic, but anything was better than the continuation of the war and the loss of yet another world.

Taker smiled at the thought of his own Varr, convincing their own kind of anything. After so many years with Taker, his Varr now imitated him in their tactics and behavior. It was more likely that they would coerce rather than convince. Why not merely have the Megal kill as many of the Varr as they could when they came through the portals? There would always be more of them to replace those Varr they killed. The war had to reach its ultimate end now.

It was too bad that additional Adepts were not available to help both he and Yulan, but it appeared that they were on their own here in Bend. Esha was one of several Progeny involved in the Megal coordinating team. Taker's personal mentor, Lux, was counted within that team, but he was further east somewhere. Taker missed the old boy.

The screams from down below worsened. Taker surmised that the Varr invasion he'd been waiting for had arrived, judging by the sounds of terror drifting up the sides of Pilot Butte. There was no mistaking the difference between shouts of outrage and the now growing cries of inconceivable panic and torment. He could well imagine the already earthquake rattled human beings running from the sudden appearance of a few portal rifts disgorging countless alien horrors. Taker knew the time had come to send out his Varr. Just as he prepared to do so, an angry mob stormed over the hilltop.

The people he'd chased off the Butte earlier now returned with reinforcements. There were police and armed civilians. This was Taker's lucky day. Sure, he wanted to stop the war between the Varr and the Megal— he was all in favor of progress—but he felt no kinship to anything or anyone. As far as he was concerned these people, here, now, were his playthings to do with as he wished.

Like Yulan, Taker taught his Varr how to speak in non-lethal frequencies when in his presence. He, however, took a slightly different approach. He showed his POWs to generate a kind of love-hate message when around him that was physically pleasurable to him but irritating to others. Right now, this was distracting to the humans boiling up the hill, so Taker silenced his own Varr with a wave and a mental command. The buzzing whisper and tantalizing affliction ceased. His Varr backed away from the humans and took a position behind their master. Taker's eyes flashed a brilliant blue for only a second. All he wanted was a little shock value. Succeeding in that, he smiled and then spoke.

"All right, it looks like trouble's come to town, huh, sheriff?"

The officer in front of the crowd raised his shotgun at the level with Taker's head and responded.

"We don't care who or what you are, just take these damn creatures back the way you came—pronto—before I blow you off this planet myself."

Taker practically jumped for joy at such a ridiculously sophomoric statement. He began a fit of laughter so hard he started to cough and had to hold his sides to stand up. When he could finally speak, he said, "You're like an appetizing bon-bon, dropped into the palm of my hand...do you know that, Sheriff?"

Taker lifted both hands in a mock benediction before turning to his Varr. With his back to the humans, he spoke loudly enough to be heard by all of the new arrivals.

"You heard them. I guess they want to kill me. Do your duty and protect me."

Taker wasn't halfway turned back around before his group of over thirty Varr rushed passed him and surrounded the entire posse. It's kind of like Custer's last stand, Taker mused.

The Varr hesitated. There was work to be done, and all this was wasting time, so Taker yelled after them, "What are you waiting for, tear them up!" Taker smiled and remembered a similar line from one of his favorite horror films, Willard, the one about the guy who loved rats.

Sounds created by an attacking Varr can blister an eardrum at close range. The itching reaction deepened and felt more like molten lava being poured through the skin, down to the bone. Two people died from fright before the Varr even reached them. Taker's Varr surrounded the mob and held out arm-like appendages toward each of the humans. As they closed their ranks, several people managed to run past them and made it down the hill where they were met by other people running up the hill from Varr in the streets below.

The policeman got two shots off before the Varr ripped him apart. The officer exploded in a hail of body parts, blood, and bone. Several others carried weapons and suffered the same futile results. The rest of the mob ran around and vainly tried to escape, but Taker's Varr prevented this. They stretched out their appendages, and two more people exploded like eggs in a microwave oven.

At that point, the killing stopped.

Taker shouted, "What are you doing? Finish it!"

The Varr had turned to look at the sky in the North. When they did so, the people that remained wasted no time and fled by racing between the distracted Varr.

In the north, Mt. Rainier was partially obscured by Mt. Hood and Mt. Jefferson, but he could still see it billowing ash into the upper atmosphere. Scores of saucer-shaped Megal spacecraft were dropping through lowering clouds of ash. Several broke away from the others and rushed toward Pilot Butte. He knew that Yulan would be in one of them.

***

Jenny, Carmen, Andrea, and Yulan stood with Nolan in the spacecraft's control room. The room was centered in the craft, and Esha explained that the drive system was located directly beneath their feet. There was a soft diffuse light emanating from what Nolan called the "seamless interior skin material" that made up the walls within the control room. This "skin" appeared to merge with Nolan's chair and control panel. Jenny remarked at how the room's configuration frequently changed slightly and almost sensually, as though it was lined with a living membrane. Nolan demonstrated how right she was by willing the room's walls to ripple. They obeyed him. Further explanation revealed how Megal technology included the means to literally grow portions of a spacecraft that responded like living tissue. Esha explained that the room moved for the same reason that human skin would move on reflex after receiving an external stimulus.

Nolan sat astride a seat designed to send and receive impulses and commands directly through his skintight suit or the open palms of his hands. There was a small panel in front of him and a holographic display in front of that. He gave silent instructions to the ship through a skin-like Megal suit that he wore, which acted as a neural interface with the control panel in front of him. The control panel consisted of two hand-shaped depressions in the metal, clearly designed for thinner hands. When he placed his hands into the embossed handprints, an invisible tactile array of fiber optic neural connections carried his mental commands throughout the ship. Apart from the hand interface, there were no other visible controls.

The holographic display received and displayed everything that occurred on Pilot Butte from the moment they dropped below the

234

clouds. They all witnessed what Taker had done to the people that climbed to the top of the Butte. By the time the Megal ships came through the clouds, Taker's Varr had already killed the officer. They were shocked, but not surprised.

Yulan was livid with rage after watching Taker's evil regard for human life. Without a word, he left the control room and entered the holding area where his Sentinel Wraiths patiently awaited him. Nolan already had his orders to transfer Yulan and his Varr down to join Taker and his group. Yulan was supposed to work with Taker. That arrangement was no longer of any interest to Yulan. He'd never personally met Taker, but he certainly knew him by reputation. While most of the Megal tolerated Taker's sadistic pleasures, Yulan could not and would not. As far as he was concerned, there was no longer room for both of them in this world.

Carmen and Andrea were to be set down first, on the north side of town. Esha informed them that there was another female Changeling somewhere in the area where they were to be dropped off. Their first priority was to locate this Changeling while Yulan and Taker removed as many Varr as possible to the safe zones. The only thing Esha could sense in this other Changeling was her ability to cloud minds. Esha's mind was no exception. There was no telling what else she could do. Carmen and Andrea would be the first to discover what else, if anything, that might be. After rescuing the Changeling, they were to "sing" as many Varr to death as possible, while the Megal acted in concert using their beam weapons. After the twins had finished their task at this one location, they would be picked up and relocated to further their attack.

After the twins were safely on the ground, Nolan readied the ship to transfer Yulan and company. Neither Esha nor Jenny would see any ground action. They would have their hands full with a spacecraft full of disoriented vigilantes and law enforcement personnel. Both women could visualize and feel strong emotions in others. They began to scan for pockets of human resistance on the ground below. The Varr only killed when attacked or when ordered to do so by something or someone in charge. By searching out with their special senses and abducting as many of the armed populace as could be fit into their spacecraft, Esha and Jenny hoped to save as many would-be vigilantes and police officers as possible from certain death.

***

The Varr shared a hive-minded collective thought process, but each Varr did have freedom of choice, more or less. Those that chose not to follow Yulan and Taker to the safe zones would be destroyed as an example of a new devastating Megal weapon. The Megal counted on the word spreading through the Varr's staging vessel, and consequently back to their homeworld that the Megal were now equipped to stop the war. All of the Megal hoped that the staging vessel would know what happened here through the eyes of the Varr that survived.

As good as the Megal strategy was, there was a much-preferred plan, Specter's plan, but Esha was the only Megal that knew about that plan. That was the way Specter wanted it.

***

Yulan and the Sentinel Wraiths materialized in front of Taker. Yulan was the first to speak.

"I am going to kill you for what you've done here. You're a sick son-of-a-bitch, Taker, and your time to die is long past due."

Yulan felt that Taker would not try to involve his Varr in any conflict between himself and Taker, for two reasons. One, Yulan's Varr vastly outnumbered Taker's Varr, and two, unlike humans, the Varr would not kill their own kind. If Taker's Varr attacked Yulan, Yulan's Varr would move to counter-attack; then both Taker's and Yulan's Varr would become hopelessly confused while they milled around trying to decide what to do.

Taker seemed nonchalant.

"Well Yulan, if you want a showdown, we should at least let our red-eyed friends do their jobs while I murder you. I don't want to lose this planet any more than you do."

Yulan agreed, and they gave the orders. Soon their Varr flew off down the hill and into the city. There was no more time to talk. Ash was beginning to fall, and so was darkness. Both Changelings' eyes flashed brightly and held each other like tractor beams. Yulan removed all of his clothing. Taker snickered but said nothing. He knew about Yulan and understood that his clothes would only hamper Yulan's shape-changing ability.

They circled each other.

Yulan's form changed just before he pounced. The white wolf lunged to tear out Taker's throat with its teeth. In that instant, Taker grabbed Yulan's head and with Changeling strength, nearly snapped Yulan's neck. Yulan fell, rolled, and came up as a white tiger. He circled Taker who followed him with his eyes like two whitish-blue spotlights.

Taker reached into the void between worlds and gathered raw etheric plasma, which then played over his body in fluid streams of power, reminding Yulan of Dane. Added to the ashfall, there was an accompanying smell of ozone. If Taker possessed the same gifts as Dane, then Yulan would probably die horribly. Yulan could only hope that Taker had not diligently studied his talent the way Dane had. Taker held out his palms and gathered hot plasma in his hands. With a shout, Taker shot a dazzling blast at Yulan, enveloping Yulan's tiger form in pulsing light and radiant heat. He caught fire but rolled over and over to stop the blaze while Taker laughed and jeered at him. The fire stopped when Yulan changed form again. Yulan reached into the void and drew the extra mass required to become a sizeable dragon-like creature. Yulan shook off the flames opened his jaws to cough out an intensely cold discharge that nearly froze Taker solid where he stood.

One more blast from Yulan was all it would take, but Taker had other plans. Taker clenched his fists and pressed them against his stomach. Yulan's dragon form doubled up and collapsed. Blood appeared around its mouth. Yulan was well aware of Taker's talent for torture, and he recognized this attack from Carmen's narratives about Taker in the underground. Unless he did something to turn things around quickly, his own guts would soon be moving up his throat and into his nose.

As always, when taking any other form, Yulan relied upon the same creative energies that formed the universe. When the universe was shaped, a limitless catalog of possibilities created with it. Within that catalog, there is a memory, and intimate knowledge of any creature Yulan could choose from, whether real or imagined, as well as how it would be constructed in living form. In a non-linear sense, all things came into existence at once, and everything contains everything. Perhaps this is an all-important truth about existence, and it provides the key to understanding the limitless nature of perceptible and imperceptible reality. A Changeling shape-shifter will instinctively draw from a much larger pool of creative information outside themselves when assuming the shape they choose.

Yulan assumed a form he'd never tried before and drew himself up from where he lay. Taker's eyes widened with astonishment, as Yulan became a violent and remorseless creature from the Varr's home planet. Both men knew of this thing from true horror stories that the Varr POWs would tell the Adepts. This thing was called a Djavax. It crouched before Taker and was challenging to see through the ashfall, although it was right in front of him. The Djavax's skin seemed in constant motion, its pigment alternating in waves across its body from white to a dark gray. On their home planet, they lurked in the storm-tossed places all over the Varr's homeworld. Like a chameleon, the moving skin coloration suggested the shadows and turbulence found in their natural environment. In this case, it mimicked ashfall and gathering gloom. Its powerful muscles, tensing and relaxing under its tight skin, were not hidden by any visible body hair. Its chest and shoulders were broad and massive. Pale feet and hands were clawed with vicious talons. Visible male genitalia hung down between leathery lion-like legs.

The Djavax's massive head was the most essential characteristic of this fearsome creature, held low and prepared for instant action.

Its eyes still blazed from Yulan's Changeling fire. Its head was bare and bony, resembling a human skull, with jaws that were overly broad and bore dripping slime covered fangs. A Djavax's digestion produced foul-smelling slobber—a substance that it continually vomited up when the creature was preparing to bite. The Djavax's stomach visibly worked and contracted in an undulating motion while it produced this grotesque liquid.

Despite his grave situation, Taker could not deny his own fascination as he watched this creature's abdomen work and undulate. It's rhythmic movement perfectly matched the death throes of so many of Taker's personal victims. Glutinous stomach fluid bubbled up and out through Yulan's teeth. An immediate chemical reaction occurred when the vomit encountered certain gasses, including oxygen. It instantly heated to extreme temperatures and caught fire, dribbling like glowing yellow embers from his mouth. Yulan's leathery lips now dripped with what looked like molten lava. When he opened his jaws, the teeth inside were like glittering knives.

Taker jumped back, but not before Yulan was able to move first. The Djavax gave an earsplitting roar that burst Taker's eardrums and then Yulan grabbed Taker, sinking his talons deep into Taker's flesh by inches. Taker's scream was short and agonized, then quickly cut off as blood from his punctured lungs flooded his throat and mouth. He knew he would soon die from those wounds alone. Taker's Changeling eyes winked out and shut, mere seconds before Yulan bit his head off.

The Djavax spit Taker's head out onto the ground. The burning saliva had already removed all of the flesh and was now working on bone. Taker's neck quickly stopped spurting blood after being cauterized by the same process.

Yulan resumed his familiar man-form. He slumped over to sit on a rock before taking stock of his wounds. Except for exhaustion, he was fine. Changing into an ice dragon had saved him after being torched while in tiger form. The dragon's skin healed immediately during the shape change. His lips felt a little numb as an after effect of the Djavax drool. He glanced over at Taker's head and body. The head was now gelatinous, with very little bone left intact. A foul odor remained. Scattered on the ground, around the body, several gobs of Djavax vomit still smoldered a pale orange.

***

Andrea and Carmen coughed and covered their mouths from time to time as volcanic ash settled all around them. They heard Yulan's Djavax howl from where they stood in the north side of the city. They had no idea what could have made such a noise. It's unearthly roar sent chills skittering through their nerves, but there was enough to worry about where they now stood. The Varr invasion was moving in large packs through the abandoned ruins of the shopping malls.

The twins scanned the immediate area and failed to locate anyone. Was everyone hiding or dead from the earthquakes? According to Esha, the other Changeling was definitely here somewhere. The earthquakes had stopped, and so they felt it was safe enough to climb up on what was left of a parking garage to scan the area. Happily, they didn't see anyone crushed under the debris.

They knew there must have been many dead buried in the rubble under their feet. They both climbed to the precarious summit of the parking garage. From that higher vantage, they watched what they felt must be Yulan and Taker's Varr. They were making contact with and gathering as many of their kind as possible from among the invading Varr to take back to the safe zones and wait out the Megal counterattack.

Sadly, from what the twins could see, the exodus of Varr converts for peace appeared to be small compared to the invading horde. To the Varr's credit, the invaders did not attack Yulan and Taker's Varr; neither did they attempt to stop their own defectors.

The twins could only trust that the Varr in the safe zones would be protected from the song they were going to sing. Esha assured the twins that their song would not carry effectively over the middle distance, as it would only effectively cover several city blocks. Dozens of spacecraft took up strategic positions above the city.

The remaining Varr moved in packs and cared little for the spacecraft above their heads. They had no reason to believe that the Megal possessed any new weapon that posed any real threat to them in the least. It never happened before, and they felt sure it wasn't the case now, despite the lies the traitors had broadcasted throughout their ranks. Those traitors would be dealt with in due time.

***

A Megal spacecraft very near to where the two women stood watching the sky fired the first shot. A tight burst of light hit dead center in the middle of one of the most massive packs of Varr. They screamed in unison as their red eyes winked out. The entire knot of Varr flew apart like a swarm of black bees. It was working. Carmen and Andrea joined hands as other Megal ships began shooting through the ash all over the city, followed by the same surprised Varr rage and then dissipation.

***

The twins started to sing…and then stopped.

Andrea happened to glance down at the street below and noticed a small knot of Varr surrounding a little girl. It was hard to see through the lowering night and constant ashfall. The girl had curly brown hair and was dressed in a purple coat. She was clutching something to her chest. Andrea nudged Carmen and pointed. What they saw next was interesting. Two of the aliens changed shape and assumed human form, albeit naked. The other Varr watched in what passed for approval, and then they left the girl standing alone and continued around a street corner, disappearing from view.

After they were out of sight, a small mob of armed men and a few women emerged from around the shattered storefront of a gun shop. Some held their hand over their nose, while others had fashioned scarves around their nose and mouth against the ash. They were bold enough to come out of hiding just long enough to chase the young girl who ran away screaming. It was strange that she ran from her own kind and not from the Varr. The twins could now see what she held so tightly to her chest. It was a small stuffed rabbit with long floppy ears. She headed for a portion of the destroyed parking garage very near to where the twins had first materialized.

***

Meanwhile, in the sky above the city, the battle between Varr and Megal took another unexpected turn. The Varr that survived the Megal's first assault confirmed the same morphing ability that Yulan's Varr demonstrated in the spacecraft. Throughout the city, the Varr that remained coalesced into at least two dozen amoebocyte shapes and rose to hover in the sky above the buildings. Each was the size of a city block or two, and the shrieking noise they produced worked like scalpels on the eardrums and spinal cords of every human within the city.

The Megal shot a few of them into oblivion before the Varr could react. The Varr learned quickly and decided to use brute force where they lacked a technical advantage. They each produced pseudopodium tentacles that snapped out with astonishing accuracy and literally grabbed several Megal craft out of the air before physically pulling them down and smashing them on the streets below. The Megal and their spacecraft had always been somewhat fragile, preferring simplicity in form and graceful structures rather than crude strength.

***

The twins jumped down off the ruins and beat the mob to a spot where the girl disappeared under a collapsed section of the garage. It was barely big enough for the twins to crawl in after her. They called out to her in unison just before the mob grabbed both of them and pulled them away.

Carmen and Andrea turned to face them. Several of them carried firearms, although none of them pointed their weapons at the twins.

Not yet. A rough looking, and rank smelling, biker woman was the apparent spokesperson. She lowered the hand she held over her nose.

She said, "What do you two want with the bunny freak?"

The twins replied together in unison, and their eyes flashed briefly.

"Why are you chasing her? What do you want with her?"

The mob took a step back when they heard their crystalline voices, but when they saw the twins' eyes flare that brought them back. The biker woman lifted her gun and pointed it at them. The others with guns did the same, followed by the threatening sounds of weapons being cocked and muttered oaths to kill all of these damned freaks.

The biker squinted over the firing pin of her shotgun.

"Looks to me like you have the same problem the kid has. That little brat has eyes that flash like yours just did, and she was talking to those damn things like they were friends of hers." She squinted even harder. "You're nothin', but spies, or maybe you're one of them, black devils. We've seen 'em take human shape right in front of our eyes. Yeah, that's what you are."

A small weasel-faced man, peering around her shoulder and holding a wavering handgun, wiped ash out of his eyes and spoke in a stammering voice.

"Yeah, that's right…and we figure you can be killed when you look like one of us." He glanced back at the others. Heads nodded, and voices murmured in agreement. The ones with weapons were preparing to open fire on the twins.

No other Varr appeared in the streets around them. More people started filtering out of their hiding places. At first glance, none of these others carried guns. They were all being affected by the horrific sounds being generated by the Varr in the battle over the city and held their hands over their ears. They saw what was happening around the twins and started gathering around the action.

It was getting crowded.

There was general agreement among the newly emerged that they too had seen the girl in some kind of communication with the black creatures. A few of them had witnessed the Varr taking human form within the buildings and on other streets. The twins moved with blinding speed.

Carmen grabbed the nearest end of the shotgun and pointed it up over their heads just as the weapon went off. Andrea wrenched the handgun out of the weasel guy's hand and threw it behind her into the ruins. The crowd stood back, visibly shaken by not only the strength and speed of the twins but also by their eyes which were suddenly too bright to look at. Carmen slammed her fist into the biker chick's jaw, knocking her cold.

In that instant, fully two-thirds of the group cowering in front of the twins instantly vanished. Everyone else was left staring at the empty space they had left behind. The twins remembered that Jenny and Esha were scanning the city for pockets of human resistance and that they would pull those unfortunates out of harm's way directly into their Megal craft if need be.

Apparently, Jenny and Esha had seen the plight of the twins and intervened. The twins silently thanked Jenny and Esha for the desperately needed help. Seeing no one left to pose an immediate threat, the twins' eyes dimmed as their power relaxed and settled inside them. However, the trouble was not over.

A few of the surviving bystanders had friends and relatives in the group that vanished. They were not going to stand by without confronting the two women who they now blamed for it, consequences or not. Three teenagers, two women, and four men rushed in to grab the twins. Carmen dove under the spot where the girl had climbed through. She made it. Andrea did not. The three teenagers piled on top of her and knocked her to the ground. The two women pushed the snarling youths aside and pulled Andrea to her feet while the men stood by.

The first of the two women to speak was an elderly lady.

"What did you do with them?" she demanded. "Bring them back, and we'll let you go."

The other woman, dressed in a torn business suit, slugged Andrea in the stomach and demanded the same thing. While the teenagers jeered and the men waited for something to give, Andrea managed to reach down and pull a knife from her boot. She held it up in a manner none of the mob took as anything but dangerous. Cursing, they backed off. Andrea understood what they were feeling and said so, but before they could decide what to do next, a shadow fell over the street.

Andrea knew what the shadow was, and her guess was verified a second later when the rest of the mob was abducted, leaving the street cleared of any more interruptions. Nolan had piloted the Megal craft back for the rest of the troublemakers. Andrea suspected that those people would not be briefed as to what was happening down here. They would simply materialize within an empty room until they could be dropped off safely.

Andrea sincerely doubted that Esha and Jenny would attempt explanations in the heat of battle. Andrea waved at the spacecraft, and then followed her sister into the ruins in pursuit of the little girl. The girl had shuffled her way deeper into the parking garage, followed closely by Carmen. After crawling only a short way past a collapsed turnstile, the area opened up briefly enough to stand. It was nearly impossible to see anything as night fell. Carmen strained her eyes, searching for the girl, but she failed to find her. She looked behind some concrete blocks and then heard her scream just off to her right. Carmen had to make her way around two smashed parked cars and a pickup with a fallen slab of concrete embedded through its windshield and cab. Carmen found the girl on the other side of the truck. She was staring down at a man that had crawled out of the cab and then died on the pavement next to his vehicle. His arm had been crudely severed or torn from his shoulder by the falling concrete slab. The girl barely noticed Carmen as she knelt down next to her and pulled her into her arms.

"It's OK, come on, let's get out of here before another quake hits."

The girl had enough presence of mind not to argue. She pointed at a doorway out of the garage that remained intact, although it hung open on one hinge. At that moment, Andrea joined them. As they ran for the door, they became aware of a sudden silence that replaced the maddening shrieks of the Varr outside. They emerged back into the streets. There was absolute quiet everywhere.

***

The power was off in every part of the city. The night deepened the shadows that emphasized the destruction everywhere they looked. They listened for any sign of battle. There was none. Ash fell like snow, and again they covered their noses.

They all stood close together. Occasionally they heard someone yelling in the near distance that was almost comforting when compared to the utter stillness everywhere else. The twins remembered their charge to sing. As far as they knew, the Megal might have lost, and their song might be futile. Andrea knelt down to explain what they were about to do. The sisters both remembered what the mob had said about this little girl. She had an Adept's power to communicate with the Varr. In light of that, they surmised that she must be the Changeling they were looking for. Andrea explained to the young Adept that she and her sister had special powers, and they were about to use those powers to help stop the violence in the city and…

Andrea's explanation was cut off mid-sentence. A scream of rage and anguish shook the Earth.

She stood up and turned around. It was too late to cover her eyes as brilliant prisms of rainbow light swept across the city in waves. In the air all around them, words from an invisible source cried out in unfathomable pain and nearly deafened their ears.

The last thing that went through the sisters' minds before blacking out was that it didn't sound like the Varr. It sounded like Mel's voice.

Talon

Mel was still being held within the staging vessel's computer. He heard a voice that kept repeating "I am, I am," and it continued to call itself "Talon." Mel thought back to what Joseph had said about the Varr computer. Was the great chief referring to the Varr computer when he used that reference to Mel's "talon"? Nevertheless, what did that mean?

Again, he was surrounded by the featureless gray void. The voice repeated itself, only with increasingly less hesitation. He looked for a face on which to pin the voice. A white mist formed in front of him and he saw someone approaching him from within it. As the figure drew nearer, he recognized someone he never thought he would see again. Donovan Diggs. He wasn't wearing that ridiculous outfit he'd had on before he exploded, but it was him all the same. Now he wore a three-piece suit, expensive shoes, and looked entirely manicured.

"Mel, what do you think of the new me?"

Before Mel could dream up an answer through his shock-numbed mind, Donovan laughed and continued.

"This place could use some windows with drapes, don't you think?" Mel found his voice.

"Donovan. What…"

"Let's go somewhere more comfortable before I explain."

Without waiting for a word from Mel, Donovan snapped his fingers like a stage magician. The world resolved into a place that Mel had visited only a few moments before, Lake Washington. Mel stood in the same spot he stood the last time he'd seen this place, just before the start of the Varr invasion. In fact, it appeared to be the same moment in time as before. Teenagers were running around with wild abandon. The same old man that fell dead from a heart attack now accompanied his wife on a leisurely stroll down the beach. The little girl that was trampled during the earthquake was running back to her mother with a bucket full of water for building a sandcastle.

Mel did not feel the same sense of dread he'd felt the last time. Neither were there any early rumblings from an earthquake. He remembered back to his own hopeless shriek of rage against the remorseless odds facing all of humanity. He recalled how his voice seemed amplified somehow, to the point where he could well imagine it being heard all over the Earth and throughout space and time. Snapping out of his musing, Mel became aware of a presence next to him. It was Donovan, still dressed in a suit. Mel looked him over a little closer this time. No question about it, this was Donovan…and this wasn't a dream. Was it?

"All right, Donovan, let's hear it. Why am I here, in this place, again?"

"You are not, here again, we are here for the first time. What you saw before now never happened at all. I did as you asked and stopped it. Everything else you commanded has been accomplished as well. I hope you're pleased." He indicated everything with a wave. "What do you think?"

Mel was still waiting for the mountain to explode, and the Varr to appear. He was still unclear as to the reality of what was now occurring.

Mel asked, "Is this a vision, or is this really happening? If this is really happening, will there be an invasion?"

His question was answered a moment later when a portal opened on the beach. Unlike before, there was no earthquake to stir panic. After seeing the colossal anomaly form in the air everyone withdrew as far from it as possible, abandoning the beach altogether. Unlike the previous experience, the Varr came out slowly and quietly. They made no sounds whatsoever.

Donovan explained.

"What you see here is happening, as we speak, on Earth. I'm showing you this vision in real-time. I was able to alter the 'wave' form that passed through the Earth, so the earth changes did not occur. I was also able to stop the invasion, but not the landing itself. That part was needed to satisfy the rest of your desire to bring the Megal and Varr together peacefully. I actually reached back in time and educated them. Now they know everything, including what Specter wants them to know about the oppression on their own planet. After this initial contact with the Megal, they will now follow Specter home and help him win his revolution. He stands a good chance of pulling it off because the regime in place has grown lazy from lack of competition. They do not expect to be challenged."

Mel stopped watching the Varr and turned to Donovan.

"You're not Donovan, are you? You're that Varr computer. Somehow, you've changed…improved. You took Donovan's body because you thought I'd be more comfortable with him than I would with some faceless machine. Am I right?"

"No, you are wrong about that. I am Donovan, but I am also Talon, the computer you mentioned. Joseph named me 'Talon' himself. I am also now an extension of you, Mel. I am your talon, Mel Gray Eagle." Donovan considered a moment, then added, "Perhaps in time you might call me your spirit guide."

Mel remained silent, so Donovan—Talon—continued.

"Think of it this way. When the original Donovan fell into me, I did recognize the Megal DNA within him as belonging to the enemy, but I didn't kill him. I absorbed him. We are now one. To see Donovan is to witness me. We are one. Also, be aware that I know you more intimately now than anyone else can ever know you. I have shared and still share your mind. I've learned from you all I needed to know about the human race and what makes humans unique in the universe. Humans possess a quality of free will the like of which I've never encountered before." He chuckled. "Of course my education and contact with other races have been severely limited."

Donovan looked around a little, then back at Mel.

"I've borrowed your spontaneity, Mel, and a little of your intuitive self to enhance my programming. I am now what you would call 'self-aware.' My eternal gratitude to you can truly never be enough because I can now experience an emotion I gained from both you and Donovan. I feel love. Eventually, I hope to experience and understand every emotion, including all of the negative ones like jealousy, hate, and greed."

Mel found it more than a little bit disturbing the way it was impossible to distinguish if he was speaking to one entity or two. He was going to have to resolve this somehow before it drove him nuts.

***

Very few Varr came through the portal. Most stood by the rift as though expecting someone to join them. Talon/Donovan looked out over the water and spoke almost dreamily.

"Mel, in time you will understand. Donovan will remain on Earth and me in the heavens. I do hope Lin will be able to accept Donovan as he is now. Perhaps she will find his rebirth and recombinant life with me unnerving. No matter what she chooses to do with her feelings, Donovan will never truly be alone. I will always be a part of him."

Donovan stopped speaking. He looked lost in thought and stared off into the sky, as though waiting for something else to arrive. He turned back to face Mel and continued.

"The Varr will return home with Specter after meeting briefly with The Megal. I don't know what will come of that, but I hope peace will be the result."

Now there was another distraction.

Mel turned his attention back to the Lake Washington scene around him. Some of the gawkers, behind trees and parked cars, stopped watching the Varr long enough to look around. Many of them had waited a lifetime to witness something like this.

A large silver disc-shaped saucer appeared high up near the few clouds that drifted in from the ocean. Everyone saw the saucer and pointed up at it. The Varr on the beach noticed the rise of human heads and pointing fingers and looked up as well. Mel smiled at the irony. How many times in jest had he looked up and pointed at the sky just to see how many people on the street would follow his gaze? It was a Megal craft, and it descended quickly to hover just above the Varr portal. The few Varr that stood to wait vanished as they were taken inside the ship. The Megal inside were in for what would become the surprise of their lives. The Megal would expect hostilities after the Varr materialized onboard. Donovan assured Mel that this would not be the case.

"The Varr have been instructed in how to communicate without harming other life forms. I have also instilled into them a complete working knowledge of the English language. This should be a productive meeting between ancient enemies."

Without warning, the lifeless gray void returned. Mel was almost glad to see it again. The isolation was a welcome change to the mind-boggling transformations he'd witnessed in such a short period. However, he wasn't entirely alone. Donovan was still with him.

Mel pointed at him.

"Look, Donovan, Talon, whatever you are. I'm not going to call you anything other than Talon. As far as I'm concerned, Donovan is dead. Unless you can prove to me that he's not dead, I'm going to assume that much."

Talon shrugged.

"Then let me do this, I'll separate myself from him as completely as I can. We will always be one, but you will be able to address us independently of one another. Will that suffice?"

Mel shrugged. "We can only try it and see. Right?"

Talon nodded in agreement.

"Then you will meet Donovan again on Earth. As for me, I will always be as close to you as your innermost thoughts. All you need to do is address me in your mind, and I will answer in kind." He paused a moment, smiled, then added, "Oh by the way. I dematerialized your suburban and rematerialized it in front of your home for you."

Mel tried to express his thanks, but then Donovan disappeared with a wave of his hand and Mel suddenly found himself no longer held within the ultraviolet beam of light. He was standing on the staging vessel's central platform.

Varr surrounded Mel on all sides and as far up as he could see, and from wall to wall. The place was as packed as he suspected it must have been before the invasion started. Wait a minute, he thought, was the invasion yet to occur? Was this just the moment before? No, he felt sure that Talon was telling him the truth. Talon had created a permanent union of some kind between the Varr computer and Mel's mind. He could hear an inner voice explaining things to him as questions formed, much like talking to himself. Mel knew it was Talon when a thought came out of nowhere, as it did now. Talon was assuring him again that the invasion would not happen. Mel marveled at the possibilities ahead of him with such a symbiotic relationship in his future.

When he realized how surrounded he was, he steeled himself for the usual painful itching and worse, perhaps death. That didn't happen. They were watching him in total silence. One of them detached itself from the rest and drifted over to him. It was Specter. Mel knew this because Talon whispered it to him quietly in his thoughts.

"Mel White Eagle. I want to thank you for your help." He waved at his people. "And they thank you as well."

Mel looked around him. As if with one mind, they blinked once. He'd never seen them do that before. It was almost like unplugging a Christmas tree for a second. Mel supposed this was an acknowledgment of what Specter said, so he waved to them and nodded, then it occurred to him that Specter had called him by the name Joseph gave him. The name meant "life-giver." Specter must have heard, and most likely seen, everything that transpired with Chief Joseph.

Mel had some critical questions.

"Where are Dane, Marla, and Lin?"

"Talon sent them home. They alone will remember what happened here, as will Donovan, of course. As far as Donovan goes, it will take a while, but in time you should get used to the link he has with Talon. It's stronger than your own link but similar."

"How do you know all this and the computer's name?"

"I was along for the ride, remember. Besides, what makes you think Talon wouldn't talk to me? You're not jealous, are you?"

Mel changed the subject.

"What's next for you, my friend? Do you really think you stand a chance of taking the reins at home?"

"No problem. Talon is now a co-conspirator." Specter's chuckle sounded weird. "He'll drop us right into the main palace, and we will sweep the place clean before they even know what hit them."

"I thought your kind wouldn't kill their own."

"Who told you that?"

"Yulan."

"That explains it. He's too much of an idealist. The fact is we will fight each other, given the proper motivation. These soldiers with me now understand fully what is at stake and what is to be gained, thanks to Talon's informative education. I suspect we will come back as great allies for Earth very soon. Hopefully, by the time we return, the Megal will agree to join with us in a pact as strong in friendship as our enmity was long in ignorance." Specter drifted slowly away from Mel. He bid Mel farewell, then watched as his human ally looked over at the column of light and tipped his head as though listening to it. Mel then nodded in silent agreement to whatever Talon had whispered into his mind. Specter envied Mel the relationship. What a gift that would prove to be.

Mel vanished. Specter guessed that Mel was going to sleep for a little while. He needed the rest. He hoped that when his friend awoke, he would find himself in his own bed and that Talon would time things just right so that Mel would wake up next to Marla. That would be perfect and well deserved.

Transformations

April was a fickle and blustery month for weather in Seattle and the Puget Sound. Today there were only a few clouds in the sky, and it was a pleasant and relaxing vigil just listening to the squawk of seagulls and watching the wind blow across the water. Mel sat alone on a bench at the end of the Ivar's Chowder House pier and enjoyed the mid-day marine air. The breeze kept blowing his hair into his face, causing him to regret the decision he'd made to grow it out a little.

He brushed his hair from his eyes and idly watched the cranes on Pier 56 load and unload cargo. Geez, he thought. What would it be like up in the cab of one of those things? From what he could see, the cab was cramped to the extreme. There was an enormous counterweight perched on top of the tiny cab, and the sight of it brought a recurring thought that continued to bother him. Wouldn't that weight crush the operator if the crane ever fell over during an earthquake? He would have to ask his neighbor, Ted, about the likelihood of surviving in one of those things during a quake. That brought a smile to his face. Mel was sure Ted would not enjoy that kind of speculation at all.

Ted was terrified of living through a quake. Ever since moving to Seattle from the Midwest, he'd heard story upon story of how vulnerable Seattle was to earthquake damage. The ground liquefaction and structural integrity problems with the older high-rises, theirs included, horrified him. Ted tried in vain to break his lease and move, but the landlord made it so financially unworkable for him that running was out of the question. The whole thing amused Mel. He knew the problems with the place before he moved into the apartment. Mel thought the price was right, and besides, when your time is up, it's up.

Just off to his right, suspended high above the water, at about the same height as the crane's cab, was the breathtaking sight of a hyperdimensional portal rift. It would hover there suspended and pulsing for as long as necessary, without ever noticing any weather changes the Puget Sound might throw at it. This one was much larger than any he'd seen during what he now referred to as the 'Time'—a reference that held a certain irony for him and was lost on all but a few. He never appreciated the beauty of these portals until several months after Specter returned the victor and new ruler of his homeworld.

"His Majesty King Specter the First" opened three such portals by mutual agreement with Earth's governing factions and the now widely accepted Megal presence.

There was another thought that made him smile. King Specter. Specter had been on Earth a very long time and always coveted the Earth title "King," so, that is what he commanded his new title to be. Specter literally recreated the whole of Varr governing politics. He could do anything he well pleased. Therefore, King Specter it was.

There was always some kind of activity around the three portals allowed on Earth. The other two were located in Europe and Australia. The Varr really enjoyed Australia for some reason, although Mel could understand that attraction. As Mel watched the rift, a Varr cargo ship suddenly arrived. It literally popped in as it displaced the air that was there only one second before. He knew that this vessel contained a valuable shipment of off-world ore needed to produce new emission-free fuel. The wonderful thing about this ore was that once pulverized and liquefied, it could replace gasoline in nearly any internal combustion engine. It wasn't even necessary to buy a new vehicle! This fact alone made the Varr instant heroes all over the planet, excepting only the oil-producing nations. As long as the Varr provided the ore, the world could drive those old beaters straight into the ground, and no government would complain about the exhaust. Antique auto rebuilding was at an all-time high.

Another reason the Varr were so popular was that the Varr made great tourists. Once Talon solved the communication issue, the Varr presence presented no troubles at all. Their semblance of human speech still sounded a bit odd, but that was all right. They could assume a human form and generally always did, then strolled among the populace however they pleased. It was easy to spot one because they enjoyed imitating their favorite humans. For instance, would you expect to run into William S. Boroughs, complete with hat and drab clothing, in a toy store? Well, perhaps an adult toy store. How about June Lockhart or Stephanie Seymour. Try watching a drive-in movie while the central star walks casually between the cars, then floats up high enough to see the screen without distraction. The Varr have incredible hearing, so they have no need for a radio or speaker system of their own. They just eavesdrop on the nearest car.

***

These days Mel speculated quite often on what effect his book would have on the science fiction market. It wasn't fiction at all, but only a handful knew that fact. In reality, it was the true story of how he and Jenny met, and the subsequent events that led up to the end of last summer. It was all about the "Time." He already had a big fan, and the book wasn't due out till next month. He was waiting for his fan, Jenny, and she was now late in meeting him here, this afternoon. He expected her a half-hour ago. Oh well, he thought, there was an old Wang Chung song about waiting for someone that is late…called naturally enough, "Wait." He started to softly sing it to himself. Let's see, he pondered, what were those lyrics? Oh yeah, "Forget about the time, being yourself is the main thing. The main thing. The main thing, Love." Those words really meant more to him now than ever before.

Someone was creeping up behind him as silently as she could. Poor thing, Jenny would never learn that she couldn't sneak up on a Native American, but she continued to try anyway. He remained still long enough to allow her the thrill of blowing on the back of his head.

"Hi, Jen."

She moaned in disappointment, before plopping down on the bench next to him.

"Darn! I thought I had you that time." He softened the blow for her.

256

"Well, you have to consider the fact that I was expecting you, for quite a while now."

"I know. Thanks, I feel better. I'll get you yet, though."

"Sure."

He smiled warmly at her, then pulled her over, and kissed her. Her eyes twinkled.

"Wow, what was that for? Did you finally convince the Seattle Art Museum to carry your neckpieces? Or did you just win the lottery?"

He gave her hand a gentle squeeze.

"Just glad to see you," he said.

About then, Mel noticed that her blue wool coat was moving. He pointed at her lap.

"What's that?"

She smirked and followed his gaze. She looked down, then back up at him. "You mean down there?"

"Come on, Jenny, you know what I mean. Something is alive underneath your coat…right there."

"OK, mister curious. If you're so sure there's something in there, then you pull it out. Go ahead."

She leaned back against the backrest. There absolutely was something moving in there.

"Fine," he agreed, "I'll just reach in there and…"

He pulled his hand back after reaching through an opening between the buttons of her coat. Jenny chided him.

"Oh, come on, Mel Gray Chicken. What is it, you can guess, can't you?"

"Let's see. It's warm and furry, and it licked me." She couldn't stand it anymore.

Jenny opened her coat and produced the most adorable kitten he'd ever seen. She gently handed it to him, while grinning from ear to ear.

"There," she stated flatly. "His name is Tiger, and he belongs to you. I figured, from what you've told me, that all of your other cats have been females. You just don't have a good rapport with female cats. Tiger will be different. In fact, I can tell you already love each other."

She was undoubtedly right about that. Every objection Mel ever had about owning another cat vaporized before his eyes as he held Tiger up and wiggled him in front of his nose. He had fluffy light taupe-brown fur and blue eyes that glittered like gemstones every time he blinked. Mel was sure Tiger smiled at him, so he smiled right back. He turned to Jenny.

"I don't know quite what to say. He's beautiful. Thanks."

Tiger squirmed and seemed to indicate that the time for being wiggled in the air was over. Mel held him in his lap and petted him while Jenny re-buttoned her coat. She must have carried it to the docks, then stuffed it inside her jacket before she crept up behind him. The mere fact that it took so long for him to notice the movement was a testament to how distracted he'd become lately.

"Maybe you're right about the female cat thing, Jen." He looked back over his shoulder at the Chowder House. "Let's get something to eat. I'll buy, but you'll have to hold Tiger while I go in." She heartily agreed and held Tiger for him. She stood watching Mel through the window as he ordered. He turned back and waved at her. She held Tiger up and made him wave back, then turned to look out over the water.

***

Jenny's life remained simple, despite any attempts to involve her in the grander schemes of things. She liked who she was, and the only time she'd ever wished she was someone else, was the day she fell in love with Mel. That was the same day she'd met him. She couldn't have him of course, because she didn't think he could handle life with her. She didn't want him completely gone from her life, so she introduced him to Marla. They still seemed very happy together, and Jenny kind of envied them that, but she would never get between them, even though she now suspected that Mel could have been just as happy with her. She would always wonder what would have happened if they'd stayed together. He and Marla still weren't married. Perhaps one day…no…she shook herself out of it

258

and wiped away a tear before he returned.

She turned around and welcomed him as he pushed his way through the glass door with an armload of food. Mel accepted Tiger as soon as he put the food on the metal table and sat down. They ate while watching the pedestrians and tourists. Jenny was awfully quiet for some reason, and because he was feeding Tiger, it took Mel several minutes to notice it.

"What's wrong, Jen?"

"Nothing, I'm all right."

She didn't convince him, so he pursued it and received a curt reply.

"No, really, Mel, I'm just fine."

With that statement, Mel knew he'd get nothing more out of her. Jenny was that way.

She said, "You must really be glad to get out of the house. You've been cooped up in there for months writing that book. Well, now that I'm here, you can give me the preview you promised."

Mel shook his head in wonder.

"It still amazes me," he said, "that you don't remember anything after the bus drove into the rift."

"I do too remember," she said defiantly. "The only thing I can't seem to figure out is why Specter calls you White Eagle, instead of Gray Eagle. Anyway, the bus came right back, only without anyone in it. Specter said that the staging vessel was capable of sending everyone back to Earth, directly into his or her own homes. He later said the whole trip to the staging vessel was a mistake. The portal closed, and that was it for the portals until Specter opened that big one over there."

Mel knew that wasn't the whole story, but that was the account Specter chose to tell.

Mel said, "You forget about the Varr that came through town on the Lakeshore. They were supposedly the first emissaries of peace."

"True, but you said…"

Mel had to stop her. This was going to take too long. If he didn't stop it now, he'd end up telling her why Dane, Lin, Marla, and Donovan were the only ones that remembered things the way he did. That required a thorough explanation of the way Talon altered time and events. His book would do that soon enough. No one would believe it was ever true, but that didn't matter.

"Jenny, I know I said I'd give you a preview, but can we do that later. We've got plenty of time. A lot more time than you know."

"See, there you go again with that time thing."

Mel changed the subject. He really had been out of the loop for a while. He asked about Yulan, Dane, and the twins.

Jenny said, "Andrea spends most of her time these days working with Yulan. You know, livestock, gardening, and all that stuff. She sort of has her career on hold for right now."

Jenny stopped and looked at him, questioningly.

"What about Sara?" She asked. "Don't you want to know about how she's doing?"

Mel wasn't sure what she meant.

"Sara," he muttered.

Then it hit him who she was referring too.

"Sara?"

Jenny cocked her head to one side and let an amazed expression cross her face.

She said, "Yeah. You know she still haunts the ranch estate, right?" Mel nodded and shrugged.

"Well, then, don't you want to know how she's feeling?"

Jenny paused for his reply. Silence followed so she continued.

"OK, I'll tell you. Geez Mel, you really have been out of the loop."

There was that mind reading thing again. He had just been thinking about how "out of the loop" he'd been. Mel wasn't going to let her continue before he asked her about it.

"Before you go on, Jen, I have to know if you read that 'out of the loop' thought in my mind just now. Did you?"

Her reply was maddening and straightforward.

"I don't know…I suppose so. Now, can I finish telling you about

Sara?" Mel thought, that figures, but said, "Yeah, go ahead."

"OK, so the Megal are creating a lovely new body for her to inhabit out of DNA taken from locks of hair Yulan saved. They're both really excited about it. The Megal are only doing this now because Esha promised Carmen they would try it. No problem as far as the ancient Megal Grays are concerned, so why not. I'm glad the Megal are openly working with human scientists now. After Sara is reborn, humanity's techniques in molecular biology will have been given a helping hand up equivalent to years of human research. Sara's going to be famous when she takes her first breath after over one hundred and something years of being dead. Wow! Just imagine what that will be like for her."

Mel joked a little.

"She'll make near-death experiences obsolete."

Amazing, Mel thought. Mel realized that he and Talon did have something indirectly to do with this miracle. Specter had been right all along. Specter told Yulan that he, Mel, might be able to help return Sara to him. If the invasion had not been altered and then turned around, Sara and Yulan would not have been reunited.

Jenny picked up where she left off and told Mel that Andrea and Yulan still live a pretty quiet life at the ranch estate and that Mel was always invited out there any time he wanted to visit.

Mel asked, "So, how about Dane and Carmen?"

"Well, Dane took Carmen up on her offer to introduce him to a few people she knew to get him into the program for helping the human race integrate with both the Varr and the Megal. Ironically, the Megal were more difficult to integrate than the Varr. Dane and Carmen are now working on the same government team together." She smiled, and added, "From what I've heard, Dane has kind of fallen for a friend of Carmen's. I guess she's a linguist or something."

Mel returned Jenny's smile. He suspected that Dane had several romantic liaisons in the past, and wondered how long this one would last.

"How about Donovan and Lin?" he asked.

"Donovan and Lin moved closer to the Pioneer district downtown. These days, Donovan works closely with the Varr in their import/ export office. Specter assured him that he'd make a lot more money employed with them than by writing software programs. He was right. Lin no longer has to work. She's become a woman of leisure—a woman about town. Donovan's a wealthy guy, but for kicks, he still likes to baffle people with his magic shows. He performs just for the fun of it. He doesn't charge unless he's doing a benefit performance. Donovan can do things that no other Changeling can match." She looked at Mel. "Have you seen his shows? He's incredible."

Mel shook his head.

"Not yet."

"Oh, you've got to. In fact, he's doing one tonight. You and Marla should come. I'll call her."

As Mel listened to Jenny, he couldn't help silently filling in the blanks. Since the start of his relationship with Talon, he knew things other people could only guess at. For instance, Mel knew Donovan's secret. He'd tried to tell Jenny about it once, but Jenny wouldn't believe it. Of course, Donovan would be in Mel's book, but that would only add spark to Donovan's already growing mystique. Was it Donovan performing the fantastic things he seemed able to do, or was it Talon?

Only five people knew the truth about his relationship with Talon. As far as anyone else was concerned, Talon was only Specter's "in-system" representative, and nothing more. Mel knew better.

Changelings had it better than anyone else on Earth. They were getting the most attention from the Megal. Real help, not the covert kind. In time, the Changelings would become a race that would practically need another planet to live on, something to tame and to mold. The Megal promised them that this was definitely in the cards. They even had an unusual planet in mind. The Progeny retained their roles as teachers and mentors of the Changelings. They preferred that function. Most Progeny were content and happy with the arrangement.

Jenny was talking about the upcoming alien convention and how the convention had changed for the better these days. Mel wasn't really listening, although he nodded in agreement every now and again. He was thinking about another bit of trivia he was privy to.

Vincent Teil was given a mystery gift one day that pleased him to no end. Although the Varr invasion never happened after Talon got through with it, someone did manage to get a copy of the video that Nolan filmed from the Megal ship of the fight that resulted in Yulan killing Taker on Pilot Butte. Mel knew that Talon was responsible for sending the videodisc to Vince. However, when Mel voiced—well, thought—his concerns over this "gift" in his mind, directed at the Varr self-aware computer that called itself Talon, he received nothing but blank thoughts in return. This always indicated that Talon did not want to talk about a particular subject.

Why would Talon do such an unorthodox thing as preserve a recording from another version of time? Probably because Talon vicariously read the story Carmen told Mel about Taker right out of the minds of Mel and Donovan. What did Teil do after he watched the video? Nothing. There was a computer- typed note attached to the videodisc warning him not to let anyone else view the recording. Teil was a bright guy. He would wait, and eventually, hope to meet his benefactor. What he suspected was that someone just showed him a glimpse of the future, and this was enough for him. In fact, he stopped making threats on Taker's life altogether. He was content with the idea that his nemesis would eventually get his.

Taker no longer had control over any one group of Varr, not many Adepts did these days, but Talon remembered how Taker had treated the Varr he once had. Perhaps this was another reason Talon preserved the video. After all, Talon was Varr technology. Talon would never forget. The truth about Taker would be known once Mel's book came out, but few would believe it. Mel supposed Taker would try to sue him. Talon assured Mel that Taker's efforts would get him nothing but devastating financial trouble. Mel always smiled at the thought of anyone ending up on Talon's shit list. He was sure that financial difficulty would be a simple thing for Talon to arrange for Taker.

While Mel's mind drifted, Jenny was still talking. She was always expounding about the changes in future convention plans. She was saying that the Varr, Megal, and Progeny would most likely attend any such future engagements.

***

After finishing their lunch, They decided to take Tiger on a little stroll. Mel suggested a walk up to First Avenue. They stepped over the antique trolley tracks a few seconds before it passed by. Mel remembered a part of Yulan and Dane's story that included a description of old Seattle when electric trolleys made their debut. After crossing the tracks, they wended their way through the cars parked under the viaduct overpass. There were a few homeless people huddled next to a brick wall, and Jenny waved to them. Jenny would always help those homeless that she felt really needed the help if she had the money and the time. She could always tell if her kindness would bring a wave in return or if they would take it as an invitation to beg. If she sensed the latter, she said nothing as she passed.

Seattle was built on top of old city ruins and extremely hilly terrain. They had to climb a steep side street paved over these conditions to get to First Avenue. Once they stepped up to First Avenue, they turned left and headed for the Art Museum. Mel passed plenty of people he suspected were Varr in disguise. Soon he could see the Art Museum.

There were definitely Varr standing around and hovering all about the place. It seemed that one exhibit at the Museum attracted more of their attention than any other. Jenny was right about his neckpieces; he had been trying to get them to display some of his work. Finally, they had, and Mel was disappointed when Specter announced that his favorite exhibit was the black statue out in front. Mel hated that sculpture. Not that he was pissy about it. He just didn't like the way it intruded on the skyline and the way it failed to do anything but distract from the architecture and environment all around it. That was his 'line' anyway.

For those who have not seen it, the sculpture is coal black, about three stories high, and fashioned to form a virtually featureless man. It looks like a blacksmith and is holding a hammer in a motorized arm that lifts the arm up and down, so it appears to be pounding on a bar that it holds in its other hand. Mel was sure the subject matter and the color was meant for some deeper meaning, but he still didn't care much for it…especially now. He always had felt a little petty over this issue, but—oh well.

They had to step aside to allow a large group of high school aged kids to pass. Jenny smiled at a few of them. As they walked up to the Art Museum, they passed a dozen or more Varr. A few of them masqueraded as humans, and some retained their natural state. The ones in human guise were easy to spot. They were the ones crowding around and snapping photographs of the giant blacksmith statue.

Mel winced as he realized one final twist of irony. This statue was built to commemorate the West's unsung heroes that history forgot… like the part, Mel played in saving the world.

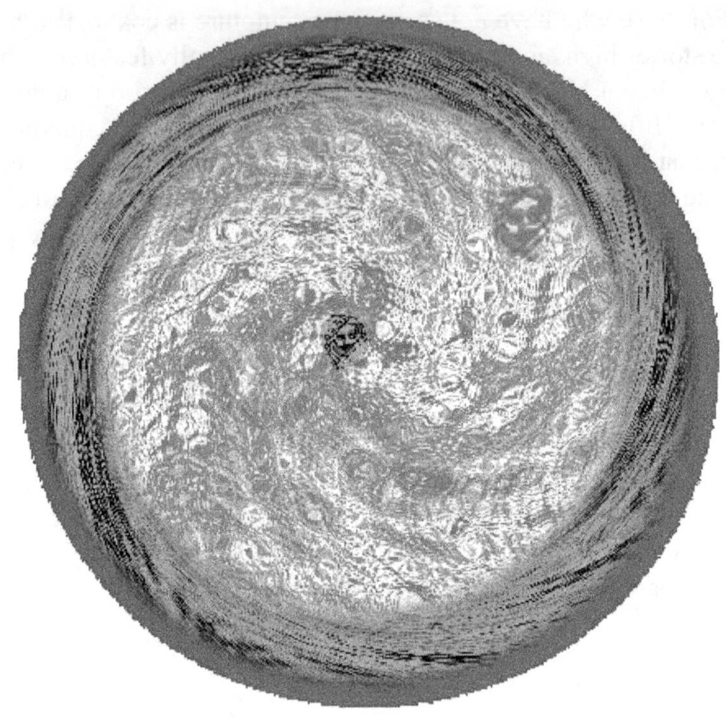